A Collection distributed by Heron Books

NEVIL SHUTE

Pastoral

NEVIL SHUTE

Pastoral

Original Illustrations by Rosemary Neale

Distributed by
HERON BOOKS

Published by arrangement with
William Heinemann Ltd.

Published in Canada by arrangement with
William Morrow & Co. Inc.

© *Illustrations, Edito-Service S.A., Geneva*

PASTORAL. *n.* a poem which describes the scenery and life of the country: (mus.) a simple melody.

Chambers's Twentieth Century Dictionary

ACKNOWLEDGMENTS

The verses from A. E. Housman's Collected Poems (pub. Jonathan Cape Ltd.) quoted on pages 9 and 81 are printed by permission of the Society of Authors as the literary representative of the Trustees of the estate of the late A. E. Housman.

The translation by Sir Henry Newbolt of the verses from the French of Wenceslas, Duke of Brabant and Luxembourg quoted on page 53 is reprinted by permission of Sir Henry Newbolt's executors and is taken from "Poems New and Old" published by Messrs. John Murray.

The verse by W. E. Henley quoted on page 153 is printed by permission of Messrs. Macmillan & Co., Ltd.

The verses by Alfred Noyes quoted on page 165 are printed by permission of Mr. Alfred Noyes and Messrs. William Blackwood & Sons, Ltd.

The poem by Rupert Brooke quoted on page 185 is printed by permission of Messrs. Sidgwick & Jackson Ltd.

The words of the song *A Nightingale Sang in Berkeley Square* on pages 209, 210, 212 and 213 are quoted by permission of the Peter Maurice Music Co., Ltd.

CHAPTER ONE

Think no more, lad; laugh, be jolly:
    Why should men make haste to die?
Empty heads and tongues a-talking
Make the rough road easy walking,
And the feather pate of folly
    Bears the falling sky.
                            A. E. HOUSMAN

Peter Marshall stirred in the broad light of day, and woke up slowly. The pale sun of February streamed into his narrow room, a gold streak crossing the foot of his bed and lighting on the deal wash-stand. He saw the sunlight through half-opened eyes, then closed them again to ease the dazzle. He could not close his ears. He heard, passing away above his head, the high scream of an ungeared engine in fine pitch, and automatically his mind said: "Harvard." He listened, tense even in his torpor, till the note dropped as the unseen pilot changed to coarse and throttled back a little; then he relaxed and pressed his head more deeply in the pillow.

It would not have woken him if it had been a Wellington. Wimpies were part and parcel of his life, the very texture of his work. He was awake now, though he lay with his eyes closed. There was a Wimpey running up one engine, somewhere away out in the middle distance of the aerodrome. It would be one of the ones up for forty-hour inspection, or else the one that hadn't taken off last night. The engine, he decided, sounded lousy.

The noise died down to a tick over, and he heard the birds. There were elm trees opposite the mess, retained for camouflage; these trees were full of rooks. He heard them cawing and disputing. He heard the twittering of sparrows. He heard a cow lowing from the meadow. He heard an A.C.2 pass beneath his window whistling: "Daisy, Daisy . . ." He opened his eyes again, and there was the pale gold sun streaming across the wash-stand. He turned his head to look at the window and saw a pale blue, cloudless sky, and felt the cold air fresh upon his face. He remembered the Met. report and the belt of high pressure that extended out into the Atlantic.

"God," he muttered drowsily, "it's going to be a bloody fine day."

9

He raised his head to look at the wrist-watch laid upon the chair beside him; it was seven minutes past ten. He closed his eyes again, calculating. It had been nearly three when he had got to bed, he thought. They had landed back just before two. Taxi-ing to dispersal and handing over to the ground crew took a bit of time. Ten minutes in the truck to Wing Head-quarters and twenty minutes over the report. Then the truck again to the mess, and a quarter of an hour, sleepy and silent, over cocoa and buns. It must have been three before he was in bed. That meant he had only had seven hours' sleep; enough for an old man, maybe, but not for a growing boy. He need not get up yet.

He stretched and turned over in his bed, savouring the com-fort of it, closing his eyes and striving to regain the warm oblivion from which the Harvard had dragged him. He could not sleep again. He lay for twenty minutes growing gradually wakeful, till he heard the batwoman banging about in the room next to his. He heard the rattle of china as she emptied the basin into her slop-pail.

The partitions were only beaverboard. He shouted: "Beatrice! Beatrice—come in here a minute."

He heard the pail go down with a rattle of the handle, and she put her head around the door. "Did you call, Mr. Mar-shall?"

"I did," he said. He turned in bed to look at her. "Have you been down for your elevenses?"

"Not yet. We aren't supposed to go before half-past ten."

"It's half-past ten now. Will you bring me up a cup of tea when you come back?"

She giggled. "Oh, Mr. Marshall! You know I'm not sup-posed to do that, not at this time of the morning. Mrs. Stevens, she wouldn't half let me know about it if she saw me."

"She won't see you."

"When are you going to get up, Mr. Marshall? I got this room to do before dinner."

"I'll get up when I've had my tea."

She said: "I never promised," and shut the door. Lying there in bed and asking for tea, she thought, and with the sun streaming in, and all. Even if he had been out late. She had heard the aircraft coming in over her hutment in the camp, in the middle of the night. Them blue pyjamas he had on were ever so nice, and he didn't half look nice in them. She went downstairs to get his tea.

Marshall sat up in bed. The room, small as it was, held all his personal belongings. He got out of bed and crossed to the corner by the door, and picked up a long green rod-bag. From a top drawer of the chest of drawers he took a little leather bag that held a reel. Carrying these with him, he returned to bed.

He had been introduced to fishing about six or seven months before by Sergeant Phillips, his rear-gunner, who came from York. In peace-time Phillips worked a complicated machine that put the chocolate on to chocolate biscuits, but his heart was in fishing. Every Sunday he would go out and sit on the bank of some slow-flowing stream, frequently the Derwent. He fished for nothing but roach. With his long green-heart roach-pole, his bag of ground bait, and his gentles he would sit all day, watchful, alert, and patient. He had developed into a very good rear-gunner in the Wimpey.

He had taught Marshall to fish for roach. He had succeeded so far as he had fired his captain with enthusiasm for fishing, but his pupil had soon deserted roach for pike. Spinning for pike was more in keeping with the quick energy of the pilot; moreover, you could eat stuffed pike. It was true that Phillips ate the roach, but it was generally conceded that roach were an acquired taste. If you happened to like eating cotton-wool stuffed with mud you liked eating roach.

Gunnar was a roach fisherman, and used to go and sit with Phillips by the slow stream two miles away, the River Fittel, that ran southwards to the Thames through the pleasant farms of Oxfordshire. Gunnar Franck was a Dane from Copenhagen, a sergeant pilot, Marshall's second pilot and navigator. In 1940 he had been a medical student in his home town; he had reached England from Norway in a fishing-boat in 1941 and had spent six weeks in an internment camp while his credentials were examined. He approved of that, and frequently told the story in the sergeants' mess. "Ver' careful, ver' good," he would say. "Soon as I got on shore at Aberdeen, officer asks me questions. I not speak English ver' well those days, and pretty soon he think I was a Nazi. I spend six weeks in prison." From gaol he had been sent to Ottawa, from Ottawa to Arizona to a flying school. Ten months later he had flown a Hudson back from Montreal to Scotland as a second pilot. He had been a second pilot ever since, though recently he had been re-mustered as a navigator.

Gunnar was a big young man with a red face and curly black hair, good-tempered, methodical, and rather slow. So far as Marshall knew, he had never made a mistake in navigation, and no emergency had ever made him hurry. He never passed a course or distance verbally, but wrote it down and gave it to his captain. He had explained this once to Marshall. "No mistakes," he had said, beaming good-humouredly. "No mistakes this way. Perhaps one day you think I say something when I mean differently, so I think it better that I write it down." He always crossed his sevens in the continental style.

These two, Phillips and Gunnar Franck, formed the backbone of the crew; the others came and went in training or dilution of the air crews, but the rear-gunner and the navigator stayed with Marshall. He had reflected once or twice that all of them were fishermen, and had once suggested that a heraldic roach, rampant in *or* upon a field of *gules*, should decorate the front fuselage of the current Wimpey. The Wing Commander had taken a poor view of that and Marshall, lying in bed in the pale sunlight, was not altogether sorry that the scheme had come to nothing. A roach was a lousy fish to put upon a Wellington. A pike, a pike with great snapping jaws and very fierce would be altogether different.

Sitting up in bed he assembled his new rod. It was a very little rod, a slender wand of steel more like a rapier than a rod, not more than five feet long. It was beautifully made and finished. The sun glinted on the chromium-plated rings above the wand; the shaped cork grip nestled in the palm of his hand. He fitted the little multiplying reel and flicked tentatively in the air above his bed. A chap could chuck a plug the hell of a way with that.

The W.A.A.F. batwoman found him sitting so when she brought in his tea, critically examining his new rod. "My," she said, "what's that you've got?"

"Fishing-rod," he said.

She said again: "My . . ." Them pyjamas were a dream. "Well, here's your tea. Now you get up, 'n let me do this room."

"I'll get up in a minute."

She said: "Don't sit there playing with your fishing-rod. I got my work to do."

She went out, and the pilot sat on in his bed, sipping the large cup of hot, sweet tea that she had brought him. He was in no hurry to get up. He had missed breakfast by the best part of a couple of hours, and it was a full hour and a half before lunch. For decency, he would have to go and look his Wimpey over; he could do that before lunch. He did not want to fly it; for the moment he was sated with flying. What he wanted most of all to do, and what he certainly would do when he had had a meal, was to take his new rod and his new reel and his new plugs, and ride three miles on his bicycle to Coldstone mill-pool, and see if he could get a pike.

He took the rod to pieces and packed it away again, and presently he got out of bed. He walked over to the window and looked out. He could not see the aerodrome. He looked out over a small valley, pasture and ploughland alternating in chequers, parted by hedges and great bushy trees. It was very still, and quiet, and sunny. Over to the right a little squad of W.A.A.F.s were standing in open order in a field doing physical jerks. The girls wore battle-dress in Air Force blue; the Section Officer who was drilling them wore grey trousers and a grey jumper with a polo neck. She stood facing them. "One —two—down—up—swing—stretch—down. Not bad. Let's try that once again." A mile away he heard the village church of Hartley Magna chime the quarters, and then strike eleven.

He rubbed his hand across his face, yawned, stretched, and went to the bathroom.

Half an hour later he was getting on his bicycle to ride around the ring runway to dispersal. He rode slowly with one hand in his pocket, savouring the freshness of the morning. He passed various Wellingtons upon their little concrete bays. One had a gaping, jagged hole at the trailing edge of its starboard extension plane, that had removed a portion of the aileron and put the flap permanently half-way down. He glanced at it casually, without much interest, as he passed. It was a big job. Nobody was doing anything about it yet.

He came to his own Wellington, R for Robert. The ground crew were working on it; the fitters had stripped the port engine of its cowling, and there was somebody in the cockpit. Marshall got off his bicycle and laid it down upon the grass, and strolled over to the port engine.

"Morning," he said. "How do we go?"

One of the fitters said: "You got an oil leak. Filter casting's cracked. Did you know?"

Marshall shook his head. "Pressure was all right. Might have been five pounds down. Is it bad?"

The man went to the engine and wiped the casting with a dirty rag; immediately the new oil showed the crack. "You were nearly dry on this side," he said. "Not more'n two gallons in the tank."

Marshall looked again. "Did something hit that?" he asked. "Or did it just go?"

"Just went, I should say." The man wiped it again. "I don't see any mark." He glanced up at the pilot. "Is that right, it was Turin?"

"That's right."

"Much stuff about?"

"Not much. Seen anything of Sergeant Pilot Franck this morning?"

"He's inside, sir."

There were several people in the fuselage: Gunnar Franck, and the corporal rigger, and one of the men from Vickers. Marshall swung himself in and said: "What's this in aid of?"

Franck turned to him. "There is little holes," he said. "In the bomb doors and the underneath of the rear fuselage, and the tail also. I have thought that it was the rats, maybe."

Marshall said: "Very likely. Couldn't have been anything else." He bent with them to examine the damage, which was no more than superficial, and heard what the technician proposed to do about it. "Strong teeth the little muggers have," he observed, fingering a buckled duralumin bracing of the geodetic.

Gunnar said: "Also, they have strong stomachs. I have found the droppings." He opened his hand and showed three tiny, jagged fragments of shell-case.

"They're not well," said Marshall.

Phillips came down the fuselage from the rear turret. Marshall said: "Everything all right your end?"

"Okay. I never fired a round all night, bar testing. I'll check up with the target this afternoon, soon as I can get it."

They got out of the aircraft and stood beside it in the warm sunlight. Before them stretched the field, criss-crossed with the wide runways, empty, idle, and still. Phillips said: "None of our lot bought it, did they?"

Marshall shook his head. "It was a bit of cake." He turned from the machine. "I'm going up to Coldstone Mill this afternoon to try and get a pike," he said. "You coming along?"

The sergeant shook his head. "If I go out, I'll go to the river." He meant, to fish for roach. "But I got a date for the pictures to-night, so I don't suppose I'll go. Wouldn't hardly be worth it."

The pilot said: "I've got a twisted wire cast that I got in

Oxford, and a single wire cast, and a sort of artificial gut cast—thick stuff. Which would you use?"

"With them plugs and the little rod? I'd use the single wire."

"Not the gut?"

"I dunno. I never used that fancy sort of stuff for spinning. If there's a fish there and he likes the bait, he wouldn't bother about wire or gut."

"They don't notice?"

"Naow—not pike don't. I knew a chap one time, in Elvington it was, used to use brass picture-wire, fishing for pike. And he got plenty. Tain't like as if it was roach." He paused, stooped under the fuselage and fingered a little rent in the belly fabric; then he straightened up again. "You should do all right this afternoon," he said. "They like the sunny days."

He glanced up at the pilot. "Will we be doing a flight test to-morrow?"

"If the riggers are through."

"They should be through with all that lot this afternoon. Them patches can have a second lick of dope first thing in the morning."

"I'll be out here at half-past nine," the pilot said. "We'll try and get the flight test off before dinner."

The sergeant said: "Okay. I'll tell the boys."

Marshall picked up his bicycle and rode off slowly down the runway in the direction of the mess. The air was very still and fresh, the sky pale blue, the distance hazy. He passed the Wimpey with the damaged starboard wing. There were men about it now; as he rode slowly past, Pat Johnson, the pilot, walked in front of it.

Marshall, riding at a walking pace in the warm sun, said conversationally: "You've made a bloody mess of that."

The other grinned. "Got to have a new wing."

"What about a noggin?"

"Right. I'll be along in a minute."

Marshall parked his bicycle and went up to his bedroom. The batwoman had done the room and made his bed; he laid out all his fishing gear upon the counterpane and looked it over. Rod, reel, plugs, traces, fishing-bag—all were there, ready to be taken in a moment after lunch. He stood a little, fingering them; then went down to the ante-room.

Johnson was there; he pressed the bell and ordered a couple of pints of beer. Few of the pilots drank anything but beer, partly from inclination and partly from economy. Marshall said: "Have any trouble getting her down?"

The other shook his head. "She came in all right. She was all right once I put the flaps down. But she was a swine to handle all the way home. One flap was out and wouldn't go back. We had to fly her all the way, in half-hour spells. Then when we put the flaps down to land, she was all right."

The beer came, two tankards on a tray borne by a white-coated W.A.A.F. "I looks towards you," said Johnson.

"I catches your eye," said Marshall.

"What are you doing to-day?"

"Going fishing."

"Bet you don't catch anything."

"No takers."

They had been together at Hartley aerodrome for nearly a year. At one time both had been novices of golf; they had laboured together round the Hartley course counting it a superior achievement to hole out in less than eight. Marshall had tired of it and turned to fishing; Pat Johnson had gone forward to a handicap of fifteen in the local tournament. In the evenings they had formed the habit of finding amusement together; they were friends. They were much the same age, and from very much the same social class. Marshall had worked for a year before the war in an insurance office in Holborn; Pat Johnson had been apprenticed to an estate agent in Croydon. Both had developed into seasoned and reliable pilots of large aircraft.

Johnson said: "Coming down to the 'Black Horse' after dinner? Take you on at shove-halfpenny."

"If it's not raining."

"It won't rain to-night."

The "Black Horse" was one of the two pubs in Hartley Magna, tacitly dedicated to the air crews; other ranks went to the "Swan." The "Black Horse" was rather more than a mere country pub; in peace-time it had been something of a road-house, with a snack-bar that still sold sandwiches. It was the only social centre within walking distance of the aerodrome; for the wider life it was necessary to catch the occasional bus for Oxford, fourteen miles away, or jump a ride if there was transport going to the city.

The pilots went and had their lunch together. A masterful, grey-haired woman of about forty-five, Flight Officer Stevens, came and sat by Marshall. "Morning," she said.

16

"I've got a bone to pick with you."

Marshall knew what was coming; he had had this one with the Officer-in-charge-W.A.A.F. before. "Really?" he said innocently. "What's that?"

"Your cup of tea. I cannot have the girls wasting their time bringing you up cups of tea in the middle of the morning. They've got their work to do, and that's not it. If you want elevenses you must come down and get it."

Marshall said: "It was only a little cup . . ."

"It was the biggest we've got on the station. She put two spoonfuls of sugar in, too, which isn't allowed, and she'd have given you a third if I hadn't caught her. Next time I'll put her on a charge."

"I wouldn't do that."

"I will. You see if I don't."

Marshall dropped the subject, uncertain if the officer was aware that he had got his cup of tea or not. Instead, he said: "If I catch a fish this afternoon can I have it for lunch to-morrow?"

Pat Johnson said: "That's what they call an academic question."

Mrs. Stevens said: "If it's one tiddley little roach, you can't. If it's a fish that will feed several people, or a lot of fish, you can."

"What do you call a lot of fish?"

"Three or four pounds."

"That's hitched his wagon to a star all right," said Mr. Johnson.

They went on with the meal in silence. The grey-haired Flight Officer felt out of things beside these inconsequential young men. They had no right to make her feel . . . old, but they did. She could no longer put herself alongside twenty-year-old youth. That afternoon while they were at their games, or flying, she would be writing to her husband in the Western Desert, somewhere near Benghazi. She wrote every other day. The war had brought him two promotions, so that he was now Air Commodore Stevens, and that was splendid; but it had broken up their home. They had had a little house at Chisle-hurst which had been convenient when he was at the Air Ministry. Three years before, they had put the furniture in store, and shut the door, and left that little house. He had gone to Egypt, she had gone into the W.A.A.F.s, the two children had been sent to boarding-school. The furniture, all that they

17

had, was burnt in the London blitz; when the war ended they would have to start all over again. In the meantime she must live with young men and young women twenty years her junior, lonely and out of it. She knew they took her for a dragon. She did not want to be a dragon, which was why she had allowed the girl Beatrice to take Marshall the cup of tea. But she could never get alongside them; she knew now that she never would. She was too old.

Marshall got away from her as soon as he decently could, and drank a quick cup of coffee in the ante-room. Then he went up to his bedroom; in five minutes he was on his bicycle riding out of the camp.

Coldstone Mill was a tall, factory-like building set in the countryside upon the River Fittel. A lane crossed the river on a stone bridge of two arches; a hundred yards below the bridge the mill stood by the weir, and below that again was the mill-pool. It was a broad, gravelly pool, scoured wide by the mill-stream and the weir, overhung by trees at the lower end. It stood in pasture fields, very sunny and bright.

The pilot left his bicycle at the mill and went down to the pool. For a time he walked slowly round the edge trying if he could see a fish; presently he sat down and began to assemble his rod. He fitted the little silvery reel and threaded the fine line, and chose the little trace with the single wire, as the rear-gunner had advised him. He spread out his collection of seven plugs upon the flat canvas of his bag and studied them thoughtfully. Finally he chose a desperate-looking parody of a small fish, more like a septic banana than a fish, and hooked it on the trace. Then, standing up, he began to cast over the pool.

He spent the next ten minutes clearing over-runs upon his reel. He was not a very skilled performer.

He fished for the next hour, supremely happy. The rhythm of the cast, the antics of the plug, delighted him; the warm sunlight, and the very fact of handling a well-designed instrument, made him content. The rush of water from the weir made a murmur that drowned the sound of the many aircraft that were in the sky, except when they passed closely overhead; the water slipping past over the green weed and the gravelly shallows was a thing remote from any of his duties.

He paused after an hour or so, and sat down on the ground, and lit a pipe. He took off the septic banana and fitted in its place a peculiar whirligig designed to represent a lame mouse taking swimming exercise, alleged to be very attractive to a

pike. He was still sitting smoking when he turned to a step behind him.

It was Gunnar Franck, carrying his roach-pole and his little stool, on his way down to the quieter reaches of the river. "Phillips, he say you have come here," he said. "Goes well?"

"Very well," said the pilot. "Marvellous afternoon, isn't it?" He lifted the little steel rod. "Have a crack with this."

The Dane took the rod doubtfully, made an ineffective cast, and produced a tangle of line massed and jamming the reel. He handed the rod back to Marshall. "I shall go catch a roach," he said. "When I come back, he will be disentangled, yes?"

The pilot began to unravel the line. "Just in time for you to muck it up again," he said. "Getcha!" He glanced up at the Dane. "None of those bits hit any of the tanks, did they? I was thinking of that just now. I ought to have looked to see."

"I looked." Above their heads, in a bare elm tree, there was a sudden flap and clatter, and a pigeon flew off. They raised their heads to watch it. "I looked, but there was nothing. Only the bomb doors and the belly and the fabric underneath the tail. It is no damage, really."

Marshall said: "It was just as you said 'Bombs away.' Just after that, wasn't it? We were running-up too long."

"One minute only. Sixty-five seconds. I had the stop-watch running," said Gunnar.

"We'll have to get it shorter. I'd hate to get shot up by the Eyeties. I should die of shame."

"Of shame?" The Dane wrinkled his forehead; there were still points of English manners that eluded him.

The pilot said: "Did you see that pigeon? This place is stiff with them. You haven't got a gun?"

Gunnar shook his head. "Sergeant Pilot Nutter, he has a rifle. A little gun, his own. Two-two."

"Bring it out with you next time you come and let's see if we can't get one or two. They're bloody good eating, pigeons."

"O—oh, yes. Pigeons is ver' good eating. In my country we eat many pigeons."

"Well, see if you can lay your hands on that gun, and let's have a crack at them."

"The farmer—it will be all right?"

"I'll see the people at the mill and see if they mind. They ought not to. I'll race around the mess and see if I can borrow a shot-gun. It's a good thing to shoot pigeons. They eat the crops. It says so in the paper."

"Perhaps the farmer does not read the paper."

"Get that rifle, anyway." The pilot wound the last of the line back smoothly on to the reel. He raised the little rod above and behind his head and flicked his arm; the plug went sailing out into the stream smoothly and with no effort.

"Nice," said Gunnar. He stooped to the bag and picked out a reddish, translucent plug bait. "I think this one will be the best." He pointed to the shallows and the backwater between beds of reeds. "There is the best place for a pike."

The pilot said: "Too weedy and too shallow." He paused. "Do you think we could get the run-up a bit shorter?"

"I will try."

Marshall reeled the plug in to his feet and drew it dripping from the water. "I'll try telling you the evasive action that I'm going to take, down the intercom. Each move, so that you know what's coming. And you can tell me which way to bias it. We'll have to waltz into position before levelling off."

"It will be ver' difficult," said Gunnar doubtfully.

"We'll have a stab at it to-morrow on the flight test."

"Okay." The Dane picked up his rod. "Now I will catch a roach for tea."

Marshall called after him: "Don't forget about that rifle."

Gunnar raised his hand, and the pilot stood watching him for a moment as he went away down-stream between the trees in the dappled sunshine. He was a damn good chap, Marshall thought. That matter of the tanks—Gunnar never missed a thing. He'd probably get his roach all right.

Marshall turned back to the pool and began casting.

A quarter of an hour later he rested again, thoughtful. There might be something in what Gunnar said; pike liked sunny spots and sometimes came into quite shallow water. He did not think he could cast in among those reeds without catching his plug and losing it eventually; still, if it wouldn't catch a fish what good was it to him? He cast the lame mouse up the backwater into a shallow swim between green beds of weed and drew it fluttering towards him. Was it his fancy, or was there something following behind the bait?

He cast to the same place a second and a third time, without result. Then he changed to the reddish plug that Gunnar had advised, and made an experimental cast or two out into the rough water of the pool. Having got his length he cast again to the same place, the gravelly, weedy shallow, and began reeling in.

In the backwater there was a sudden splashing gulp upon
the surface. The line tightened and the little rod bent suddenly; he gripped it with both hands and heard the reel scream as
the line went out. He knew at once that it was a bigger fish than
he had ever hooked before; indeed, he had only caught two
pike in his life, both very small. In the backwater there was a
thrashing turmoil in the weeds with quick jerks on the line. He
grasped the handle of the reel and got in line. The fish dashed
from him up the backwater taking out line as he went; the pilot
reeled him in again. Then, in the manner of a pike, the fight
went out of him, and Marshall drew him through the swift
water of the stream without a kick. He woke up when he saw
the pilot and made a short run; then he was finished and came
up to the surface as Marshall pulled him in. The great snapping mouth, cream-coloured underneath, was open, the red
plug hooked firm in the lower jaw.

The young man breathed: "God, he's a bloody monster."

He had neither gaff nor landing-net nor priest. He had too
much sense to touch the fish; he towed it with the rod, limp
and supine in the water, to a little beach and pulled it up the
sandy mud, wriggling and snapping the great jaws. Then with
a stone he hit it gingerly upon the head, divided in his anxieties
to kill it before it could escape, to kill it without injuring the
look of it, and to avoid being bitten. Presently it lay still, and
he pulled it up on to the grass.

He was excited and exultant; it seemed to him to be a most
enormous fish. As soon as he dared put his hand near it
he measured it with his thumb, which he knew to be an inch
and a quarter from knuckle to tip; it was thirty-three inches
long.

His heart was fluttering with excitement. Mechanically he
began to take down his rod and pack up his gear; he would
fish no more that afternoon. Anything after this magnificent
experience would be an anti-climax; there was a time to stop
and rest upon achievement, and this was it. Gingerly and
timorously he poked a bit of string through the gills and made
a loop. He slung his bag over his shoulder, and with the fish
in one hand and his rod in the other went to find Gunnar.

A wet fish thirty-three inches long suspended by a bit of thin
string is not a convenient burden if you want to keep its tail
from dragging on the ground. Carrying it with his arm
crooked Marshall found the muscular exertion quite considerable and it spread its slime all down his battle-dress

trousers; carrying it over his shoulder upon the butt end of the rod was easier, and it spread its slime all down the back of his blouse. In the open air, and while the slime was fresh, this did not seem to matter very much; it became important to him later in the day.

Gunnar saw him coming in the distance and stood up from his little stool, and came to meet him. "That is ver' good," he said genially. "It is a ver' good fish, that one."

Marshall said: "Thirty-three inches."

"So?" The Dane felt the weight of it. "With which plug?"

"The red one—and over in the shallows."

Gunnar nodded. "He pull ver' hard?"

Marshall said: "He gave up pretty soon." He paused. "Have you done any good?"

"Two." The sergeant pilot opened his bag and showed two quarter-pound roach lying upon a bed of grass.

"Coming back to the camp?"

Gunnar shook his head. "They are feeding well; I shall stay here." He grinned. "I think that they have heard the news; so they come out to feed."

Marshall glanced down at his fish. "I bet this one's eaten a few roach in his time."

He left Gunnar and walked up the bank towards his bicycle, carrying his awkward burden. He speculated as he went how much it weighed; his estimates showed a tendency to rise as he went on, so that the buoyancy of his spirits offset the fatigue of his arm. He reached the mill at last and spread the fish, now stiffening, across his bicycle basket and tied it insecurely there with string. Then he rode back to the camp.

The guard at the gate grinned broadly as he rode into the camp with a very large fish drooping at his handle-bars, and took occasion to salute him very formally. Marshall returned the salute and rode on to the mess past laughing groups of air-craftmen and W.A.A.F.s; nobody in the camp would ever say again that he could not catch fish. He parked the bike and, carrying the fish, went through into the kitchen and induced the W.A.A.F. cook to put it on the scales. It weighed eleven and a quarter pounds.

"My!" she said. "That is a nice bit of fish now, isn't it?" Her words were like music to him. "Will you have it stuffed, Mr. Marshall, like we did the other?"

He agreed, and she gave him a dish for it and arranged it stretched out at full length, and he carried it through into the dining-room and put it on the table for display. Then he went through to the ante-room to see whom he could find to show it to.

It was half-past five. There were half a dozen officers sitting reading in arm-chairs, and two W.A.A.F. officers looking at the illustrated papers. Marshall looked around for Pat Johnson to confound him, but Pat was not there, nor Lines, nor Humphries. Davy would have to do. Davy was reading about Lemmy Caution and his gorgeous dames, and detached his mind with an effort as Marshall said:

"I caught a bloody fine fish this afternoon. Come and have a look at it."

"Where is it ?"

"In the dining-room."

"See it some other time, old boy." The dame had brunette chestnut hair that fell down on a bare shoulder, and slim bare ankles thrust into white mules, and grey eyes, and curves in all the right places, a small black automatic pistol that pointed straight at Mr. Caution's heart. It was asking too much to leave that for a dead fish.

Slightly damped, Marshall looked around. None of the old sweats of the Wing, the men that he had known for many months, happened to be in. There were only new arrivals that he did not know so well, officers who had been drafted to the station in the last month to replace casualties. There was a Canadian that he had hardly spoken to since he arrived a week before, just getting to his feet. Marshall said: "Like to come and see my fish ?"

"What kind of fish ?"

"Pike. Eleven and a quarter pounds."

"I guess that's pretty big, isn't it ?"

"Not bad."

"Pike. Is that the same as a muskie—what we call a muskellunge in Canada ?"

"I think it is. Come and have a look—it's in the dining-room."

The other said: "I'm real sorry, but I've got a date. I'm late for it already. Say, you want to come to Canada one day. I'll take you where you can get a muskie, thirty pounds, any day of the week. Gee, I wish I was back there!" He waved his hand. "Be seeing you."

The glamour was fading fast. Outside the light was going; the sun was setting behind trees in a clear sky. A W.A.A.F.

mess waitress came in and put on the lights and began to draw the black-out. Marshall lit a cigarette and looked around.

He saw Pilot Officer Forbes sitting pretending to read the *Illustrated London News* and staring at the coal-scuttle. Pilot Officer Forbes had been sitting and pretending to read things for three days now, since Stuttgart. They all knew what was wrong with him; it was Bobbie Fraser. But what could anybody do?

Marshall hesitated, and then crossed over to him. "I caught a bloody nice fish to-day," he said gently. All the conceit had gone out of his voice. "Like to come and have a look at it? It's in the dining-room."

Forbes said without moving: 'I don't think so."

Marshall said in a low tone: "Come on, old boy. Snap out of it."

Forbes raised his head. "If you don't muck off and let me alone," he said, "I'll kick your bloody face in."

Marshall moved away towards the table with the periodicals upon it. Section Officer Robertson looked up from *Punch* as he passed her. He looked like a little boy, she thought, disappointed because nobody would play with him. It was too bad.

She got up from her chair. "I'll come and see your fish," she said, "if I may. Where did you say it was?"

CHAPTER TWO

Come, let us go, while we are in our prime,
And take the harmless folly of the time!
   We shall grow old apace, and die
   Before we know our liberty.
And, as a vapour or a drop of rain,
Once lost, can ne'er be found again,
   So when or you or I are made
   A fable, song, or fleeting shade,
   All love, all liking, all delight
   Lies drowned with us in endless night.
Then, while times serves, and we are but decaying,
Come, my Corinna, come, let's go a-Maying.
            ROBERT HERRICK, 1648

Marshall turned to her in pleased surprise. "Would you really like to see it ?"

"I don't mind," she said.

"Will you listen if I tell you how I caught it ?"

"Not for very long. But I'd quite to like to see it."

"Okay," he said. "I've got it in the dining-room."

It was the first time that he had spoken to Section Officer Robertson. She had been with the Wing for about a month, but the W.A.A.F. officers kept themselves very much to themselves. They used the ante-room and lunched with the officers, but they had their own sitting-room in their own quarters to relax in. In the mess and in the ante-room they were carefully correct, and brightly cheerful, and rather inhuman; when they wanted to read the *Picturegoer* or mend their underwear they went to their own place to do it. It was suggested to them when they took commissions that good W.A.A.F. officers did not contract personal relationships with young men on their own station. As candidates for commissions they were serious about their work and desperately keen about the honour of the Service, and so some of them didn't.

Marshall took the girl through into the deserted dining-room. The fish lay recumbent on its dish, its sombre colours dulled. Death had not improved it; it leered at them with sordid cruelty, and it was smelling rather strong.

Section Officer Robertson said brightly: "I say, what a lovely one! How much does it weigh ?"

25

"Eleven and a quarter pounds."

"Did you have an awful job landing it?"

"Not bad. I had it on a wire trace; I was spinning for it."

"In this river here?"

He nodded. "Up at Coldstone Mill."

"Oh, I know that," she said. "A great tall building in the fields."

"That's the place," he said. "I got it in the pool below the mill."

"It must have been lovely out there this afternoon," she said. "It's been such a heavenly day."

Recollection came to him suddenly: the black-haired girl in the grey jersey. "I saw a lot of W.A.A.F.s this morning out in the field doing physical jerks," he said. "I saw them from my window as I was getting up. Was that you drilling them?"

She nodded. "I took them out because it was so lovely. Were you just getting up then?"

He said indignantly: "I didn't get to bed till three!"

She laughed. "Sorry." She turned back to the fish.

"It really is a beauty." That, after all, was what she had come to say.

She had overdone it. Marshall looked at it with clearer eyes. "I don't know that I quite agree," he said. "I think it looks ugly as sin, and it's starting to ponk a bit. Be better with a lemon in its mouth."

She laughed again, relaxed. "Well—yes. We'd better open a window if you're going to leave it here. What are you going to do with it?"

"Have it for lunch to-morrow. Mollie, in the kitchen, said she'd stuff it for me. Would you like a bit?"

"I'd love it. I've never eaten pike."

"All right—I'll tell them." He hesitated. "I say, what's your name? Who shall I say, to give it to?"

"Robertson," she said. "I do signals."

"Mine's Marshall," he said.

She raised her eyebrows. "Oh, I know—R for Robert."

"That's right," he said. "R for Robert."

She turned away. "I've got to go now. You must have had an awful lot of fun this afternoon."

"Well, yes," he said. "I did."

She looked up at him quickly, about to say something; then she checked herself. She turned towards the door. "I've got to go now," she said politely. "Thank you ever so much

26

for showing it to me."

"Not a bit," said Marshall. "I'll tell you when I catch the next one and you can come and see that."

She laughed self-consciously, and went.

Marshall went back into the ante-room, lit a cigarette, picked up a copy of *The Aeroplane*, and sank down into a chair before the fire. He was pleasantly tired, and utterly content. He had had a lovely day in the sunshine in the middle of the winter, he had caught the biggest fish he had ever caught in his life and landed it without a net or gaff, and a young woman that he had never spoken to before had been nice to him. She had black hair that she wore in coils above her ears; she had a very clear complexion with slight colour, and a nose that turned up a bit. Section Officer Robertson. He wondered what her Christian name was.

He opened *The Aeroplane*, and there was a full description of the new Messerschmidt 210, with a double-page skeleton drawing. He was still poring over it twenty minutes later when Pat Johnson came in and looked over his shoulder.

"Bloody interesting, that," said Mr. Johnson. "See the barbettes?"

Marshall looked up. "Do any good?" He restrained himself from blurting out his own news.

"Ninety-three." Bogey was seventy-two. "I fluffed the twelfth and lost a ball, and then I couldn't do a thing."

"Marvellous afternoon."

"And how. You do any good?"

"I caught the biggest fish in the river."

"Better not let Ma Stevens see it, if you want to get it cooked."

Marshall threw down his paper. "You don't know who you're talking to. When I catch fish, I catch fish."

Flight Lieutenant Johnson looked at him doubtfully. "No, really—did you get one?"

Marshall heaved himself up from his chair. "Come and see."

He led the way through into the dining-room and snapped on the lights. "God!" said Mr. Johnson. "What an awful-looking thing."

"What d'you mean? That's a bloody fine fish. It's eleven and a quarter pounds."

"Maybe. It looks like something out of the main sewer."

Marshall glanced at the clock; it was five minutes past six.

"I was going to buy you a noggin," he said, with dignity. "Now I shall buy myself two."

Johnson said: "Has anybody else seen it?"

"Only one of the Section Officers."

"Which one?"

"The new one, with black hair."

"The one that runs the signallers?"

"That's the one."

"She came and had a look at it?"

"That's right. I said she could have a bit of it for lunch to-morrow."

"You did?" Mr. Johnson considered for a minute. The dead fish leered at them from the plate. "You offered her a bit of that?"

"I did. And what's more, old boy, she said she'd like to have it."

Johnson looked at the fish again. "Must be in love with you."

Section Officer Robertson walked down the road to the small house that was the W.A.A.F. officers' quarters. She went into the little sitting-room. Mrs. Stevens was at the writing-table, finishing a letter. The Section Officer said: "I've just seen the most enormous fish."

The Flight Officer said: "Fish? What fish—where?"

"It was a pike—about *that* long." She measured with her hands. "One of the pilots had it on a dish in the dining-room."

"Peter Marshall? A Flight Lieutenant? He was going fishing this afternoon."

The girl nodded. "That's the one." So his name was Peter. "He said he was going to have it for lunch to-morrow."

"Oh, he did, did he? Well, I did say that he could if he caught a big fish that would feed several people."

"It'll do that all right," said Miss Robertson. "Probably make us all sick."

The older woman turned back to the table to address her letter; the girl took her novel from the mantelpiece and sat down to read for an hour before supper. She lit a cigarette, opened the book where the turned wrapper marked the place, and began to read. The book failed to hold her. She sat there smoking by the fire, turning a page from time to time, reading without taking in the meaning of the words.

She disliked being at Hartley. She had held a commission for about a year after a period in the ranks; that year had been spent at a training station in the north of England. She was a north country girl from Thirsk in Yorkshire, country-bred among the moors and streams of the North Riding. She did not like it when she was transferred to Bomber Command and sent down to the south, to Oxfordshire, far from her home. She liked it less when she had been at Hartley for a week. In two raids during that week the Wing lost four machines. She was on duty for one of those raids. She attended at the briefing of the crews, handing the C.O. lists of frequencies and D.F. stations and identification signals for him to read out to them. She was on duty all the night. From midnight onwards she was in and out of the control office till dawn, trying to locate the missing two machines. When she walked back to her quarters in the grey morning it was with the knowledge that two young officers that she had messed with would not return. She was tired and cold and numb as she walked through the station to her quarters; in her bed she wept for a long while in her fatigue and misery before sleep claimed her. Next day she was pale-faced, and very quiet.

In Training Command the casualties had been very few; here they happened necessarily again and again. They did not permanently depress her because she was young; they were, rather, recurrent bouts of a sharp misery that she associated inevitably with Oxfordshire and Hartley aerodrome. Moreover, she had come alone to Hartley; for the first week or two she knew nobody and made no friends. She longed for the cheerful atmosphere of her last station, instead of the grey unhappiness of this operational place.

She sat looking, unseeing, at her book. It had been amazing to hear that young man admit that he had enjoyed his day. And what was more, he obviously had. She had been about to take him up, and ask how anyone could have fun in such an awful hole as Hartley, but she had checked herself. One didn't say that sort of thing.

Peter Marshall. He looked as if he enjoyed doing things. He said he had been spinning for the pike. After Turin in the black night he must have had a very happy day, and, queerly, she was happy that he had.

She stirred herself to fix attention on her book, and presently she was reading it in earnest.

Marshall and Johnson dined together in the mess, and afterwards walked down with Humphries to the "Black Horse". It was a fine, windy, starry night and rather cold; they walked quickly through the black lanes, arching a tracery of fine bare branches overhead. In the dark night from time to time they heard the noise of aircraft in the distance; they speculated upon whether an operation was in progress and, if so, who was doing it. They talked shop and only shop all the way down to the "Horse".

In the saloon-bar there were lights and cheerful talk, and shove-halfpenny, and a table of bar billiards ticking away the sixpences. The room was full of smoke and noise. Most of the men were air crews from the station; there were one or two W.A.A.F.s with them sitting in corners rather diffidently in so masculine a place, and one or two civilians from the district. After an hour or so Marshall found himself telling one of these civilians about his pike.

"Eleven pounds?" the man said. He was a delicate-looking chap about thirty years of age, dressed in a golf coat and grey trousers. "That's a good weight. Not many pike that weight in the Fittel." His words were like music to the pilot. "A chap at Uffington got one last year that weighed fifteen and a half pounds—that's the biggest that there's been in recent years."

"Have a beer," said Marshall. And when he had provided it, he said: "You've lived here a long time, I suppose?"

The other laughed. "Eighteen months," he said. "I come from London. I'm in the motor trade—Great Portland Street. Now I'm in tractors. I run the service depot up the road. Now and again I flog a second-hand Morris, but it's mostly tractors."

Marshall said: "A bit quiet after London?"

"God, no. I love it down here."

"I should have thought it would have bored you stiff."

The man said: "Well, you might think so. But—what I mean is, up in London you arse around and go to the local and meet the boys and perhaps take in a flick, and then when you go to bed you find you've spent a quid and wonder where in hell it went and what you got for it. Down here there's always something to do."

"What sort of thing?"

"Well—shooting, for example. I know most of the farmers because I keep the tractors turning over for them, don't you see? And any time I want to take a gun and shoot a rabbit or a pigeon, they like to have me do it round the farm, see? And it's all in the day's work, because you see the tractor at the same time and have a chat with the driver and show him

30

how to change the oil in the back axle, and then you go on and take a pot at a hare or anything that's going, see? I got a hare last Thursday—no, Friday."

The pilot said: "Do you know the people out at Coldstone Mill?"

"Up the river—where you caught the pike? It's on Jack Barton's land. I don't know the people in the mill, but I know Jack Barton."

"Would he let me have a go at the pigeons in the trees below the mill?"

"Sure he would. I sold him an eight-horse-power Ford last June."

"If you know him, would you like to ask him for me? Or give me a chit to him?"

The man said: "Give me twopence for the call, and I'll give him a tinkle in the morning."

"That's awfully good of you."

"What's your name?"

"Marshall. What's yours?"

"Ellison. If I don't see you to-morrow night, I'll leave word with Nellie there, behind the bar."

They lit cigarettes. Eillison exhaled a long grey cloud. "There's always something to do here. We had a fox shoot last month, all through the woods. They can't keep them down, now that the hunt's packed up."

"Are there many foxes here?"

"The woods are stiff with them." The tractor salesman leaned forward impressively. "I tell you, I could guarantee to take you and show you a fox and a badger both within a quarter of an hour."

The pilot, fifty miles from London, stared at him incredulously. "You couldn't!"

"I could." Neither of them was drunk or anywhere near it, but their inhibitions were relaxed by beer. "I'd take you and show you a fox and a badger both within a quarter of an hour."

"Where?"

"Never you mind."

"But wild?"

"Sure—out in the woods. A wild fox and a wild badger, both within a quarter of an hour."

"Bet you couldn't."

"Bet you ten bob I could. What about it?"

"It's a bet. What do we have to do?"

"Let's get this straight," said Mr. Ellison. "If I show you a wild fox and a wild badger both within a quarter of an hour, you give me ten bob. And if I don't, I give you ten bob."

"That's right," said Marshall. "What do we do?"

"Christ," said Mr. Ellison, "the missus won't half tear me to bits. We meet in Hartley market-place, by the cross, at four o'clock in the morning."

"Christmas!" said the pilot. "All right. But it's pitch dark till seven."

"That's right—that's what we want. Come on your bike. If either doesn't turn up, he loses the ten bob."

They discussed the detail of their plan and drank another beer or two; then it was closing time, and the "Black Horse" vomited its occupants out into the dim, moonlit street. Marshall walked back to the station with his companions and went up to bed. Lying in bed before sleep, he thought that he had had a splendid day. He had got up in the middle of the morning, and it had been fine and bright and sunny. He had gone fishing with his new rod. He had caught one of the biggest fish in the river and landed it without either net or gaff. He had showed it to a girl, quite a pretty girl, and she had been nice to him about it. He was well on the way to a day's pigeon-shooting, and he had contracted to be shown a wild fox and a wild badger both within a quarter of an hour. A splendid day.

Quite a pretty girl. He wondered how he could find out her Christian name without calling attention to his curiosity.

He slept.

He was out next morning at dispersal soon after nine. Gunnar was there already, preparing to start up; the ground crew were plugging-in the battery. Marshall walked up and inspected the fabric patches on the fuselage, still red with dope. His rear-gunner joined him.

"Come up nice and tight, haven't they?" he said. "It's the dry weather does it."

Marshall straightened up. "They want a lick of paint now. We don't want to go around like that." He liked things to be neat and tidy and good-looking, like that Section Officer.

Sergeant Phillips said: "I'll get hold of some paint and give them a lick this afternoon, after we come in."

His captain said: "Hear about my pike?"

The sergeant grinned: "Aye. The young lady I took out last night, she saw you riding into camp with it. How much did it weigh?"

"Eleven and a quarter pounds."

"My young lady, she was just coming off duty in the signals office. She said they didn't half have a good laugh to see you riding with it on your handle-bars."

"They'd laugh louder if you did that with a roach," said the pilot.

Sergeant Pilot Franck came up to them. "I have been thinking about what you say yesterday," he said. "It is I that should tell you how to weave. Right weave . . . Left weave . . . So. If every time you weave exactly in the same way, then we run up for ver' short time."

"All right if I could weave the same each time. I think you'll find I go thirty degrees one way and fifty the other."

"If you were German," said the Dane severely, "you would always weave the same."

"If I was a German," said the pilot equably, "I'd be flying a Heinkel and kicking your bloody arse because you didn't say 'Heil Hitler' before you spoke. All right, let's have a crack at it that way, and see how it goes." He turned round to the crew of four, gathered around him in their flying kit. "We're going to practise a few run-ups this morning, taking the gasometer at Princes Risborough as the target. Eight thousand feet." He turned to the wireless operator, a pale lad from Stockton-on-Tees. "Leech, you can do the navigation, and Phillips, you can help him if he gets it wrong." He did all he could to ensure that everybody understood the wireless and the navigation and the guns.

They took off presently, and went climbing away into the distance. It was nearly two hours later when they landed back again, taxied in, and wheeled round into wind at the dispersal point with a grinding squeal of brakes. In turn the engines died and came to rest.

Marshall stood up beside Gunnar, who had landed the machine, with Sergeant Phillips' notebook in his hand. "Take out runs three and seven, when you weren't on," he said. "The rest go fifty-two seconds, fifty-four, forty-four, forty-four, forty-one, forty-five, thirty-nine, forty-two, thirty-nine. It's not bad."

They discussed their practice for a few minutes, standing crouched and cramped beside the pilot's seat. Then they got out of the machine down on to the concrete beneath the nose, slipped off their harness, and stretched cramped limbs. The corporal fitter went into a huddle with Sergeant Pilot Franck

33

over the engine temperatures and pressures. Marshall turned
to the fuselage and had another look at the patches. Sergeant
Phillips walked up and joined him.

"Nice and tight," the sergeant said. "I'll get a drop of paint
this afternoon."

The pilot nodded. "When you spoke of your young lady,
that saw me with that fish—did you say she was a signaller?"

"Telephonist," the other said. "Works on the board all
day."

"Does she come under that Section Officer Robertson?"

"That's right. A new Section Officer with black hair."

Marshall said carefully: "I knew a Flying Officer called
Robertson at my last station, who had a sister called Sheila
who was a W.A.A.F. Section Officer. I was wondering if this
was her. Ask your young lady if she knows her Christian name,
will you?" He spoke with elaborate carelessness that did not
deceive the sergeant for one moment.

Phillips said: "Oh aye, I'll find that out for you."

The pilot said: "Thanks. It was just an idea I had." He
left the machine and, carrying his parachute and harness,
walked down to the control office.

Half an hour later he was in the mess with a pint of beer.
The ante-room gradually filled before lunch. The Wing Commander came in, and Marshall crossed the room to him, beer
can in hand.

"May I go off the station at four o'clock to-morrow morning, sir?" he said. "I'll be back before breakfast."

"What for?"

Marshall grinned. "I met a chap in the 'Black Horse' last
night who said he'd take me to see a fox. A fox and a badger,
both within a quarter of an hour. I've got a bet on that he
can't."

The Squadron Leader (Admin.), a grey-haired man called
Chesterton with wings from the last war, laughed sharply.
"Lady into fox?" he said.

The pilot flushed a little. "No, sir. Honest-to-god fox—
beast what smells." There was general laughter in the group.

The C.O. said: "Smell him when he comes back, Chesterton; let me know if it's fox or Coty."

The laugh grew loud. Section Officer Robertson turned to
see what it was all about. She saw Marshall talking to the Wing
Commander in the centre of a laughing group. She thought
that it was something to do with the pike, the pike that she was

to have a bit of for her lunch. She drew near, smiling at their mirth without understanding it, wanting to know what was going on.

The C.O. said: "A badger and a fox? Where are you going for that?"

"I don't know—somewhere in the woods. It's got to be before dawn. I said I'd meet him in Hartley at four o'clock—if that's all right with you, sir."

The Squadron Leader said: "I don't believe there are any badgers here. Plenty of foxes. But it's too close to London for a badger."

The C.O. said: "It's all right with me. Better go to bed early, or else get in some sleep to-morrow. We may be on the job to-morrow night."

"Thank you, sir."

Chesterton said: "I'll have the guard warned that you'll be going out."

The pilot turned away, and found himself face to face with Miss Robertson. She said: "Did you say you were going to see a *badger*?" There was a quality of breathless interest in her voice.

Marshall grinned. "I don't know," he said. "Chap in the 'Black Horse' said he'd show me a badger and a fox both within a quarter of an hour, and I bet him ten bob that he couldn't."

"They don't come out in daylight, do they? Badgers, I mean."

"I don't think so. I think they stooge around all night."

"Where are you going for it?"

The pilot glanced down at her face turned up to his. In one fleeting moment in the crowded ante-room he saw the colour in her cheeks, her parted lips, her eyes bright and sparkling. He withdrew his glance quickly, because of the crowd about them. He had not known before that she was beautiful.

"I don't know," he said casually. "Somewhere in the woods."

"Oh." She thought for a minute. "Will there be a moon?"

Marshall said: "Yes, if it's a fine night. The moon rises about two o'clock."

She said: "I think it will be fine. Three-tenths cloud or something. We got the message in this morning."

There was a little pause; slowly the animation died out of her face. "It'll be awfully interesting," she said. Queerly, it

35

seemed to Marshall that she was disappointed about something, or depressed. Perhaps her boy friend was giving her the run around. If that were so, it was a shame; she was a nice kid.

"I didn't forget about that bit of pike," he said kindly. "I told them in the kitchen, and I told them to give Ma Stevens a bit, too."

She said: "You're sure you can spare it ?"

He said: "Lady, I eats hearty, but not eleven and a quarter pounds."

She laughed. "I suppose not."

He moved away from her, though he would rather have stayed talking to her and have taken her in to lunch, in the hope of seeing her look again as she had looked when he was telling her about the badger. He had lived in a mess too long to risk being seen to talk much with one W.A.A.F. officer. In a society predominantly masculine with just a few young women, gossip ran rife; Marshall had caused embarrassment to too many young men from time to time to risk himself as target. He went in to lunch with Pat Johnson, choosing strategically a seat that gave him a view of Section Officer Robertson eating pike, twenty feet away.

He was relieved to notice that she ate it all, in happy distinction to Mr. Johnson, who took one mouthful, put it out again, said a rude word, and went and fetched himself a plate of beef.

Marshall watched Section Officer Robertson covertly all through the meal, timing the progress of his lunch to synchronise with hers while talking to Humphries about accelerated take-offs. He followed her out into the ante-room for coffee. He asked her how she had liked the pike.

"I liked it," she replied. "It's different to most other fish."

"So Pat thought," he said. "He told the maid to give it to the cat, if the cat would have it."

"What a shame!"

"I'll go out this afternoon and try and get another," Marshall said.

She turned to him. "Mr. Marshall, do let me know what happens about your badger. You must be awfully well in with the country people here, to get a chance like that."

He shook his head. "This chap sells motors in Great Portland Street."

She wrinkled up her forehead in perplexity. "Sells motors ? But you have to know the country frightfully well to find a badger."

36

"I know that." He paused. "Anyway, it should be rather fun."

It was the second time that he had spoken to her about fun at Hartley aerodrome. She dropped her eyes. "Tell me about it when you come back," she said quietly.

"Okay," he said. "I'll give you all the lowdown on the sordid side of country life, lunch time to-morrow."

She took her coffee and the *Daily Express*, and crossed the room to a chair. Presently she got up, and went out to the signals office, and sat down at her bare deal table garnished with messages and signal forms in bulldog clips.

She was deeply disappointed. She was a country girl from the North Riding; her father was an auctioneer in Thirsk. Her uncle was rector of Thistleton, a little village in the hills near Helmsley; she knew country matters very well. She had a considerable knowledge of foxes; she had followed the hunt on various farm ponies, and she had crept out several times into the woods to stalk a vixen playing with her cubs before the earth; for one of these expeditions she had a blurred Brownie photograph to show. In all her experience of the country she had never seen a badger. This expedition in the moonlight night before the dawn was in her line exactly; she ached to be going out with Marshall in the morning. The very suggestion had been like a breath of fresh air to her, a reminder of a sane, decent, country world that she had left behind her in the north.

That was not possible, of course. A good W.A.A.F. officer, mindful of the honour of the Service, did not get out of bed at four o'clock in the morning to go roaming in the moonlit woods with an officer from her station. She spent an appreciable portion of her time endeavouring to restrain her aircraft-women from that sort of thing, though it was true that none of them had ever thought to plead that they had a date with a badger.

She stared disconsolately at the signal pad before her. The fault, she felt, in some way lay within herself. Hartley was a rotten station to be in, but there was fun to be got there, good country fun, if you knew your way about and had the wit to find it. Peter Marshall seemed to have a lovely time; the pike yesterday, and now this "fox and badger in a quarter of an hour" business. All she had managed so far was to go for rides upon her bicycle and, since the country was flat and she came from the hills, she didn't think much of that.

It was a very quiet afternoon, with little flying in progress and nothing in particular happening. She took a little walk around her duties; passing the main telephone switchboard she looked in to see how L.A.W. Smeed was getting on. L.A.W. Smeed was sitting with headphones on her hair and microphone upon her chest eating her black-market sweets and knitting a jumper for her next leave. She slipped the knitting down beside her chair when her officer appeared in the doorway.

"Afternoon, Elsie," said Miss Robertson. "Let's see your book."

The girl handed her the log-book, written in pencil between ruled pencil columns; there were not many calls upon it. "Not very busy," said Miss Robertson.

"No, ma'am. Real slack it's been to-day."

They chatted for a few minutes about the work. Then L.A.W. Smeed said: "Mind if I ask a question, ma'am?"

"What is it?" said Miss Robertson. She knew what it was likely to be: something to do with late leave, an attempt to short-circuit Flight Officer Stevens.

Elsie said: "Your name's a funny one, isn't it, Miss Robertson? Some of the girls were having an argument."

The Section Officer said: "Gervase. It's not a very common one."

"Gervase. I never knew anyone called that before. I think it's ever so nice. What's the other one, Miss Robertson—the L?"

"Laura. There are plenty of those about."

"I know ever so many Lauras," said the telephonist, "but I never met a Gervase before. I do think that's pretty. Are there many girls called Gervase where you come from?"

"I don't think so. I don't think it's a Yorkshire name particularly."

"Is that where your home is, Miss Robertson? I live in Clapham, just by Clapham South Underground."

The officer said: "I come from a little place called Thirsk, in Yorkshire. But I don't think Gervase is a Yorkshire name at all. Mother got it out of a book—Tennyson, or something."

The telephone buzzed, and put an end to further confidences. Miss Robertson went on with her round.

Out in the country, by the river below Coldstone Mill, Marshall was assembling his little rod. He worked more absently than on the previous day, his mind equally divided between fishing and Section Officer Robertson. He wondered if the red plug would do the trick again or whether he should use a narrow-bodied thing that simulated a little alcoholic fish, unable to swim very well. He wondered if Section Officer Robertson really had a boy friend who was doing her dirt. It was quite possible that she had got mixed up with somebody at her last station; indeed, it would be rather queer if she had not, being as attractive as she was. Anyway, she was going to get mixed up with somebody on this one; he knew that very well already.

He wondered whether it was any good casting to the same place in the millpool for another pike, and he wondered very much what her name was. He had already discovered her initials from the file of postings to the station. He wondered how old she was; he was twenty-two himself and he was pretty sure that she was younger than that. If he could find out how long she had been a Section Officer, that might give him a line. But he could ask her that.

He began casting in a desultory way over the running water, but soon gave it up, and sat down on a stone and lit his pipe. Over his head the pigeons flapped and fluttered in and out of the trees, small clouds sailed slowly past on a blue sky, and once an early bee flew past his ear. Presently he got up and, smoking still, began to walk down the river, rod in hand. It was no good flogging the same place two days running, he thought.

He passed a couple of aircraftmen fishing where Gunnar had been on the previous day, and went on towards a pool at the next weir. Just above the pool he came on Sergeant Phillips sitting on a little stool, his float between the weed beds in mid-stream. The pilot paused beside him.

"Done any good?" he asked.

The sergeant shook his head. "Don't seem to be nowt stirring. I reckon Gunnar must ha' caught them all yesterday."

"How many did he get?"

"Four."

The pilot glanced back up the river. "I told Gunnar to see if he could borrow Sergeant Pilot Nutter's little rifle, and we'd have a crack at those pigeons up by the mill."

"Aye, he was talking about that. He's got the gun."

"We'll have a crack at them one day."

The sergeant nodded. "Make a change to get a pigeon for tea."

Marshall left him, and went on to the weir. He cast for an

hour above it and below but rose nothing; either there were no pike there or it was an off day when they would not feed. Presently he walked slowly back up-stream towards the mill, casting here and there as he went. At the mill he took down his rod, got on his bicycle, and rode back to the station.

He had packed up early with a vague hope that if he got back to the mess by half-past four he might, quite accidentally, see Section Officer Robertson drinking a cup of tea. He did not find her there; either she was having tea in her office or else in her own quarters. He lingered for some little time until hope died; then he went up to his room to write his weekly letter to his mother.

He got out his pad, squared his shoulders at the deal table at the end of his bed, and began to write. He never knew what to say. His mother, he knew, lived each day in an agony of fear for him, a gnawing pain that she had suffered and concealed for nearly two years now. He could not write to her about the difficult raids, the ones that had not been so good, and he had long ago exhausted all that could be said about the uneventful ones. He wrote:

My darling mother,
We had a lovely flight the night before last, over to Turin and back. The moon got up as we were getting to the Alps and it was frightfully pretty with snow on the mountains and lakes and everything. They don't have any black-out there and you could see the street lamps in the towns, and cars going along the road and everything. We went up to seventeen thousand and it was frightfully cold, but it was dry and there wasn't any icing. I wore your leather waistcoat under everything else, and it was fine.

He paused, and then he wrote:

I've seen Switzerland three times now and I'd love to go there one day for a holiday, ski-ing and skating. I don't think I want to go to Italy much.

He paused again; there really wasn't much else to say about flying. He went on presently:

I caught a pike yesterday on one of the plugs, in the river here; eleven and a quarter pounds, it was awful fun. I

40

brought it back and a lot of us had it for lunch to-day, stuffed.

Dare he say that Section Officer Robertson had liked it ? Better not. He went on:

> The biggest one caught for years was only fifteen pounds, so mine was a pretty good show. I got it on the new rod with the multiplying reel; it's fine to use. A chap I met says he can show me a fox and a badger both in a quarter of an hour and we're going out to try it to-morrow very early, about four. Next week I hope we shall be able to go pigeon-shooting.

He drifted into reverie. G.L. . . . Gertrude Lucy? He took up his fountain-pen again and wrote:

> I like being on this station more and more; there are some awfully nice people here. Has Bill got his second pip yet? All my love to Daddy and to you, darling.
>
> PETER.

It exactly filled the double page, which was his statutory length. He read it through and put it in the envelope, and took it downstairs to the post.

He rang up Ellison and confirmed their meeting in the morning; then he retired into the ante-room with a can of beer. He was called to the telephone five minutes before dinner.

"Marshall speaking," he said. "Who's that?"

"Sergeant Phillips here, sir. I don't think that Section Officer can be the one you meant. What did you say her name was? The one that was the sister of the chap you knew?"

Damn it, what had he said? Cynthia? Sylvia? What on earth was it?

"Sylvia," he said. "It was just a thought I had, that it might be the same. What's this one called?"

"You said the name was Sheila this morning, Cap. I suppose he had two sisters in the W.A.A.F.s. But it's not the same family at all."

Marshall said very slowly and emphatically: "What—is—this—one—called?"

"Gervase, Cap. Uncommon sort of name." He spelled it

out. "Gervase Laura. Did your friends live in Thirsk?"

Marshall said: "No, they lived near—er—Reading."

"Cant' be the same, Cap. This one comes from Thirsk in the North Riding."

"Oh well—thanks."

"Okay."

Marshall put down the receiver, conscious that he had had his leg pulled by the sergeant. Still he had got the information that he wanted.

He went to bed early that night, having thoughtfully secured a packet of sandwiches from the kitchen. He ate these as he was dressing in the middle of the night. At ten minutes to four he was riding out of the station on his bicycle, yawning and rather cold, and wondering if it was really worth it.

He met Mr. Ellison, a dim shadow with a bicycle, in Hartley market as they had arranged. "Couple of bloody fools, we are," said Mr. Ellison. "This isn't worth ten bob of anybody's money. Let's get going."

"How far?"

"Seven or eight miles. Kingslake Woods, over by Chipping Hinton."

They rode off down the main road leading north. The sky was practically clear; a half-moon was rising, making it light enough to see the detail of the countryside. They rode on steadily for nearly an hour, growing warm with the exertion. In the end Ellison slowed down.

"Steady a moment," he said. "There's a gate just here somewhere."

They found the gate and left their bicycles inside it, and went on up a muddy track that wound slowly uphill through the woods. The leafless branches made a fine tracery over their heads, screening the white clouds drifting past the moon. There was little wind; the woods were very quiet. From time to time a rabbit shot away before them; once an owl swooped low over their heads with a great whirr of wings.

Ellison led on steadily for a quarter of an hour or more. Once Marshall asked: "How in hell do you know where to go?"

The motor salesman said: "I came here last month, that time when we were shooting foxes. Then old Jim Bullen brought me here again to see a badger, because I told him that I'd never seen one." He paused, and then he said: "They're a bit scarce where I come from, around Great Portland Street."

The pilot nodded. "There aren't so many down in Holborn, where I used to work."

In the end they paused on the edge of a clearing, full of dappled moonlit shadows. Ellison whispered: "This is the place—keep damn quiet now. If we have any luck we'll see the badger here." He pointed across the clearing to a little earthy cliff. "There's an earth there. . . . See ? And there's another one about a hundred yards along. . . . There."

Marshall strained his eyes, but could see nothing but the dappled moonlight. The wind was blowing to them from the earth; it was as good a place to watch as any. "Take your word for it," he whispered. "How long shall we have to wait ?"

Ellison said: "It must be close on six. We'll give it an hour before we call it off."

"We'll be bloody cold by then."

They settled down upon a log to wait and watch, motionless. The silvery radiance that filled the clearing, ebbing and flowing with the passing clouds, was nothing novel to Marshall; he knew moonlight very well. For many hours he had sat patterned in black and white within the moonlit cockpit, uneasy and vigilant for night fighters; home to him was the appearance of a moonlit landfall seen through gaps of cloud, faint, silvery, ethereal cliffs and fields. He had seen so much moon in the last fifteen months that he had absorbed a little of its serenity, perhaps. At the beginning of his career as a bombing pilot he had been confused and distressed and bewildered by the casualties, by the deaths of friends that he had known and played with in their leisure hours. The casualties had less effect upon him now; they were things that happened, that must be accepted as they came. One day he would probably go too; the thought did not distress him very much. Life in the R.A.F. was real, and exciting, and great fun —better by far than the life he had known in his insurance office before the war. Everything had to end some time. It was undesirable to be killed, but it was also undesirable to go creeping back into the office when the war was over.

In the quiet glamour of the night his mind was full of Section Officer Robertson. Gervase, Gervase Laura Robertson. Thinking of her, he discovered his own mind. She was attractive, and neat, and pretty as a picture; she was a friendly girl and, he thought, rather an unhappy one. He wished very much that he knew what it was that worried her, whether it was some prune that she had left at her last station. He liked her very much indeed; he knew himself already to be half in love with her. Quite suddenly he realised that much of the fun of this attempt to see a badger and a fox within a quarter of an hour would be in telling her about it.

A stave out of the theme song of a picture came into his mind and set him smiling at his own foolishness—

> Moonlight becomes you, it goes with your hair—
> You certainly know the right things to wear . . .

He could not remember any more words, but the tune stayed with him, and Fred Astaire. For him the moonlit glade was filled with music as he sat there waiting for the badger. Gervase, he thought, was pretty enough in uniform, but in civilian clothes—say in a cotton summer frock—she must look wonderful.

Forty minutes passed, and his only knowledge of the drift of time lay in his chilling feet and legs. Then Ellison pressed him very gently on the arm, and pointed stealthily to the far hedge.

The pilot followed his direction. It was a true bill; some animal was there. It trotted along the hedge, seen dimly in the variable light; then it came out into the glade making towards the earth. It was greyish-black in colour with a long black-and-white face that it carried close down to the ground. It went purposefully and fairly fast, pausing for an instant now and then to snuffle at some delicacy of the woods, then going on.

Near the entrance to the earth it paused and froze, warned by some sixth sense. Ellison stood up, clumsy with the cold, making a slight noise of clothes and crushing leaves and twigs. "Badger," he said. "See it ?"

There was a quick scramble on the far side of the glade, and it was gone. Marshall stood up stiffly. "I'll give you that one," he agreed. "Damn good show." Then, remembering their bet, he peered down at his wrist-watch in the dim white light. "Six twenty-three," he said. "Now—fox before six thirty-eight."

Ellison said: "It don't seem so long now as it did back in the pub." He turned, and led the way back down the track towards the road.

In a few minutes they branched off, and came to a piece of open pasture, rough and uncared for. There was a streak of grey light over towards the east, but it was still moonlight.

44

Ellison paused. "Over in the corner there's an earth," he whispered. "Old rabbit burrow."

They waited for nearly half an hour, but nothing happened. By then the grey light was spreading over the whole sky; they gave it up, and started down the track towards their bicycles. "Bloody swindle," said the motor salesman. "I made sure that I'd be able to produce the fox."

The pilot said: "Maybe you shot him the other day."

"That might be."

And as he spoke, a big dog fox crossed the track a hundred yards ahead of them. In the half-light they saw it loping steadily away between the trees, red, furry, and with a bushy tail held level with the ground. Both said: "Fox!" at the same moment, and stood watching it till it was out of sight.

"Well, there you are," said Ellison. "Bit late, but what's the odds?"

"None of that," said the pilot. He looked at his watch; it was two minutes past seven. "You took thirty-nine minutes, not a quarter of an hour. Tell you what. Buy you a drink at the 'Black Horse' to-night."

"Okay."

They recovered their bicycles and rode back to Hartley with the light wind behind them in fifty minutes. Marshall left Ellison at the road junction and turned off for the camp, arriving back in the mess in comfortable time for breakfast. He was lighting his pipe and reading the comic strip in his paper when the Tannoy sounded metallically above his head. All ranks were to remain within the camp till further notice. All crews of serviceable aircraft were to muster at their machines at 10.00.

Marshall passed by Pat Johnson on his way up to his room. Mr. Johnson said: "Did you go out this morning?"

Marshall nodded. "Saw the badger, and the fox, but not in a quarter of an hour."

"Was it cold?"

"Awful."

"Must be crackers," said Mr. Johnson. "As if we don't get enough of running round in the dark."

"Where's it to be? Have you heard?"

The other shrugged his shoulders. "I don't know and I can't say that I care. It'll look just the same as all the others when we get there, laddie."

The morning passed in a routine of checking the aircraft, its engines, guns, instruments, and equipment. Then they got into it and took it off for a quarter of an hour's final test. When they taxied back to their dispersal point the Bowser was waiting to tank up the Wellington and the armourers were waiting, sitting on their little train of bombs. Bombing up began as the tank lorry drew away. When they dispersed for lunch there was only the de-icing paste to be put on, and the perspex to be polished for the night.

Marshall went into the ante-room for his beer before lunch. The Adjutant came up to him sniffing pointedly and loudly. Marshall said: "Fox and badger, sir. Not a particle of Coty, more's the pity."

"Did you see them ?"

He had to tell the story of the night, much aware of Section Officer Robertson listening from across the room. He did not speak to her before lunch, but contrived to take his coffee from the urn immediately after her.

She said: "You saw them both, a badger and a fox ?"

He nodded, smiling. "Not within the quarter of an hour. But we did see both—the badger first and then the fox."

"Where did you go ?"

"Place called Kingslake Woods—somewhere near Chipping Hinton. I'd never been there before."

The name meant nothing to her. "Was it very wild country —in the woods ?"

"Not specially. They were lovely woods."

There was a short pause. Then she said: "You must be tired, aren't you ?"

He grinned. "Sleep a bit this afternoon."

"I shall, too," she said. "I'm on to-night."

"Are you ?" A thought came to him, sly and subtle and altogether bad. "Could you let me have the frequencies and D.F. stations ? I like to get those in my mind before the briefing."

She had been operational for too short a time to know the idiosyncrasies of all the pilots. She said: "Of course. If you'd like to walk over to the office I'll give them to you now."

They left the mess together and went over to Headquarters, to her little bare office with the ink-stained deal table, the two hard chairs, the bulldog clips and the buff papers. She read out to him the information that he wanted; he wrote it all down carefully in his notebook, asked a question or two, and slipped the book back in his pocket.

"Thanks awfully," he said. He paused, and then said rather shyly: "It was lovely in the woods this morning. Perishing cold, but it was awful fun."

She said: "It must have been. Did you have to wait very long?"

"A fair time." He launched into a description of the expedition. For ten minutes they talked badger and fox. "Foxes often make their homes in old rabbit-burrows," she said presently. "I think most of them do that. But I don't know about badgers. Did this one have an earth of his own?"

"I don't know," said Marshall. "We didn't go to it. We were chasing off after the fox, because of the time."

The girl said: "I've never seen a badger, or even a badger's earth."

Elaborately casual, Marshall said: "I can show you this earth any time you like. Show you the badger, too, if you like to put your hand in and pull him out."

They laughed together. "Would you like to do that one afternoon?" he said. "You've got a bike, haven't you?"

She hesitated for a moment. "I'd love to see it," she said. "If I met you out there, would you show it me?"

His heart warmed to her for her discretion. "Sure," he said. "It'll take you about an hour to get there on your bike. What about half-past three to-morrow afternoon?"

She was suddenly frightened at his confidence. Between then and half-past three to-morrow afternoon there lay an operation, a thing of darkness and of terror, of bombs and fire and flares and flak and death. Beyond that, he was making an assignment to go walking in the woods with her.

"All right," she said. "Half-past three to-morrow." That wouldn't bring bad luck, would it?

He said: "That's a date. Have you got a map?"

She had a map, a map on which in lonely absorption she had traced in red the solitary cycle rides that she had made around Hartley Magna. He studied it for a minute or two and then drew a little pencil circle at an intersection of two lanes. "There," he said. "Half-past three to-morrow."

She smiled up at him. "I'll be there."

He went back to the mess and she went over to her quarters and up to her room. She undressed partially and lay down on her bed, pulling a blanket over her. Life for her had suddenly become very full of incident. First there was the operation immediately ahead. She took her work very seriously. She had

47

been bored with the work of training at her last station; she had wanted to be more closely in contact with the war. Now that she was at an operational station the war terrified her. From time to time when the machines were coming back from the target she had to bear quite heavy responsibilities in the fleeting moment. There had been a terrible occasion ten days previously when a crippled aircraft running short of petrol over the North Sea had appealed for a W/T fix, and when she gave it had complained, in a thin whisper of Morse, that their transmission had been weak and undecipherable. For a desperate half-hour she had laboured with a flight sergeant and two wireless mechanics to check the station transmission and to get in touch again with C for Charlie, while a stream of signals from the other aircraft were passing in and out. There had been nothing wrong with the transmission. The fault must have been some damage to the receiving set in the aircraft, but they were never to know that. That last whisper of Morse haunted her, making her more vigilant and serious about her work than ever.

Beyond the problems and the perils of the night there lay this matter of the badger's earth, and Flight Lieutenant Marshall. At her last station she had been out from time to time with young officers, had been kissed once or twice at dances, and had taken it all with an air of detachment that showed her lack of interest. None of them had ever touched the Achilles heel, her interest in country matters. To her this little expedition to see the badger's earth was like the opening of a door. It was a return to the sane, pleasurable matters that she had abandoned as a schoolgirl, when she had first joined the W.A.A.F.s. For the last couple of days she had been well aware that the things she liked to do were to be found at Hartley and that a young man called Peter Marshall was doing them. Now she was to join him in them, for an afternoon at any rate. For her that made an enormous difference to the Hartley scene.

She lay for some time wakeful, thoughtful and feeling herself to be much occupied, very much involved. Presently she dozed a little. She was called at half-past four and went down for a cup of tea before the briefing.

Marshall also lay upon his bed, reviewing the many calls upon his time. He was consciously and absurdly happy; this week, he felt, had been a splendid week. First there had been the big pike; he still got a thrill from the memory of the first

48

snatching take, and the scream of his reel in the first rush. It must, he thought, be rather like catching a salmon, only in the case of the salmon it went on for half an hour or so. It was always in his mind that one day he might be transferred back to Coastal to fly Liberators over the Atlantic; if that should ever come off he would try to get to a station in the West of Scotland or the Hebrides, where he could have a crack at salmon. Then there was the badger and fox business, which had been wizard.

To-morrow afternoon there would be this expedition to the badger's earth; he looked forward immensely to that. Everyone else upon the station seemed to think him crackers except his own crew, who had similar interests, and possibly the Wing Commander, and now Gervase Robertson.

This operation, he thought, was a bloody nuisance. Certainly it was his job and one had to do a spot of work sometimes. Still, but for that he might have been walking through the woods with Gervase at that moment, showing her things, talking to her, and watching her smile. She would have come with him that very afternoon; he was sure about that, but for the raid. Still, it was something to look forward to, to think about till to-morrow. He wondered anxiously about the weather, would it keep fine for them? He was not concerned that afternoon about low cloud in the night, or ground mists, or icing; it was only important to him that the sun should shine in Kingslake Woods at three-thirty the next day.

And, after that, there was the chance of pigeon-shooting, and he simply must contrive an afternoon to have another go at the pike before the season for coarse fish ended in a week or so, and there might possibly be other afternoons with Gervase Robertson which would take precedence over everything.

He lay for a while revolving his many occupations pleasantly in his mind, and presently he slept, to be awakened in time for his high tea before the briefing.

Section Officer Robertson was on duty that night in the control office. She had taken over from her predecessor, and she was now in charge of radio and telephone communications at Hartley, working closely under the control of a flight lieutenant at Group Headquarters, Charwick. Three stations formed the Group: Charwick, Wittington, and Hartley Magna. There was a Group W/T station at Pilsey, a hamlet three miles from Hartley; this was manned for operations by the signals officers from the three stations working in rotation.

In the control building on the aerodrome a radio and tele-phone room opened out of the control office; this housed the R/T sets and the more secret equipment, and a small tele-phone switchboard. Four girls were normally on duty in this room upon an operations night, with Section Officer Robert-son in charge of them, unless she was on duty at the Group W/T station, when Section Officer Ford took the control. The work was not very difficult. It mainly consisted of taking signals as they came in and marking up a very large black-board, showing the position of each aircraft in the successive stages of its flight in order that the Wing Commander and the control officer could see the operational position at a glance.

That night the aircraft took off for Dortmund in succession between seven-thirty and eight-fifteen. Miss Robertson was busy with her chalk upon the blackboard while all that was going on; then there was a lull as the machines were winging outward to the target. At ten o'clock she gave the Squadron Leader who was serving as control officer a cup of tea and a piece of cake, and had a little meal herself, sitting at her desk in a corner of the control-room. At 10.35 the first "Mission completed" signal came through, and began another round of duty for her with her bit of chalk.

One by one she marked them up as the messages came through upon the telephone from the W/T station. D for Donald—that was Sanderson. L for London, Humphries. S for Sammy, Johnson. N for Nuts, Davy. R for Robert, Marshall.

She chalked up N for Nuts and R for Robert on the board. The bare office room seemed suddenly more cheerful; she looked through into the radio-room and asked the W.A.A.F. corporal for another cup of tea. From his desk the control officer glanced up at the board. "Davy and Marshall," he re-marked. "I wasn't losing any sleep for them."

She was curious, and vaguely resentful. "Why not, sir?" she enquired. "The risk's the same for all of them, isn't it?"

He said briefly: "Those two have been at this for years. They know all the answers."

He sat thoughtful for a moment, his eyes fixed on the black-board, studying the ciphers and figures written neat in the lined spaces. "Check back to Group," he said quietly, "and see if they've got anything from H for Harry."

H for Harry was Pilot Officer Forbes, the second aircraft to take off that night. A minute later Section Officer Robertson said: "Nothing yet from H for Harry, sir."

The control officer said absently: "Okay."

At one-fifteen the first aircraft, D for Donald, was heard making a wide circuit overhead, and the operation of landing the machines began. By two o'clock they were down and parked at the dispersal points, all except the one. Gervase Robertson stayed on with her sergeant and her corporal in the control-room till after four o'clock, combing by telephone the aerodromes and W/T stations throughout the country for some news of H for Harry. In the cold hour before the dawn she walked back grave and sleepy to her bed, unsuccessful.

CHAPTER THREE

Long ago to thee I gave
Body, soul, and all I have—
  Nothing in the world I keep:

All that in return I crave
Is that thou accept the slave:
Long ago to thee I gave
  Body, soul, and all I have.

Had I more to share or save,
I would give as give the brave,
  Stooping not to part the heap;
Long ago to thee I gave
Body, soul, and all I have—
  Nothing in the world I keep.

Translated into English by SIR HENRY NEWBOLT
from the French of Wenceslas,
Duke of Brabant and Luxembourg, 1384

Gervase Robertson woke up in the middle of the morning and got up shortly before lunch, feeling stale and jaded. She looked into the sitting-room of her quarters before going over to the mess. Flight Officer Stevens was writing at the desk. Gervase asked: "Has anything been heard of H for Harry yet? It was missing when I went to bed."

The older woman said: "It was shot down over the target. Several of the others reported it." She had found, from two years in the Command, that the harder and more matter-of-fact you were about these things, the easier it was.

The girl said: "Oh. . . . Did any of them get out?" Sometimes there were reports of crews who had been seen to bale out, and to drift down in the glow of flares and fire.

"I didn't hear of anything like that." The Flight Officer folded her letter and put it in an envelope. "There are two more officers coming in this afternoon. I've just been putting Pilot Officer Forbes' things together. We shall want that room."

Gervase winced a little. "It's pretty awful," she said quietly. "His best friend was killed at Stuttgart—only last Saturday."

"Bobbie Fraser. Forbes was very much upset about that—

53

there was a diary." The middle-aged Flight Officer lit a cigarette and flipped the match away. "It's not uncommon, that," she said in her hard voice, "when two boys are great friends. First one goes, and then the other."

There was nothing to be gained by discussing it any further, nor did either of them want to do so. Gervase went over to the ante-room. Peter Marshall was there looking as fresh as a daisy; when he saw Gervase he came over to her, beer-mug in hand.

"I say," he said cheerfully, "have you seen Ma Stevens ? She gave my batwoman the hell of a raspberry this morning, just because she went to get a cup of tea for me. I'm going to have an up-and-downer with her about it."

Gervase said: "I wouldn't do that to-day, if I were you. It's not one of her best days."

"Why not ?"

She could not enter into that with one of the pilots. She said: "She's a bit off colour this morning. Leave it till to-morrow if you want a fight with her."

"All right," he grumbled. "But I take a pretty dim view of it. I sent the girl down; if she's got anything to say about it she can say it to me."

"Did she put her on a charge ?"

"No," the pilot said. "She made her cry instead."

"Silly little fool," said Miss Robertson unsympathetically.

Marshall glanced at her. "Okay for this afternoon ?"

She nodded. "I've been looking forward to it."

He moved away from her, fearing to call attention if he stayed talking with her for very long. He began a chat with the Equipment Officer about sea-markers that did not mark, a subject cheered beyond all reason by her last words.

They met that afternoon at the intersection of the lanes by Kingslake Woods that he had marked down on her map. The girl was out there first; the weather was kind to them, and she sat for ten minutes on a stile in sunlight waiting for Marshall. He arrived presently, apologising for lateness.

Gervase said: "You aren't late. It's only just half-past three now. I was early."

Marshall said: "How long did it take you to get here ?"

"About three-quarters of an hour." She paused. "It's a lovely ride."

He said: "I don't think three-quarters of an hour on a bike could be a lovely ride, but have it your own way. We've

54

got about half a mile to go."

They went on together down the road. Presently they got off at the gate, put the machines inside, and went forward up the track between the trees.

Gervase asked: "Is this the way you came?"

He nodded. "It looked all different then, but this is the place. It was dark, of course—moonlight."

She glanced around her at the bare trees and the low undergrowth. "It must have been sort of eerie," she said.

Marshall said: "It was damn cold."

The girl laughed: "I forgot. I suppose being in the woods at night doesn't mean anything to you."

He said: "Well, I usually try and keep above the tree-tops, matter of fact. The boys don't care for driving through the woods at night."

She said: "But you do get accustomed to the darkness, don't you? I mean, more than I should be?"

Marshall said: "Yes, I think one does. I don't think I find the black-out so difficult as I used to."

"Have you been flying bombers very long?"

"Fifteen months," he said. "I was with Coastal before that."

"All the time at Hartley?" she enquired.

"Well—yes. I did my thirty operations here and then I was grounded for three months and sent to Stamford, and then I came back here again. I've done all my bomber flying from here."

Gervase glanced at him. "How many raids have you done?"

"In all? Fifty-one, if you count four I did as second pilot when I came from Coastal."

He turned to her. "You came from Training Command, didn't you?"

She nodded. "I was at Hornby for a year after I got my commission. Then they sent me down here."

"Do you like it?"

She said: "I thought at first it was the foulest hole I'd ever seen, but I'm getting to like it a bit better now."

He was surprised. "But why?" he said. "I think Hartley's a good station."

She was not sufficiently accustomed to him to be able to shed reticence. She could not tell him yet that the grim anxiety of operations, and the casualties, had made her loathe the place. She said vaguely: "I don't know. Some places

55

you like, and some you don't."

"I know," he agreed. "But I like Hartley Magna. There's always something to do here, not like Northolt or one of those places. I think they're deadly."

She was with him in that. "Were you brought up in the country? I mean, how did you get to find out about the things you do?"

He said: "I'm not country-bred. My home is in Northwood, a sort of suburb place north-west of London, about forty miles from here. I worked in Holborn, in an office, for a bit. No, my rear-gunner taught me how to fish, and Gunnar got keen on it, too. He's my navigator."

She thought of the fifty-one raids that he had made. "You must have an awfully good crew," she said.

He nodded. "I'm frightfully lucky. Gunnar and Phillips were with me in my first turn, and then when I came back here after the three months I managed to get them with me again. We've been together for the thick end of a year."

"What are they like?" she asked. She was wondering what sort of supermen these were, who took a Wellington on raids all over Europe in the dark night fifty-one times without mishap, and apparently thought nothing of it. The risks were real enough; she had to look no further than Forbes and Bobbie Fraser to see that. What sort of supermen manned R for Robert?

He said: "Gunnar's a Dane; he was a medical student in Copenhagen when the Germans walked in. Phillips worked on a machine in Terry's chocolate works in York. They're grand chaps to be with."

He began to tell her all about them as they walked up through the woods towards the badger's earth. She listened, a little bewildered. There was no explanation to the point that puzzled her about the incidence of casualties. These were ordinary young men, competent and likable perhaps, but not outstanding figures. Was it just luck that kept the flak away from R for Robert?

He studied her furtively as they walked. She had a firm chin, he decided, beneath a kind mouth; she had rather large, intelligent eyes. Such station gossip as he had been able discreetly to collect led him to believe that she was a good officer, cool in emergency and well liked by her girls. It would be a disaster if she got a transfer to another station.

"Is your job interesting?" he asked. "What do you do,

apart from the control office?" He knew about her supervision of the R/T; it had been in his mind intriguingly as he was coming in to land soon after half-past one.

She told him what she did. "It's interesting enough," she said at last "A bit too much so sometimes."

He glanced down at her. "What does that mean?" he asked.

She wanted to confide in him. She walked on for a pace or two in silence. Then she said without looking at him: "It's awful sometimes. Do you remember about C for Charlie?"

He wrinkled his forehead. "You mean that chap Sawyer? The time we went to Kiel?"

She nodded. "He asked for a fix," she said. "And when we gave it, he couldn't make it out and said our transmission was all wrong. That was all we ever got from him."

He said: "I remember. But there wasn't anything in that, was there? I mean, the station was all right. We got a bearing from you that night, I think."

Gervase said: "Our strength was quite all right. But he thought it wasn't, and we tried and tried to get it up and make it stronger for him." She hesitated, and then said: "It was beastly."

Peter Marshall looked down at her, and said kindly: "Did that worry you a lot?"

She glanced up at him. "Yes, it did," she said. "I suppose one gets accustomed to that sort of thing in time. I've been in Training Command, and I'm new to it."

He was immensely sorry for her. "Look," he said. "Sawyer went in just ahead of me, and I saw him going away after he dumped his load, and he seemed to be quite all right. Sawyer may have been hit, of course, or else the navigator. But, anyway, he went hundreds of miles away off course."

She said: "That's true. He was right over by the mouth of the Skagerrak."

"That's what I heard." He looked down at her, smiling. "It's just plain crackers to go worrying over that."

She forced a laugh, colouring a little. "I suppose it is. But it's difficult not to."

He said: "I used to worry about things a bit. But then I took up golf and found what worry really meant. It got me down, so I gave it up and took up fishing."

She laughed. "Counter-irritant!"

He grinned down at her. "That's it. You find yourself a nice new worry and stop bothering about fixes that are all right, anyway."

She walked on for a pace or two in silence. "When I was in Training Command," she said, "I wanted to be on an operational station, so as to be doing a bit more for the war. I never thought how anxious it would be."

Marshall nodded. "When I joined the R.A.F. I thought it would be lovely, all flying about in sunshine and blue sky among the dear little fleecy clouds, like a lamb gambolling in the fields." She laughed. "Honestly, I did think of it like that."

"Like the posters in Wings for Victory Week."

He said: "Just like that. You aren't the only mutt round here, if that's any comfort to you."

They came out of the woods into a clearing. They had been walking up a gentle slope for some way, and now they found that they were on a piece of rising ground looking away towards the east. The clearance in the trees showed them the country over towards Princes Risborough and its range of hills, sunny and hazy.

"This is the place," said Marshall. "We waited just here, on this log."

The girl stood and looked out over the low, flat country. "It's lovely to be looking down on something, for a change." She glanced up at him. "I come from a hilly part of the world," she said. "I've been awfully bored with this flat country here."

"Where do you come from?" he enquired. He knew already, but he wanted her to tell him.

"We live at Thirsk, in Yorkshire," she said. "Just by the Clevedon Hills."

He wrinkled his forehead. "Helmsley way?"

She nodded. "That's not very far. Do you know that country?"

"Only by flying over it," he said. "It looks as if it would be interesting country on the ground."

She nodded. "I like it. But I suppose you always do like the place where you were brought up."

They turned to the badger's earth. It showed as a scrape and a hole beneath the root of an oak tree, at a place where the soil had broken away, making a little earthy cliff. There was a fairly strong smell of animal about. "Stinks like a badger," said Marshall complacently. "Now I know what that means."

She laughed. "It does, rather."

58

They stooped down together by the hole, one on each side. The sun shone on the dead leaves and the budding shrubs above them, on the pale blue of their uniforms, and glinted on their brass buttons. "Do you think he's in there?" she enquired. She looked up at him, merry and keen.

"Must be," he said. "An empty hole wouldn't ponk like this."

"Let's get a stick and poke about, and see if we can get him out."

They got up and went and found a chestnut branch and broke a long stick off it, and went back to the earth. Gervase took it and began rattling it about down the hole; once she thought that she touched something soft that backed away. They tried in turns to get the badger out, and presently they desisted and stood up, muddy and cheerful.

"He won't play," said Marshall. "Too bad."

"I do wish we could get him out," said Gervase. "I just want to see him."

"The only thing to do would be to come back with a pick and shovel."

"He'd dig away from you," she said. "I bet he can dig faster than you can."

"I'm not going to try," said Marshall. "If you really want to see a badger I'll take you to the Zoo."

She said: "I've never seen the Zoo."

He noted that for future reference and said: "Well, that's all I can show you here to-day. Would you like to walk on for a bit and see where this track goes to?"

She said: "Let's." So they started on over the hill, walking on the dead leaves between the trees, talking about the badgers and the foxes and all the little creatures of the woods. And presently she stopped. "Look—there's a primrose!"

He was mildly interested. "There's another one over there —and there's another."

"It's frightfully early for them."

"It's the second of March. Is that early?"

She laughed up at him. "Of course it is. You don't know anything. Let's see if we can get enough to take back."

She stooped down to the leaves and began to pick the occasional blossoms. He stooped down with her, strained and awkward where she was lissom. He was not really interested in primroses, but he thought that he had never seen a sweeter sight than Gervase picking them.

With some difficulty they found sufficient for a little bunch; they bound leaves round the posy with a bit of fine string from his pocket and went on through the woods. And presently he said: "I say, what was wrong this morning with Ma Stevens?"

Her face clouded; she thought quickly and carefully before replying. "It wasn't anything to do with you or your bat-woman," she replied. "It was just she was a bit upset."

He was no fool, and he had lived a long time on a station. "Forbes?" he enquired. "Does she take things hard?"

The girl said a little testily: "Of course she does. Nobody's at their best after a thing like that."

Marshall said: "I didn't know she got cut up about things. She always seems so tough."

"I think that's her way." She turned to him. "Do you think any of them got out?"

He shook his head. "I don't think so."

A dreadful curiosity made her enquire: "Did you see it happen?"

He nodded. "I was stooging around outside a bit before going in, and so was Davy. We both saw it. It was a direct hit; I don't think any of them got out." He did not expand upon the matter. He had long passed the nervous stage of wanting to tell people what it looked like, how the fire spread and the bits fell off as the machine went down. Being shot down was like getting cancer, a sad, painful business that you did not labour to describe.

She was still puzzled. "Was it just bad luck?"

He found some difficulty in answering her. "He was running up for a damn long time," he said, "and it was pretty hot. He was making sure of getting his bombs just exactly where he wanted them. Of course, it's always bad luck if the flak gets you."

She said doubtfully: "I suppose so."

He smiled down at her. "I always stooge around a bit outside and wait a quiet time to go in," he said. "I don't know that it makes any difference really, but the boys think it does. And we like to do a different sort of approach every time, just on principle. I don't think that makes any difference, either, but it's another thing. Sometimes if you sit outside a bit and have a damn good look for five minutes or so you get a hunch what's the best way to tackle it." He laughed. "I don't think we're really yellow—just cream. We generally put our load down on the target in the end."

They came to the top of the rise, and the track ran down before them through the woods. In front of them, through the bare trees, there was the glint of water. Marshall said: "I say, there's a lake or something."

Gervase nodded. "There is a lake here," she said. "I saw it on the map. There's a house somewhere near."

The pilot said: "I wonder if there's anything in it?"

They went on briskly to the water's edge. Across the lake, no more than a hundred yards in width, there was a mown lawn fringed with rhododendrons, and at the head of this there was a house, low, long, and covered in creeper. "That's Kingslake House," said Gervase. "I remember that. The drive runs from the other side of it back on to the road where we left the bikes."

Marshall said: "Nice place. Do you know who lives there?"

She shook her head. "I suppose the wood belongs to the house."

They turned to examine the lake. It was artificial and very shallow, created by a concrete and timber dam across a little stream that ran down through the trees. With one eye on the house they made their way towards the dam and the deep water by it, and walked out upon it, fascinated by the tinkle of running water at the overflow. Gervase looked out over the small sheet of water and smiled. "I suppose this is the King's Lake," she said. "He must have been a very little King."

The pilot grinned. "Because it's a very little lake?"

She nodded, laughing up at him. "Boy's size."

They walked on round it presently, being careful to keep out of sight of the house as much as possible. "I bet there are some fish in it," Marshall said thoughtfully. "It's been dammed up so as to hold them."

Gervase agreed with him. "I've seen places like it," she said. "You buy trout and put them in—stock it. Then you have a lot of fun getting them out again."

He was interested. "How much do trout cost?"

"About a shilling each, I think."

They came to the stream that ran in at the top end and stood looking at the water. "There's a fish!" said the pilot suddenly. He touched her on the arm and pointed. "By that bit of weed."

She saw a grey shadow moving slowly over the bottom. "That's a trout," she observed. "I said there'd be trout here."

"How do you know it's a trout?" the pilot asked.

She stared at him. "Well—it's a trout. Haven't you ever seen one?"

He shook his head. "I come from High Holborn, lady. I've only fished for roach and pike so far."

She said: "It looks grey now, but if it was to turn suddenly you'd see it was a sort of goldy colour underneath. It's got spots on it, too. They're much brighter when they're out of the water."

"How do you know all that?" he asked. "Have you fished for them?"

She said: "I go out with my uncle sometimes, when I'm staying up at Twistleton. He's the rector. He fishes up and down a little river between Twistleton and Helmsley."

"Fly fishing?" She nodded. "Have you ever done it?"

She said: "The line always catches up in trees and things with me. I never caught anything." She glanced around them. "It would be different here," she said. "There's plenty of room behind. I expect they arranged the trees like that on purpose."

He stared down at her with new admiration and respect. "I never fished with fly," he said. "I don't know how to."

She was still staring at the fish. "He's awfully sluggish," she said. "I suppose it's early in the season, and cold. Let's get a stick and tickle him up a bit."

They got a long stick and thrust it very quietly down into the water at the fish. Before they reached it it flicked round and shot off into deeper water.

The pilot said: "See it flash? Sort of bronze colour. Let's see if we can find another."

They walked all round the little lake, stick in hand. They saw one or two more fish, but well out of reach of their stick. Over their heads the light began to fade and a little chill wind of March blew through the leafless trees. Presently, regretfully, they left the lake and the long house beyond the lawn and walked back over the rise, down past the badger's earth towards their bicycles.

At the gate Gervase said awkwardly: "I think we'd better go back independently . . ."

The pilot nodded. "It'll be all over the station in ten minutes if we don't." He grinned at her.

She turned to him. "I have enjoyed this afternoon," she said. "It's been like old times at home. Thank you so much for letting me come."

62

Marshall said: "Thank you for coming." He hesitated for a moment, wondering how to put what he wanted to say. She stood waiting for him. "If I could find another badger, or something," he said, "would you like to do it again?"

The afternoon had shown her that he was simple and honest. He had promised to show her a badger's earth and he had shown her just that; he had not tried to kiss her or do any of those things. He had helped her to pick primroses.

She said: "I'd like to, some afternoon when you're not fishing."

She smiled at him, got on her bicycle, and rode off down the lane towards the station. She went very happily. The wind was behind her; the evening was fine and blue. For the first time since she arrived at Hartley Magna she felt a mitigation of the bleak ugliness of life upon the station; her world was no longer made up solely of defaulting airwomen, grey wooden huts, anxiety, and grief, and death. She had had an afternoon with a young man that she liked and respected; a carefree afternoon. She knew quite well that the young man was getting to be very much interested in her, and she liked that, too. There might be difficulties ahead, but she shut her mind to those.

She got back to her quarters in the last glimmer of daylight, parked her bicycle, and went indoors to the sitting-room. Section Officer Ford was there, a fair-haired girl who was second-in-command to Flight Officer Stevens. She said: "Two pilot officers and two sergeant pilots came in this afternoon from the Pool."

Gervase rang the bell and ordered herself a cup of tea. "What are the officers like?"

"One's a South African called Harkness. He calls you 'my dear' every time he speaks. The other's a boy called Drummond."

"Do you know who they'll be put with?"

Jane Ford said: "They'll get crews of their own before very long, now that they don't carry second pilots. They might be put with Davy or Marshall or Johnson for a trip or two."

Gervase said: "Marshall has a second pilot—a Dane."

"Only because he's a Dane and they don't feel like giving him a crew of his own. They've regraded him as navigator. You mean Gunnar Franck."

Peter Marshall got back to the ante-room about the same time and ordered a pint of beer. Pat Johnson was there. He said: "Been fishing?"

63

Marshall shook his head. "Rode out on the bike to look at a pond," he said. "I don't know that it's any good to me." He paused and then said: "Did you go round to-day?"

Mr. Johnson said: "I did a lovely fifth in four."

"What did you do the thirteenth in?" That was the hole with the stream.

"Eleven," said Mr. Johnson.

"You're coming on. Have a beer."

The beer came presently. Johnson said: "I've got to have a prune with me next trip."

"Have I?"

"Not that I know of. Lines has got the other one."

"What's yours called?"

"Drummond."

Pilot Officer Drummond came into the ante-room soon after that; Johnson called him over and introduced him to Marshall and Davy. Pilot Officer Drummond was young, about nineteen; he was small and dark-haired and pale-faced, with a keen, lively manner. "I say," he said to Johnson, "I found a razor in my room. What had I better do with it?"

Johnson said equably: "Give it to Flight Officer Stevens, officer in charge of W.A.A.F.s. She'll post it on."

They gave him a can of beer. "I'm awfully glad they sent me here," he said. "They were going to send me to Coastal, but I asked for Bomber Command, and they let me change." He had been for a few weeks at an operational training station.

Marshall said: "What's wrong with Coastal? You can have a damn good time at one of those places."

The boy said: "Spend all day out over the sea and see nothing but a lot of mouldy ships. No, thanks." If he had been honest he would have said that he wanted above everything to drop bombs on Germans, but he was not quite so young as that.

Presently he asked: "When's the next operation?"

"Give us a bloody chance," said Mr. Johnson. "We had one last night. If they take my advice they'll have the next one about three months from now."

"No, seriously. You've been doing one every three or four days, haven't you?"

Marshall said: "We have for the last fortnight, but we can't keep that up. All the machines are running out their time. We'll be laying off for a bit pretty soon."

"I hope we have another first," the boy said.

"Ruddy little fire-eater," said Davy. "Don't let Winco hear him, or he'll get us into trouble."

Presently they went and dined, and afterwards they walked down in the quiet of the moonlit night to the "Black Horse." Marshall met Mr. Ellison in the lounge bar. "Sorry about last night," he said. "We had to go out on a job. What's it to be?"

The tractor salesman said: "Pint, please. It said on the wireless to-night we raided Dortmund." He raised an eyebrow enquiringly.

The pilot nodded slightly. It was not to talk about Dortmund that he had come to the "Black Horse," but to forget it. He said: "Take you on at bar billiards. Loser buys a round."

"All right." They put in sixpence and began to play as the table started ticking. "I saw Jack Barton about those pigeons, by the way. He said, go right ahead, any time you like."

"Fine. You got a gun?"

Mr. Ellison said: "Sure."

"We've got a two-two rifle, and I think I can borrow a twelve-bore. What about to-morrow afternoon? A hundred and sixty-six."

The other marked it up. "All right."

"I'll have Gunnar Franck and Phillips with me. Nice work —pretty to watch."

"'Bout three o'clock? Two hundred and forty."

"Make it half-past two. It gets dark so early."

"Okay. If we have any luck we'll take a brace along to Jack after. Maybe he'll give us some tea."

"There'll be four of us."

"Ninety. I'll let him know we're going out to-morrow afternoon. Maybe he'll come and join us."

Marshall left at closing-time and walked back to the station and went to bed. He lay in bed for some time before sleep, deeply happy about Gervase Robertson. He felt that she was a kind, generous girl; she was physically very attractive, almost unbearably so at times. Moreover, she was interested in the things that he was interested in, and talked sense about them. He wondered very much what he could ask her to do next. He knew that her position as an officer upon the station must inevitably constrain their meetings; if she got talked about too much she might be transferred away. What they did must be done discreetly, and well away from the station.

He drifted off to sleep, his problem still unsolved, thinking about her smile, the poise of her head, the slim line of her figure.

He told Gunnar Franck and Phillips about the pigeon-shoot next morning. Sergeant Phillips said he could produce an air-rifle, guaranteed to kill a rat at fifty yards, and to give it a great fright at a hundred. He promised to bring that along. Marshall went back to the ante-room before lunch and asked the Wing Commander if he could borrow his gun.

The Wing Commander was a man about thirty years old called Dobbie; he came from Scotland and had been in the regular Air Force before the war. He said: "All right. Got any cartridges ?"

Cartridges at that stage of the war were in short supply. They argued for a little time about replacement; finally Marshall sealed the loan of ten cartridges with a pint of beer.

Dobbie asked: "What other guns have you got ?"

Marshall said: "The tractor chap's got a gun, and Sergeant Pilot Franck's got a two-two, and Sergeant Phillips an air-rifle. He wanted to bring along the turret, but I said I thought you wouldn't like that, sir."

"Where are you going to do this ?"

"Coldstone Mill. Up the river."

Section Officer Robertson was near them, listening; Marshall was very conscious of her. The Wing Commander said: "Darned if I don't come out to see the fun myself, if I can make it."

The pilot said carefully: "We'd love to see you, sir, if you bring another ten cartridges. Better bring the box, perhaps."

There was a laugh. Section Officer Robertson drew near. "Is this your pigeon-shoot ?" she said. "May I come too ?" It seemed to be developing into a public party, making it possible for her.

Marshall said: "Fine. I'll race around and see if I can get one or two more guns."

There was a Jeep upon the station, acquired mysteriously by Wing Commander Dobbie and retained by him for his personal use. Gervase rode out to Coldstone Mill in this with him; as they went he justified to her the expenditure of Service petrol by a dissertation on the weight of pigeons (food) that would require to be transported back to camp. They reached complete agreement that the use of motor transport for this purpose was not only justifiable, but wise and prudent.

They got to Coldstone Mill a little late, in time for the first fusillade, which they witnessed from the bridge. A cloud of pigeons shot out from the trees with a great clatter of wings, a blue-grey cloud of birds against a pale blue sky. The sharp crack of Flying Officer Davy's Service revolver was unmistakable. One pigeon came down with a solid thump, and two more fluttered down wounded.

"I hope nobody's brought out a Sten gun," said the Wing Commander. "I'd have to take notice of that."

They shot all afternoon under the direction of Jack Barton, moving about the farm from clump to clump. They finished up with sixteen pigeons and a cup of tea at the farm in the fading light of evening.

Gervase had shot a pigeon with Gunnar Franck's borrowed rifle. She went up to him at tea. "It was terribly nice of you to let me shoot," she said. "It has been fun."

The broad, red-faced young man went redder than ever. "You shoot ver' well," he said. "How did you learn?"

She said: "We live in the country. My father has a rook rifle, and I take a pot at things sometimes."

"Where I live," he said, with a touch of nostalgia, "my sister also shoots with bow and arrow."

"Archery?"

"*Jo*. She was in the Ladies' Championship for all Denmark, but she was beaten three turns before the last, the final contest. We were very sorry."

"She must be very good to have got so far. Where is she now?"

"In Denmark. I have not heard for seven months."

He began to tell her about his home and his sister and his mother. She listened to him quietly, letting him talk, helping him every now and then with a question. It was obviously a pleasure to him. In five minutes she learned much of his family history and a little of his loneliness.

"I like being in England ver' much," he said bravely. "I have now many English friends to go to for my leave, and Danish too. But I like being here the best."

A thought crossed her mind: this simple red-faced boy with the curly black hair was one of the supermen who went fifty-one times over Germany and Italy. "Which aircraft do you go in?" she enquired. She knew well enough, but she did not want to let him know that she had been out with his captain.

He beamed. "I am with Flight Lieutenant Marshall," he said. "R for Robert." He glanced around; the pilot was some

67

way off. "I am ver' happy to be with him. He is good pilot, good navigator, good captain, good altogether. We have been now together for eleven months."

The girl said: "That's marvellous."

He nodded. "Always he is ver' careful," he said. "And practise, practise, practise all the time. Each day we practise some new thing that we have learned from the last op. Sometimes it is on the firing teacher that we practise, sometimes the Link trainer, sometimes in the air. And so when we go out," he laughed, "sometimes it is quite dull!"

She nodded. Dimly she was beginning to appreciate the hard, slogging work that lay behind good luck on operations. Good luck and safety did not come unless you reached for them, it seemed.

She said: "Aren't you the crew who are all fishermen?"

He beamed down upon her. "I like ver' well to fish," he said. "The Cap, he likes only spinning; he has caught a ver' beautiful pike last week. Have you seen it?"

"I saw it and I ate a bit of it," she said. "It was a beautiful fish."

The Dane said: "I like better to fish for roach, and Sergeant Phillips also. Now we teach Corporal Leech. The flight engineer—he changes almost every flight." He turned to her. "I think it is ver' good when all of a crew like the same things, all together," he said.

If he had been more articulate, less shy of her, and more eloquent in English, he would have said what he meant: that common interests made a bond between the men, a slender, elusive thread making for good team-work in the air. Such crews were generally lucky.

The party broke up presently, and Wing Commander Dobbie drove her back to the camp in the Jeep. On the floor behind them were three pigeons, two of his and one of hers. "Remind me to ask that farmer to the next Ensa show," he said. "We'll give him dinner first in the mess. And that chap Ellison, too. Do you know where he lives?"

Gervase said: "I don't. I think Flight Lieutenant Marshall knows, sir; I'll get the address from him."

They reached the camp and parked the Jeep; she thanked him for the lift and carried her pigeon over to her quarters to show it to Section Officer Ford. The sitting-room was empty, so she took it over to the mess and gave it to the cook. As she was coming out of the kitchen Marshall came in, flushed from riding back upon his bicycle. His hands seemed full of pigeons.

She stopped, and was glad to do so. "How many did you get ?" she asked.

He said: "I got three and Davy got two."

"Not with his revolver ?"

"No—that wasn't much good. You got one, didn't you ?"

She nodded. "It was fun. Who are you giving your other two to ?"

He said: "Anyone who stands me a beer."

She hesitated, and then said: "What about Mrs. Stevens ?"

He stared at her. "She never gave me any beer. All she did was to make my batwoman cry."

She said: "Be a sport—give her one."

There was a momentary silence. "Would you like her to have one ?" he asked.

"I think it'd be a nice thing."

The pilot said: "Heap coals of fire upon her head." He picked the pigeons over. "That's the biggest coal." He gave it to the cook for the Flight Officer's lunch. "And I hope it bloody well burns her."

Gervase said: "It'll probably get you your tea."

They went out of the mess together, she to go to her quarters and he to put away his bicycle. In the windy darkness outside the mess they paused together for a minute.

"I talked to Gunnar Franck at tea," she said. "He seems an awfully good sort."

He nodded. "He's a very nice chap, Gunnar." He hesitated, and then said: "I'm glad you came this afternoon. Did you enjoy it ?"

She said: "It was wizard. I had an awfully good time."

They talked for a little time about the events of the afternoon. In the end he said casually:

"I was thinking of going into Oxford on Satuday to see a flick." He hesitated for a moment. "Would you like to come ?"

To gain time while she thought, she asked: "What's on ?"

"Something with Irene Dunne and Cary Grant. I forget its name." He paused, and said: "We could go in independently and meet there for a cup of tea, and throw our flick, and have supper, and come back independently."

She realised that he had got it all worked out before he spoke to her. She liked him very much; she knew that she would enjoy the afternoon that he had planned for her. She had a momentary sense of something enormous looming up ahead of them that she really ought to pay attention to, but she put it from her mind.

"I'd like to do that," she said. "I've got some shopping that I want to do in Oxford."

"Okay," he said. "Where shall we meet ?"

"There's that place in the middle where the cross-roads meet. Carfax, they call it."

"All right. Four o'clock ?"

They agreed on that. And then, for no special reason, in the dim light he put out his hand, and she took it, and shook hands with him, and it seemed a perfectly natural thing to do.

He turned away. "I'll see you then," he said.

She nodded. "I'll be there."

He did not see her to speak to for the next two days, though he was very conscious of her in the mess. He made opportunities to sit where he could see her; every attitude and movement that she made seemed to him to be delightful. He was clever and discreet in this surveillance; it passed unnoticed in the ante-room and even Gervase herself was scarcely aware of it.

On her side, she was interested to find out what bits of information were available concerning R for Robert and its captain. She did not add a great deal to the knowledge that she had. The aircraft had been going for a long time; it had done over four hundred hours. The same crew had flown it most of the time; they came and went with regularity and despatch. She found that there were several crews of that sort operating from Hartley. Nothing ever seemed to happen to Davy, or Lines, or Johnson, or Sergeant Pilot Nutter; those machines appeared to be immune from all disaster. It was not really an immunity. She did not realise how much depended upon the skill and quickness of the captain in the split second of emergency, upon the perfect understanding of the members of the crew between themselves. Johnson had come back with a great hole in one wing and one flap down. She did not yet understand the quick appreciation of the damage and the re-action of the pilot, dazed and stunned by the explosion, that had brought about the instant, sure, and violent movements upon wheel and rudder pedals that had kept the machine out of a spin. All she knew was that these crews were lucky, and went on and on.

They met for the next time at Carfax in the middle of Oxford, under the shadow of an old church at the intersection of two shopping streets. He was there first by ten minutes; she came to him as the clock above his head struck four, carrying a little attaché-case that held her purchases. She smiled at him. "Have you been waiting long?"

"Not long," he said. "I went and had my hair cut."

She said: "What'll we do now? Have you had tea?"

"No—I was waiting for you. What about Fuller's?"

She said: "That's all right." So they walked together through the crowded streets towards the café, each wondering whether they would find it full of officers, W.A.A.F.s, and airmen from Hartley Magna. Marshall for his own sake was unconcerned; it would not have worried him if the whole air station had seen him taking tea with the bearded lady from the circus, but he knew that Gervase was sensitive to station gossip. Gervase, however, was taking it phlegmatically. There was no earthly reason why she should not spend an afternoon in Oxford with a pilot. She did not want the buzz to get around the station much, but if it did—well, that was just too bad. Whatever you did caused gossip at a place like Hartley, where there was nothing else to talk about except the work.

They took a table in the window overlooking the Corn-market and ordered tea and what passed for sweet cakes and pastries, a thin shadow of the peace-time days. At the beginning of the little meal they talked about the picture they were going to see together; by the end of it they had thawed out and were talking about themselves.

He said presently: "I say, what's your name?" He knew that perfectly well, but was afraid to tell her so. "I mean, it's silly to go on calling you Miss Robertson."

She said: "You could call me Section Officer."

He said: "If you aren't damn careful, I will. Look, I'll do a deal over this. I'll tell you my name if you tell me yours." They were immensely young.

"I know yours," she said equably. She bit into a bun. "It's Peter."

He stared at her. "You've been peeping! That's not fair."

She laughed, and choked. "I've not been peeping," she said when she got her breath. "Mrs. Stevens always calls you Peter Marshall."

He nodded. "They all fall for me," he said. "It's my fatal attraction."

She laughed again. "I wouldn't bank too much on that."

Their eyes met, and he smiled at her. "What is it, anyway?"

"Gervase," she said, and wondered why she had given in so easily.

"That's rather pretty," he said. "What's the L ?"

She told him, and he offered her a cigarette, and they sat by the window over the remnants of their tea, smoking and telling each other about their brothers and sisters and their homes. And as they sat a half-hour passed unnoticed; they would have sat there indefinitely together, learning about each other, but for sheer decency that made them get up at the time the programme started at their picture-house.

They walked together through the crowded shopping streets to the cinema, not now caring whether anybody saw them or not. In the large dimness of the hall they sat together for three hours, very conscious of each other. They sat through the news, and shook with laughter at Donald Duck, and wondered at a picture about Russia, and thrilled with Cary Grant and Irene Dunne. And at the end they stumbled out into the black-out, and he took her up the street to the George restaurant for supper and gave her a gimlet to drink before the meal.

They talked about Oxford across the table. It meant nothing to them academically and they did not clearly understand what went on there in peace-time. Now it was stuffed full of Americans from the Army and the Army Air Corps.

Marshall said: "There was some talk of my brother coming here to one of the colleges. But now he's been in the Army for three years; I don't suppose he'll want to when it's all over. He'll be too old."

Gervase said: "What a shame. What do you think he'll do ?"

He told her about Bill, who wanted to be a solicitor and probably would be one day. And then she asked:

"What will you do when it's over ?"

He said: "I can always go back to the office—they said they'd keep the job for me." He was not really interested in what might happen to him after the war was over; for most people in his way of life that was an academic question.

He glanced at her. "What about you ?" he asked. "What would you do if the war ended now ?"

She said: "I did a course of shorthand and typing just before I joined up, and I did a bit of that at first before I was an officer. Then they let me go into signals, and then I got my commission. I think I'd try and get a job as secretary to somebody in the radio business."

"That means working in a town," he said. "Would you like that?"

She grimaced and shook her head.

"There's only one thing for it, then. You'll have to marry a farmer and settle down in the country." He did not want her in the least to marry a farmer; already he had other plans for her.

"I don't know about marrying a farmer," she said. "I'd like to settle down in the country. But I don't want to do that yet."

"Why not?"

She said: "I think when people are young they ought to do an honest job of work. There are lots of beastly things that have to be done, like working in towns, in offices. I don't think anybody ought to shirk that side of life."

"I suppose that's right," he said. "But most people never get beyond the office and the town."

She nodded. "I don't want to get stuck in a groove. I'd like to work in some business for seven or eight years and then marry and go back to the country."

He said: "I'd like to go on flying with Imperial Airways, or whatever they call it, after the war. But I don't suppose I'll be able to. There'll be an awful lot of us milling after just a few jobs."

They talked for some time about Hartley Magna, and the people on the station, and the life. He found that Gervase was much more reconciled to life there than when he had talked to her last. "You get to like it," he said. "At least, I did."

She nodded. "I'm liking it a bit better now. I suppose it's because I'm finding more to do, like you and your fishing."

Peter said: "The fishing ends in a week's time."

She knew vaguely that the coarse-fishing season came to an end some time in the middle of March. She said: "You'll have to think of something else to do."

"So will the boys," he said. "I want to go farther up the river one day in the next week, though, and see if I can't get another pike."

"How far?"

"There's a place about two miles farther up, by Riddington, where there's a little sort of pool. Sergeant Phillips went up there one Sunday after roach. He says he thinks there are pike there. It's a good long way to go."

73

"Five miles," she said. "That isn't much."

He said: "It may not be to you, but I took to biking very late in life."

She laughed. "How old are you?"

"Twenty-two," he said. He glanced at her. "How old are you?"

She said: "I'm twenty-one." Then they told each other all about their birthdays.

They ate with one eye on the clock, watching the time to catch their bus back to Hartley Magna. Peter said: "Look, Gervase—would you rather that I didn't come on this bus? There's that other one at half-past ten; I could come on that."

She said: "That means you'd have to wait about here for an hour, though."

"I could go and get drunk," he said.

She laughed. "You needn't do that for me, unless you want to for your own evil purposes. It doesn't matter our going back on the same bus if we don't sit together. After all, we might have come here quite independently." She paused, and then she added: "It doesn't matter a bit, anyway, if people do see us."

He paid the bill and they left the restaurant and walked towards the market-place, where the bus started. In the dark, crowded street they jostled against people in the black-out; he took her arm to guide her and they walked so to the bus, each thrilling with the contact.

In the darkness, fifty yards from the dim-lighted oblong of the bus, they paused. "We'd better say good-night here," he said. "It's probably full of people from the station."

She turned to him; he reached for her hand, and held it. He did not think that she was ready to be kissed. She said: "It's been a lovely afternoon, Peter. Thank you for bringing me."

She had called him by his Christian name. He said thickly: "Thank you for coming, Gervase." He stood there in the darkness caressing her hand. "You'd better buzz along and get a seat," he said at last. "I'll come on in a minute."

She left him, and he followed her a little later, and they rode back to Hartley Magna at opposite ends of the bus.

He did not speak to her again, alone, for several days.

A string of circumstances prevented them from meeting in the afternoons; one or other of them had duties to perform except for one day, when it rained. For five days Marshall had to watch her without talking to her. It was impossible for him to avoid her even if he had wanted to, and he did not want to; at the same time it was impossible for them to meet and talk without starting gossip all around the station, and he was unwilling to do that.

He found himself continually seeing things that he wanted to tell her about. He saw a blue tit on a branch one day; he did not know what it was, except that it was blue. Gervase would know; he suffered a sudden mad impulse to go to the signals office and ask her to come out and see it. He saw a Halifax without a front turret and heard from the pilot why it was given up; he wanted to pour out to her this vital and most interesting news. Down by the river, standing very quiet, he saw three tiny water-rats learning to swim; it irked him that she was not there with him to see. Gunnar Franck received a letter from his mother that had come via Switzerland and Spain; he was unable to talk to her about it. He could only catch her eye occasionally across the table or the ante-room and smile.

He slept badly during that five days; that is to say, instead of sleeping solidly for nine hours as he was accustomed to, he slept for seven and lay awake for two, and got up in the morning stale and tired. After the third such night it seemed to him that they could hardly go on as they were; they would have to work out some means of meeting—if she wanted to. He was not sure of that, however. Gervase might be quite satisfied with their relationship, for all he knew. He was uncertain and upset; in those five days his friends found him sharp and irritable. Even his crew found him to be difficult to please, a novel and unusual trait developed in their captain.

Gervase saw nothing of this restlessness because she did not meet him. When circumstances allowed, she knew she would go out with him again; the two afternoons that she had spent with him had been happy ones, the happiest she had spent since she had been at Hartley. She was not in any hurry for the third. She knew, with a little glow of wonder and of pride, that this casual, competent, and kind young man was coming to be very much in love with her. She knew that this would raise enormous problems for her in the future that she did not in the least know how to tackle. She was grateful for the respite that prevented them from meeting. Her whole instinct was to take it slowly; when it rained on the one afternoon when they were both free, she was almost glad.

They did an operation on the fifth day: Essen. It was a

massed raid of more than six hundred aircraft, Lancasters, Halifaxes, Wellingtons, and a few Stirlings. The Wellingtons from Hartley were scheduled to arrive in the last quarter of an hour; they got there when the target was a sea of flame with smoke-clouds rising up above ten thousand feet. Most of the searchlights had ceased functioning and the flak was weak and inaccurate; for the Wellingtons it was an easy raid. There were night fighters over the target, but a layer of cloud at thirteen thousand gave them cover for the journey home; Phillips got off a couple of bursts at one as they climbed up beside Lines in the dim light, covering each other. Then they were in the cloud and sheering apart, and so they came home, and landed back at about three in the morning. There were no losses, though Sergeant Pilot Nutter came back swearing like a sergeant pilot with the fabric missing from one elevator and his rear-gunner wounded in the shoulder from a burst beside the tail.

Throughout this raid Marshall was absent-minded and *distrait*. He took the machine off and flew it normally, checked his instruments with his usual care, talked to his crew down the inter-com, did all his normal duties. But there was no life in his work that night; he performed it automatically, thinking about other things. All the way from Hartley Magna to Essen and back from Essen to Hartley Magna his mind was only on Gervase. The vast glow of smoke and flame that they saw fifty miles away did not excite him; he was oppressed with the feeling that the present position with Gervase was intolerable; the artificial constraint that life upon the station placed between them must be ended as soon as possible. The target was too far obscured by smoke and fire for him to be able to identify the engine assembly shops that they were detailed to destroy. Gunnar Franck took over and from the river bend guided him across the inferno for about the right distance, and they dropped their bombs and fell into formation beside Lines as they climbed up towards the clouds, and Marshall was free again to think about his trouble. He would have to reach an understanding with Gervase. They could not go on like this.

He got to bed at about half-past three, and slept restlessly and late. He woke up at about half-past eleven; there was no tea for him in spite of the pigeon that he had given to the Flight Officer, and his batwoman had gone downstairs. He lay for half an hour in bed rather unhappy and resentful of the circumstances of his life; then he got up and shaved and went downstairs to drink his pint of beer before lunch.

He saw Gervase in the ante-room and crossed over to her, can in hand.

"Morning," he said.

She turned to him. "Good-morning. Did you get your cup of tea?"

He grumbled: "No, I didn't. Fat lot of good giving her a pigeon."

The girl said: "But she told the girl that you could have it! I know she did." In fact, he had been asleep at the time when his batwoman might have brought it to him.

"It doesn't matter," he said gloomily. "Beer is best."

She laughed. "What's the matter with you?"

He yawned. "I stayed up too late last night."

Gervase said: "It's going to be a lovely afternoon. You'd better get out and get some exercise."

He nodded. "I thought of going out to that place Ridding-ton up the river, that I told you about, to try and get another pike. Like to come with me?" He paused, and added persuasively: "I'd let you have a crack with the little rod, if you like."

She said: "All right. I'll meet you out there."

He fixed details of the time and place with her, and left her almost immediately, conscious of Flying Officer Davy watching them across the room. He went in presently to lunch, and then up to his room to collect his fishing gear. He rode out of the station on his bicycle ahead of Gervase; when she reached the river he had already fitted up his rod and made a cast or two with the red plug.

The river here swelled out into a wide pool, rather black and muddy, and overhung with trees. At one time it might have been a millpool or perhaps a reservoir; now nothing remained to show its purpose save the stone retaining wall and rusty sluice. Gervase found him at the deep end of it; she came to him by a little path through beds of nettles.

"You do find nice places," she said. "I think this is fun."

The sun shone on them through the bare trees; the shadows of the branches made thin pencilled lines upon the water. "It's nothing like that Kingslake place," he said. "I was just thinking it looks pretty grim." He glanced at the dark water and the black sunken branches sticking out of it up at the shallow end.

77

"We won't spin too deep," he said. "We might bring up the body."

She made a little gesture of distaste. "Loathsome ideas you have."

"Well, I didn't want to spoil our afternoon."

He showed her his rod, reel, and tackle. She had never fished in that way; indeed, she had never fished at all except for one or two abortive trials with a fly, as she had told him. They stood there together on the bank of the dark pool as he explained the tackle to her; he stumbled once or twice during his explanation, confused by her proximity. The tension communicated itself to her, because she moved away from him a little and said:

"All right. Go on, and let's see you do it."

He cast out over the still pool; the plug went flying thirty yards and landed with a little splash; he began to reel in slowly. "That's nice," she said. She watched as the little red fish wiggled up towards them as he reeled it out and cast again.

Presently he handed her the rod and showed her how to do it; it was necessary to adjust her hand upon the handle and her thumb upon the reel, and that was difficult for both of them. She cast, and got an overrun that tangled up the line; cast again when he had straightened it for her and got another. The third time the plug sailed correctly up the still pool a little way, giving her the thrill of achievement.

They fished on for half an hour and caught nothing, which was not surprising. Their minds were not upon the job but on very different matters; a fish, if fish there were, might have looked out of the water at them brandishing the rod above his head and wondered at their few, constrained remarks and the long, difficult silences.

For Gervase, the afternoon was a disappointment. For some reason that she did not clearly understand it was not working out so well as the day in Kingslake Woods. That and the evening in Oxford had been sheer pleasure; this was different, and awkward. She became aware that she wanted to get away, and quickly too, before something frightful happened.

She handed him back the rod. "Thanks ever so much for letting me try," she said. "I've got to go back now—I said I'd be back for tea. I hope you catch a fish."

He smiled at her. He had felt the awkwardness between them as much as she had; if she wanted to escape he would not try to stop her. "There's a dance in the Town Hall to-morrow night," he said. "Would you like to come to it?"

She said, to gain time: "You mean the one in Hartley Town Hall?"

He nodded. "That's the one."

She hesitated, and then said: "I think that's a bit near the station, isn't it?"

There was a long pause.

"I'm not so struck upon this hole-and-corner business," he said at last. "I think we ought to give ourselves a chance."

She realised in panic what was happening and tried to laugh it off. "We wouldn't have much chance if we went to the Hartley dance together." She moved away. "I really must go now."

"Just one more thing," the pilot said.

She glanced at him and realised that, as she saw him then, so he must look over the target just as Gunnar Franck said "Bombs away, Cap."

She said weakly: "What's that?"

"I think you're a grand person," he said quietly. "I'm working up to ask you if you'd like to marry me."

The date was March the fourteenth, the last day of the season for coarse fishing.

CHAPTER FOUR

Now hollow fires burn out to black,
    And lights are guttering low:
Square your shoulders, lift your pack,
    And leave your friends, and go.

Oh never fear, man, nought's to dread,
    Look not to left or right:
In all the endless path you tread
    There's nothing but the night.

A. E. HOUSMAN

There was a long silence between them. Now that the worst had happened, Gervase found that all awkwardness had disappeared; his frankness seemed to give her licence to speak freely herself. "Look," she said at last, "that's perfectly absurd. We've only met twice or three times."

He said: "Well, that's not true, because we've been meeting almost every day in the mess. But if it was true—so what? Do you think that matters?"

She thought for a moment. "No, I don't," she said. "I think you're right there. I think if you wanted to marry anybody you'd probably know in the first five minutes."

Their agreement only served to deepen the message of her words. "Well, I did," he said quietly, "even if you didn't. I knew I wanted you to marry me that first day of all, when we went to see the badger."

She said helplessly: "I'm frightfully sorry . . ."

They were still standing by the edge of the pool. Marshall said: "Let's go and sit on that stile."

She said: "I've got to go back soon."

"It won't hurt you to wait ten minutes." He smiled at her. "I won't try any of the rough stuff."

They left the pool, and carrying the rod and case they went towards the stile and sat upon it, one at each end so that there was a yard between them. As they went Marshall had time to collect his eloquence, and when they were settled he said:

"Look, Gervase. When I said we ought to give ourselves a chance, I meant just that. I hate this lousy hole-and-corner business, snooping about in the bushes in case an A.C.2. sees

81

us and starts gossiping on the station. If we were both in civil
life I wouldn't have asked you to marry me the third time we
went out together. But here, it's either that or go on creeping
round the hedges, and I take a dim view of that."

She said: "There's nothing else to do, is there? If you don't
want to set the whole station off talking."

He grinned at her. "I'd rather set the whole station off
talking and have done with it."

"I don't see what good that would do," she said. "It'd just
make things difficult."

He pulled out his cigarette-case and offered her one; she
refused, and absently he lit one himself, flipped the match
away, and blew a long cloud.

"I think I've been a bloody fool," he said. "I'm sorry if I've
upset you, Gervase."

She said: "You've not upset me." As she spoke she knew
that it would be months before she would be able to stop
thinking about what was going on between them.

He glanced at her, and saw that her face was troubled, and
her cheeks rather pink. "Would you like to hear my side of it?"
he asked.

She said: "I don't think I would, Peter. It won't do any
good."

"Maybe, but I'd like you to know." He glanced up at her,
smiling faintly. "Children may go out before the sermon."

She flushed. "I'm not a child."

"Then you can stay and listen to the sermon," he said
equably.

He blew another cloud of smoke, considering his words.
"I know we don't know much about each other," he said
slowly. "But I do think this. I think we know enough to justify
us in taking a chance together. When we know each other
better we may get to hate the sight of one another, and then
everything will come to an end, and we'll be well out of it."

"In that case," she observed, "we'd better not start."

"If I thought it was going to end like that," he said, "I
wouldn't want to. But what I think is this. I think you're the
finest girl I've ever met, Gervase, or that I'm ever likely to
meet. I think I could make you happy, not only now but when
we're old. In fifty years' time, when you've got rheumatism
and I'm stone deaf, I think we'd still be happy together. That's
what I think."

She did not speak.

"It's pretty early to speak to you about getting married," he said, "and you've got every right to shoot me down. But I'm glad I did."

There was a long silence. In the end she broke it. "When you said you wanted us to take a chance together," she said, "did you mean you wanted us to be engaged, or something?"

He thought for a minute. "If you like. What I really meant was that we should say, 'To hell with the station.' That we should meet as often as we like, and when we like. In the middle of the parade ground, if we like."

"We wouldn't go on like that for very long," she said practically. "One or other of us would get shifted. It would probably be me."

He said: "I'm sorry, Gervase. I didn't think of that."

There was a pause, and then he said: "I don't think I object so much to dodging behind hedges to kid the people on the station, so long as it's all right between ourselves. But I'm not going to kid you any more, Gervase. I think you're a lovely girl, and I think when we know each other a bit better we'll want to get married." He glanced at her. "I don't want there to be any misunderstanding about that."

She said: "There couldn't be now, Peter. You've said it about six different ways already."

He blew a cloud of smoke. "I'm pretty eloquent when I get going," he said. There was a pause, and then he added: "Mind if I ask a question?"

She shook her head, wondering what was coming now.

"You haven't got a boy friend tucked away anywhere, have you?" he asked. "Somebody you knew at your last station?"

She thought rapidly of simulating an impassioned separation, and abandoned the idea as too difficult to improvise. "There's nobody like that," she said.

Marshall said: "I didn't think there was. And I might have known I'd get a straight answer." He glanced at her and met her eyes, smiling. "You really are a wizard girl," he said. "I'm doing this all wrong. I ought to be holding you clutched to my manly bosom, whispering hot words of love into your shell-like ear."

She said nervously: "You promised to cut out the rough stuff if I stayed."

He glanced at her. "Don't worry," he said gently. "I know when I'm not wanted."

The sun shone down upon them sitting one at each end of

83

the stile, and a little wind of March blew across the plough behind them, fresh and stimulating. Gervase sat mustering her thoughts, trying to think of ways to say the things she had to say without hurting him too much.

"You're not wanted," she said quietly. "Not in the way you mean." She glanced at him, sitting staring at the dead leaves on the ground before him, smoking quietly. "I don't want to be beastly to you, saying that. You've been very nice to me, Peter. You've done me a great honour, saying you wanted to marry me. But I couldn't marry you just because of that."

He said: "I wouldn't want you to. But there's more to it than that. I think you like me a bit, too."

"I do like you," she said. "I like coming out with you. But I don't want to marry you. I don't want to marry anybody, not for six or seven years."

"Why not ?" he asked.

She said desperately: "That's not what we're here for. When I joined the W.A.A.F.s I didn't do it to get married. When I was trained in Signals, it was because they expected me to do some work in the R.A.F. It was a sort of bargain, and I do the best I can. It's not such important work as yours, but it's the best I can do. I couldn't give it up as soon as I'd started, just for a personal reason. I'd feel awfully mean if I did that."

There was a pause. Marshall said nothing, because he could not think of anything to say except that he loved her, and that seemed hardly relevant to what she said about her work. And presently Gervase went on:

"I don't think I'm a bit in love with you, Peter." She glanced at him, and glanced down again, troubled, and she said: "I'm sorry, but I'm not going to pretend. I like you awfully, and we do get on together, but that's different to being in love."

"Quite sure ?" he asked.

She nodded. "I think I can tell you. People who fall in love and want to get married always think that matters more than anything else—they all do. And I suppose it does, if you're in love. I don't feel in the least like that. I think my job here matters more than getting married, or not getting married."

"I see," he said quietly.

She knew that she had hurt him, and the knowledge hurt her in turn. "We've both got jobs to do," she said. "We're on an operational station, Peter, after all. And there hasn't been much wrong with the R/T, or the W/T either, has there?"

He shook his head.

She said: "That matters frightfully to me. Much more than anything personal."

Marshall said slowly: "Suppose that when we knew each other better we did decide we wanted to get married. You might still go on in the W.A.A.F.s while the war is on."

She shook her head. "If ever I did want to marry, I'd want to do it properly, not half and half. We wouldn't be able to be on the same station, probably. I don't think there'd be much point in getting married if we couldn't be together." She paused, and added cautiously: "Even if we wanted to."

There was a long silence between them. Presently she said: "Look at it the other way round—suppose it was you instead of me. Suppose you went to Wing Commander Dobbie and said you were going to stop flying and leave the R.A.F. because you were in love."

He glanced up at her, grinning. "That's all different."

"It's not different at all," she retorted. "The only difference is that you can't do it and I can, if I care to go the whole hog. But that doesn't change the fact that we've both got jobs to do."

"That's how you feel about it—honestly, Gervase?"

She met his eyes. "Honestly, Peter—that's how I feel. That's why I know I'm not in love with you."

He said heavily: "Well, that just about puts the lid on it."

She looked despairingly out over the glade. There was a chaffinch on a bush not far from them; she would have liked to have pointed it out to him and shared it with him, but it didn't seem to be quite the right time for that. With a sad heart she got down from the stile; it was time, she felt, to wind this up.

"I'm sorry, Peter," she said quietly. "Perhaps we'd better not come out again together, for a bit."

He cocked an eye at her. "Just what do you mean by 'for a bit'?" he asked.

She searched her mind for words to express what she did mean. "I mean, until you can forget about what you've just told me," she said at last.

He stared at her. "Are you trying to say that you'd like to be a sister to me?" he enquired. "Because that's crackers." He hesitated, and then said more gently: "I think that'd be like trying to put back the clock."

85

"If you feel like that about it," she said, "then we'd better not meet at all."

He nodded. "That's how I do feel about it," he said. "I shan't change my mind. If we can't meet on the basis that I—I'm in love with you, then I think we'd better not meet at all."

She turned to him. "I'm sorry about this," she said. "Frightfully sorry. I have enjoyed going out with you." And then, feeling that the courtesies were complete, she turned away awkwardly, saying: "I really must go now."

"Okay," he said. "Find your way back all right ?"

She said: "Oh yes—thanks." He watched her to the turning of the path, till she disappeared from view.

For half an hour he sat there mooning, staring at the black, sinister pool, trying to recover his nerve before going back to the station. Presently he lit a cigarette with fingers that shook a little and began to take down the little rod that he had been so proud of; there was no joy in it now. After a time he followed down the path to where his bicycle was lying in the bushes, and rode slowly back towards the station.

Gervase rode back ahead of him, her mind a blank. She felt tired and exhausted, as she felt when she stayed up all night upon an operation. She could not summon up the energy to think of what had happened; she only wanted to get home to her quarters, and rest.

She felt better when she was sitting in a chair before the fire in the W.A.A.F. officers' sitting-room, sipping a cup of tea. She smoked a cigarette, sitting very quiet and recovering from the strain; she was rather moved and rather sorry for herself, but confident that she had done the right thing. Presently she stirred and stubbed out her cigarette, and reached out for her novel, and began to read.

It was all about Love; she had thought it good when she had been reading it in bed the previous night, but now it seemed to her to be a rotten book. She put it away with distaste, and got up and went over to the bookcase for another. She ran her eye over the titles. Most of them seemed to be about Love in one form or another; the rest were detective stories and books about Hitler. She picked an intricate and badly-written story about Scotland Yard, lost the thread of the tale in the first three pages, and spent a dull and restless evening over it, smoking a great number of cigarettes. She went to bed with a dry mouth and a worried mind, and slept accordingly.

86

Marshall spent a troubled evening in the mess and went to bed early, to lie awake most of the night. It seemed to him that he had been a most almighty fool to raise the point of marriage with Gervase so soon, however certain he might be in his own mind; a quarter of an hour later he was thinking that he had done right to tell her plainly what he thought, that it was better to end it quick and face the pain, if they had no future together. Again, he was chivalrously and desperately sorry that he had caused her trouble and worry; in turn he was incredulous that there should be no future for them when they got on so well together.

He fell asleep at about three in the morning, and woke, heavy and dull, at seven. The short sleep had rested his mind; he now felt that it was better for them to be quite apart. It seemed to him that the right line was to see nothing of her for the next six months; if then they met again she would know, at any rate, that there was something solid that she could depend upon in his regard.

In this decision he was probably correct; the difficulty was that it was quite impracticable. He met her immediately after breakfast as she went from her quarters to the signals office, as he went to the Link trainer hut; it was genuinely fortuitous, and it was impossible to pass her without smiling and saying "Good morning." He went on troubled and depressed, and put up an unusually poor performance on the Link trainer. He met her again at lunch and sat opposite her, talking absently to Lines, watching her eat roast beef and cabbage and plum tart. He saw her again in the ante-room taking coffee, and again at tea time, reading the *Illustrated London News*. In the circumstances of their life upon the station it was inevitable that they should meet the whole day through; it was not at their option never to meet again.

In the next thirteen days he met her sixty-one times. He counted them.

In that thirteen days they did no operation. They did several long training flights at night and spent a large proportion of each day upon their various trainers and firing teachers. The machines were overhauled, a few engines were changed, and some of the crews were re-formed. Flight Lieutenant Johnson got rid of Pilot Officer Drummond, who was given a new Wellington, C for Charlie, and a new crew of his own.

"He's all right, sir," Johnson told the Wing Commander.

"A bit too conscientious, if you know what I mean. But he'll be all right."

Dobbie visualised the keen eagerness of the young man. "I'll give him Sergeant Entwhistle as navigator," he said. "He's very steady. And Murdoch as rear-gunner."

Johnson said: "I don't know Murdoch."

"Chap with a face like a burglar—came in with the last lot from the Pool. A regular Commando type. He ought to be good."

Johnson went away and found Drummond sitting in his bedroom, graph paper and pencil before him, working at a book of Weems' upon condensed celestial navigation. He told him about his crew. "You erks get all the lucky breaks," he said. "Entwhistle's done about twenty raids; he knows the routine backwards. And Winco's picked the toughest rear-gunner on the station for you. God, I wish I'd had a crowd like that for my first crew. We none of us knew arse from elbow when they pushed me off. Talk about going to sea in a sieve!"

He went off and played a round of very bad golf, confident that his apprentice was well launched upon his independence.

In R for Robert things were not so satisfactory. Corporal Leech, the wireless operator, had been taken roach-fishing by Gunnar Franck and Phillips, and to their delight had proved himself an apt pupil, keen and interested, and naturally skilful. On his first day he had caught a roach with Sergeant Phillips' rod, and on the next day he had caught another with Gunnar Franck's. He had then gone off to Oxford and bought himself a new roach-pole, and reel, and line, and floats, and tackle for the three remaining days of the coarse-fishing season.

The period after March 15th was irritating and troublesome for them. Fishing gear was taken down and packed away for three months, and they had nothing much to do with their spare time, which was considerable. Leech was a footballer, and that season was also at an end; he hung about the canteen bored and idle, and finally commenced a slap-and-tickle intrigue with one of the station cooks. Sergeant Phillips took to lying on his bed for most of his leisure time and reading thrillers; the balance he devoted to L.A.W. Elsie Smeed. There was little to do, in fact, at Hartley at that time of year except to play cards and make love. Gunnar Franck did neither, but took to going for long walks through the country lanes, browned off and thinking of Denmark and his lost life as a medical student.

Gervase met him one evening, travelling back from Oxford in the bus. The bus was nearly full; in the half-light she saw a seat by him and sat down in it. She liked Gunnar Franck; she liked him because he had lent her his rifle to shoot a pigeon with, and because he was a Dane and had given up his life's career to escape to all the hazards of the R.A.F., and because by doing so he had become a lonely man. She smiled at him and said: "Good evening. Have you been to the pictures?"

He said: "I have been to the Regal, to see the movie with Bette Davis. Always I like a Bette Davis picture. To me a Bette Davis is good, *overordentligt*."

Gervase said: "I like her, too." They talked of films and film actresses while the bus got under way and rumbled out into the darkness of the country roads, dim-lit and crowded with R.A.F. and American soldiers. Presently she said: "Do you still go fishing?"

He shook his head. "It is now the season when they breed the little fish. It is not allowed to fish now, till the middle of June."

She said: "That must be rather a blow—you're all fishermen in Robert, aren't you? What do you do instead?"

He was silent for a minute, long enough for her to look at him curiously. Then he said: "It is ver' dull. I think I would like to go away now, to another station."

She exclaimed: "But I thought you were so happy here!"

He said bitterly: "I think now perhaps it is time I have a change."

"But why, Gunnar? Has anything happened?"

She was an officer and he was a sergeant, but she was a girl, and friendly, and very young. It was nearly dark in the bus. He said: "The Captain, he has been difficult to please. It must be ver' difficult for an Englishman to have in the crew a foreigner. I think perhaps it is better that I ask if I may go to another station."

She said: "But, Gunnar, Flight Lieutenant Marshall thinks the world of you. I know he does. You mustn't think of anything like that. What's the trouble?"

There was a pause, and then he said in a low tone so that she had to bend her head to catch his words: "He say I cross my sevens so he cannot read the numbers that I write, and I must write in English if I want to stay with him."

She said: "Cross your sevens?"

"*Jo.* Always in Denmark when we write the number seven

we make a line across the tail, but in England you do not do that. And now he says that I must write in English."

She said: "But that's silly! It doesn't matter a bit, does it, if you write a seven like that?"

"Nine months we have been together," said the big young man a little sadly, "and over forty ops. And now he is angry because I write my sevens as we do at home."

A lump of apprehension rose in the girl's throat, and she said: "I thought you all got on so well together. Is this something new?"

Gunnar said: "It is the last week only. Always before he has been sympathetic; we were all very happy together. Now for a week everything has been wrong, and he finds fault with all that we do, and it is trouble all the time. It is not only me; it is Sergeant Phillips and Corporal Leech. They are quite fed up with him."

The girl said: "I *am* sorry." She relapsed into silence, worried over what she had unearthed. This was another side of Marshall that she had not seen before, this apparently unreasonable irritation with his crew. From what she had heard she felt that he had been unfair to them; certainly Gunnar Franck considered that he had been hardly used. She felt that Flight Lieutenant Marshall deserved a reprimand and she felt that she would have liked to give it to him herself, and that she could do so in a way that would improve matters. She felt, sincerely, that it was a very great pity that they were not upon speaking terms; she would have liked to tell Peter Marshall just where he got off.

It was perfectly true that Marshall was bad-tempered. He was sleeping very badly; that is to say, no more than six hours in each night, which seemed to him to be fantastically little. Most of the rest of the time that he spent in bed he spent in self-depreciation, thinking what an almighty fool he had made of himself with Gervase. He felt that he made himself ridiculous; each time they met he felt that she must be smiling inwardly at the memory of their last meeting in the wood, and he didn't blame her. This happened to him three or four times every day. The recurring humiliation mingled strangely with his admiration, which was quite unchanged. He still noted every movement that she made, each characteristic gesture, each light in her hair.

If you take a large, hungry dog and tie it up, and feed it very little, and tease it with large lumps of meat just out of reach, it will soon become very bad-tempered indeed. It will snap not only at you but at everybody else. You can make it good-tempered by giving it the meat, or you can make it good-tempered by taking away the temptation altogether, when the dog will adjust itself to its meagre diet. While you continue teasing it with the unattainable it will remain restless and bad-tempered. Scientists prove this sort of thing by practical experiment, and they say science is wonderful.

Sergeant Phillips was no scientist, but merely an observer of phenomena. He told Elsie Smeed about it in the darkness of the country lanes as he walked her back from the pictures, his arm comfortably about her waist. "Fed up, I am," he said. "Real nasty he's been lately."

"Why, whatever about?" she asked.

He said: "We got a target, what we line the guns on after firing, see? This is what he said yesterday, an' I don't care to be spoken to like that. Great big white board."

"I see them using it," she said. "Big white board on legs with spots on it, what they put up behind the aeroplane."

"That's right," he said. "You put the sight on the one in the middle and lines the barrels up on the other four, 'n there you are, see? Well, that's the way they tell you to do it, but that's for two hundred yards, 'n I like two of them to be splayed a little bit more for three hundred and two of them, the bottom two, pulled in a bit so's they're right for hundred and twenty, hundred and fifty, see?"

"I see," the girl said. She didn't see at all, but it was all very dull and didn't seem to matter anyway. "What happened?"

"Well, I got them nicely fixed, 'n he comes down the fuselage and says he wants to see. So I gets out of the turret 'n he gets in, and then he says I'm not lined up. Well, I was lined up, but not the way it was on the target. So then he didn't half start carrying on."

"You don't say!"

"Real nasty, he was," said the sergeant. "Said if I didn't want to obey orders 'n do it like it was on the target he'd chuck me out of the crew and get another gunner what'd do as he was told. I said it was the way I had them when I got the night-fighter over Rostock, 'an he asked if I had them like that when we got shot up at Hamburg, 'n I had to say it was. Then he got sort of sarcastic, so I told him the Armament Officer said I could have them my way if I wanted."

"What did he say to that?"

91

"Said I could go and fly with the Armament Officer on the firing teacher, if I wanted to. It wasn't so much what he said as the way he said it, if you take me."

She breathed sympathetically: "Oh I *say*! What happened in the end ?"

"We got them fixed like on the target," the sergeant said. "He come and checked them over again after I finished, as if he didn't trust me not to do it my way after all." He sounded hurt and aggrieved. "So that's the way we got 'em now."

There was a short silence. "I don't like 'em that way," he said uneasily. "I don't think it's as good as the way I had them. It only gives you one chance, like."

"I'd like to give him a piece of my mind," the girl said decidedly. "What's it got to do with 'im anyway ? He ain't the one that's shooting."

"He's the Cap," said Sergeant Phillips justly, "and what he says goes, if you take me. But he's quite changed lately. What I mean is, we was all matey together up to not so long ago, but now it's as if he was the officer and everybody else was so much dirt."

"What's happened, then, to make him go like that ?"

"I dunno," said the sergeant. "I can't make it out."

L.A.W. Smeed had a simple, elemental mind. To her, and at her age, there was only one explanation for the unusual. "Maybe he's in love," she said.

Sergeant Phillips considered this for a moment. Everybody at Hartley aerodrome was deeply interested in Love, except perhaps the Adjutant and Flight Officer Stevens, and one or two others more than twenty-five years old. For the majority of the Wing, Love was as essential a commodity as petrol, and much more interesting.

"With that Section Officer of yours ?" he said. "The one you asked her name ?"

"Might be," the girl said. "I haven't seen them about together, though, have you ?"

"No," said the sergeant thoughtfully. "It could be that, though. He wanted to know her name all right."

"She's been sort of pale and quiet the last day or two," the girl said hopefully. "Think she shot him down ?"

"If she did," he said, "he's got no call to take it out on us."

In the darkness outside the gate into the station they exchanged expressions of mutual esteem, then broke away and walked in separately past the guard. There was a prejudice at

Hartley against walking past the guard arm-in-arm, even when returning from the pictures.

It was true enough that Gervase was not quite herself. Like Marshall, she had not foreseen that the clean break they had arranged would be impracticable. She saw him every day in the mess, and she was troubled to observe that he seemed moody and depressed. Previously, in her experience, Marshall had been the fount of new amusements; he had always seemed to have some new diversion for the ante-room, catching a fish or chasing a badger or shooting pigeons. It troubled her to see him sitting bored and listless with a newspaper.

It troubled her still more that he was watching her so closely. She was not angry with him; he was quite nice and unobtrusive over it, but whenever they were in the room together she knew that his eyes were on her. It made her feel as if all that they had settled in the wood was nugatory and worthless; nothing was changed between them, after all. She thought that by the line that she had taken she had extinguished the fire; it was now clear to her that she had merely smothered it, that it was still as much alive as ever, secretly. She felt as if she was sitting on a volcano, and it worried her.

She took to spending longer hours than usual upon her work, staying on after duty in the signals office. She did this partly from an instinct to avoid the ante-room so far as possible, partly for the diversion for her own mind that her work could give, and partly from a sense of duty. There were indications, clear to all the station, that their spell off operations was coming to an end; she was concerned that when raids started up again her operators should be all on the top line, that there should be no inefficiency in the radio service if a girl went sick and a reserve girl had to be pulled in. She sat on in her office after tea each evening thinking out contingencies, planning for troubles and emergencies that might arise.

She was sitting so one evening at the end of the slack period. It had been announced on the Tannoy at tea time that there would be no leave off the station until further notice; this meant, in effect, a warning for an operation the next night. She was sitting conning over the last details of her organisation for the tenth time, when there was a knock upon the office door. She raised her head, and said: "Come in."

The door opened, and a very young Pilot Officer came into the room. She had seen him in the mess for some time, but did not know his name; he was small, and rather pale-faced, and

93

bright-eyed. She said "Good evening," and sat looking up at him.

He said a little nervously: "I say—my name is Drummond. There are one or two things I want to know, and Flight Lieutenant Marshall said I'd better come to you. Could you spare a few minutes?"

She said: "Of course. Shift those papers off that chair and bring it over." She shoved a packet of cigarettes lying on the desk towards him. "Will you smoke?"

He said: "Oh, thanks awfully," and fumbled in his pocket. "Won't you have one of mine?"

To put him at his ease she took it, and he lit it for her. "What's your machine?" she asked.

He said: "Red C. C for Charlie."

For a moment she was unreasonably disturbed. She had had a very bad half-hour with the last C for Charlie, and she did not care for the association. New machines had to have a letter, and it was impossible to keep vacant the identification letters of the lost machines. To fill in time she wrote down 'Drummond—C' upon the pad before her.

She said: "What can I do?"

He looked at her confidingly. "Just one or two things about the stations and the frequencies. You see," he said, "it's the first time I've been allowed to go alone."

She started giving him the information that he asked for. At the end of ten minutes she began to realise with some misgiving that he wanted to memorise all the information that his wireless operator would carry with him on a card of reference in the machine.

She said: "You can't possibly remember all you've written down. In any case, your operator will have it—Corporal Macaulay."

The boy said: "Yes, but if he got hit or something there'd be nobody."

Gervase said: "But then you'd just take a look at his card. It should be in his satchel."

He said: "Well—yes, but I'd rather memorise the more important ones. You see, the satchel might get lost, or something."

It was in her mind to tell him that if the operator were wounded and the satchel lost, the odds were that the set would be unserviceable anyway. She did not say that. She had learned that pilots were to be humoured; it was not for the ground

94

staff to say how the air crews should do their work. She went on with him and gave him all the information that he asked for; it took them another quarter of an hour. By that time he had lost his diffidence and was talking with her freely.

She said presently: "Have they given you a good crew ?"

He said: "Oh yes—they're splendid chaps. Sergeant Entwhistle's done over twenty ops, and Sergeant Murdoch is awfully tough. He boxes; he's a welter-weight, from Birmingham." He glanced at her, troubled. "I'm frightfully anxious not to let them down," he said. And then, because she was a girl, and kind, he added: "They're bound to be watching to see if I know my stuff."

She said: "You know your stuff all right. You'll probably find that they don't know theirs as well as you do."

He said, troubled: "They're so much more experienced than I am. If I forgot anything or did anything wrong they'd know at once."

The girl said: "You won't do that."

He smiled at her shyly: "Not on the wireless, with all the help you've given me." He got up to go. "It's been frightfully nice of you to give me so much time."

She was two years older than he was, being twenty-one; she felt almost motherly to him. "If there's anything you want to-morrow," she said, "come along again. I'll be in and out of here all morning. But I'm sure you'll find that it'll be all right."

He said: "Of course it will. It's just a bit worrying, that's all." He turned to her. "Flight Lieutenant Johnson told me that when he was pushed off alone he had a completely raw crew, as new to it as he was."

Gervase said: "I suppose they did that sort of thing in those days—they had to. But it's much safer to have an experienced crew like you've got."

He said uneasily: "I hope to God I don't make a fool of myself."

She smiled at him. "You won't do that."

He went away, and she sat on at her table, worrying. She knew Sergeant Entwhistle slightly, the navigator of C for Charlie. He was a young man with a superior smile and an upper lip that curled a little, very conscious of the prestige that his experience had given him. Abruptly she thought, how much happier Drummond would have been with a completely raw young man as navigator, whose mistakes he could have

95

checked with his abundant energy. But that, she reflected, was absurd. It would never do to send out aircraft with completely raw crews. That might have been all right in Pat Johnson's time, but not now.

She did not see Pilot Officer Drummond again. The operation the next night was against Bremen; all the machines that could be mustered from the station took off for it between eight and eight-thirty. Gervase was on duty at the control office. By ten-thirty the first 'Mission completed' signals were coming in; she marked them on the big blackboard in chalk, covering half of one wall. L for London, R for Robert, Q for Queenie. . . .

By eleven all the machines were accounted for in her neat writing on the board, except O for Orange and C for Charlie. With a sick heart she sat there at the little desk beside the blackboard, waiting; from time to time she went through to the telephone and R/T room next door. There was nothing she could do to assist the crews; she must wait till the machines began to arrive back again, when she would hear them overhead and they would begin talking on the R/T if they were in difficulty. Orange and Charlie might quite well be with them, their radio sets and damaged and unserviceable.

At a quarter to one the roaring of the first aircraft was heard faintly in the distance; the control officer and his flight sergeant went out on to the balcony with the Aldis lamp, and the operation of landing the machines began. In a few minutes the flight sergeant put his head in at the door. "O for Orange signalling for permission to land."

That was one of them, at any rate. Gervase marked it with a tick in chalk upon the blackboard; there was now only C for Charlie unaccounted for.

With a sick heart she began the long routine of searching the aerodromes all over England for a missing aircraft. She very soon discovered P for Percy at an aerodrome in Essex, and later in the night she found that M for Mother had been wrecked in a field near Dover, the crew having baled out of the disabled aircraft as soon as they were over land. She found no sign of C for Charlie. At four in the morning, two hours after all fuel must have been exhausted, she handed over to a flight sergeant and went back to her quarters, exhausted, white, and hurt.

She took three aspirins to assist sleep, but for a long time she lay awake, sweating and distressed. When at last she did fall asleep, she had a terrible dream.

She dreamed that Flight Officer Stevens had gone away on leave, and Section Officer Ford had gone sick, and she was left as the senior W.A.A.F. officer in the camp. She was in her office, and the telephone rang. She picked it up to answer it and it was Chesterton, the Squadron Leader (Admin.). He said: "Oh, Miss Robertson. We've got two more officers coming in this afternoon. Will you please get Flight Lieutenant Marshall's room cleared and have his things packed up to be sent to his home ? I'm afraid he won't be coming back." And she had said: "Very good, sir."

She had gone out of the office and walked slowly to the officer's block; she did not want to go; it was as if some power were pushing her from behind. When she arrived before the cheap, painted door of his room she paused; she did not want to go in, but she had to, and presently she opened the door.

The room was neat and bright and sunny; the bed was turned down and a pair of blue pyjamas laid out on it invitingly, but it had not been slept in. In a corner of the room she saw the long green bag that held the little spinning-rod that he had taught her to use, and on the dressing-table she saw the little multiplying-reel that went with it. And in her mind she said in agony: "Oh, please, I can't do this. Somebody else must do it for me," and behind her someone said: "But you must. This is the job you've got to do."

So she went forward into the room, and to the little bare table that served both as dressing-table and as writing-table, and she opened the little drawer beneath it, and took out what first came to her hand. It was a blotting-pad, and in among the doodles her own name was written, Gervase Laura Robertson. She put it down quickly, her eyes full of tears, and the next thing that she took out was a snapshot photograph of herself standing at the door of the R/T office talking to her flight sergeant, the photograph taken furtively from the window of the control office. And she said, weeping: "Please, I can't go through with this. Somebody else must do it." But behind her someone said: "It would be a waste of manpower for a man to do a simple little job like this."

She put down the photograph, and the next thing she picked out was a lock of hair, and it was her hair. And the next thing was six inches of shoulder-strap ribbon—her shoulder-strap ribbon—and she said sadly: "I never gave him that." And the next thing was a letter, sealed, and on the envelope

97

was written her own name, 'S/O G. L. Robertson'.

And while she stood irresolute, fearing to open the letter, there was a knock at the door, and she said: "Come in." And the door opened, and Beatrice the batwoman came into the room with a large cup of tea in her hand. And she said: "Oh, beg pardon, ma'am. I just brought Flight Lieutenant Marshall his cup of tea."

Then she woke up, and she was in bed, trembling and shaken, and her pillow was wet with tears. She did not sleep again that night.

She met Flight Officer Stevens at breakfast next morning. She had no appetite for sausages, but she poured herself out a strong cup of coffee, and asked:

"Has anything come in yet about Charlie?"

The older woman said: "No. Nobody appears to know anything about it."

The girl said bitterly: "Well, I do. I know something about it."

The Flight Officer looked up at her. "What's that?"

Gervase said: "The captain came to see me yesterday—Pilot Officer Drummond. He wanted to know the stations we should be working. He didn't like his crew."

Mrs. Stevens said sharply: "Were they quarrelling?"

Gervase thought for a moment. "No," she said. "I don't think they were quarrelling. But they weren't together as a team. I think he was a bit afraid of them. He felt that they were watching him to see if he made a mistake."

The Flight Officer said: "Well, they would be. That's only natural for a crew when they get a new captain."

The girl was silent, sipping at her coffee. Mrs. Stevens glanced at her, and said: "Was he very worried?"

Gervase said in a low tone: "I think he was."

There was a long pause; the Flight Officer helped herself to toast and marmalade. "There's nothing to be done about a pilot's worry when he goes out as a captain for the first time," she said. "That's one of the things that we can't help them in. If you ever hear of a crew quarrelling amongst themselves, let me know, quietly, and I'll have a word with Wing Commander Dobbie. But nervousness the first time is inevitable."

Gervase said doubtfully: "I suppose it is."

They said no more; she ate nothing, but drank two cups of coffee and smoked three cigarettes; presently she left the room and went over to her office at Headquarters. There was no news at all of C for Charlie; she felt that bad news would have been easier than suspense. She moved through her routine work all day, anxious and troubled. It was true that Drummond had not quarrelled with his crew, but she was not so sure of Marshall. When she had talked to Gunnar Franck he had been very sore indeed, very much hurt and upset at his captain's attitude. She wondered unhappily if she ought to do something about R for Robert; if so, what could she do?

Her reason told her that she had much better do nothing. A team that had done so many sorties together was not likely to disintegrate because one member of it had become irritable; that was absurd. Irritation with each other was not quarrelling; in R for Robert nobody wanted to murder anybody else. There was minor friction in that crew, but that was not a matter that could go before the Wing Commander.

Gervase pulled herself together, remembering that she had slept very little during the night, and that she had suffered a nightmare in the short time that she was asleep. In the late afternoon she got upon her bicycle and rode out of the camp, and rode steadily through the country lanes till dusk, covering about fifteen miles and returning to the camp tired out with exercise and lack of sleep and nervous strain. There was no news of C for Charlie; nobody knew what had become of that machine at all. With a sad heart Gervase ate an early supper and went to bed immediately; she slept heavily the whole night through.

The weather remained good. In spite of the loss of two machines in the Bremen operation the wing was at good strength after its fortnight's rest. Next day the station was closed again and the crews made their final preparations for another operation; when the briefing came it turned out that it was to be Mannheim.

Marshall had been to Mannheim twice before; he knew the appearance of the city from the air, and the landmarks in the immediate neighbourhood. He listened to the briefing idly, with only half his mind upon the job, staring at the familiar air photographs in absent meditation, making a desultory note or two about objectives. He was feeling stale and tired and fed-up with the whole business. For many nights now he had slept badly; with the close of the fishing season all the savour had gone out of life at Hartley Magna. He had reached the settled opinion that he had failed with Gervase because he was himself an unattractive fool, and this mood of self-depreciation, like an infection, was spreading into his work. He knew that his crew had become annoyed with him; it was only natural, he felt, for an air crew to become annoyed with an inefficient captain. In recent weeks, he felt, all the zest had gone out of the work; flying and operations now were just another duty to be got through somehow or other before he could return and see Gervase eating buttered toast in the ante-room, and suffer again.

Gunnar Franck sat beside him. He also had seen Mannheim several times before, but he was not in love. He sat with his attention concentrated on the briefing; it was in the back of his mind that, since Marshall was obviously not himself, much more might devolve upon the navigator than usual. In plain words, if the pilot were in a day-dream all the time, the navigator would have to push him through his work in the interests of their common safety. Gunnar Franck was quite prepared to do this and was concentrating hard upon the briefing with that in his mind, but he was resentful that it should be necessary.

The crews dispersed after the briefing, to take off in a couple of hours' time. Marshall went back to the mess for a light meal; he felt tired and depressed. He sat next to Pat Johnson, who said: "Take you on at golf to-morrow if it's fine. Give you half a stroke a hole."

Marshall said morosely: "I can't play that bloody game."

The conversation lapsed, and they ate on in silence. Half an hour later Marshall went down to the crew-room; his party were already there, getting into their flying clothing. Listlessly he began to dress: boots, scarf, Sidcot, harness. With helmet, 'chute, and gloves upon his knee he sat down on the bench and waited, silent and irritable. Gunnar Franck and Phillips in turn tried him with a casual remark; he snapped back at them shortly, and they let him alone.

The truck came presently and they piled into it, and drove off round the ring runway in the darkness, stopping from time to time at the dispersed machines to drop the crews. They came to Robert, and Marshall got out with his crew; the sergeant rigger came forward from the darkness to meet them. "All ready, sir," he said.

The pilot said sharply: "Have you got the windscreen clean this time?"

The sergeant said resentfully: "I had a man doing nothing

else but polish up the perspex and the windscreen for an hour, sir."

Marshall turned away. "I'll see if he's made a job of it."

He climbed up into the nose of the aircraft behind his crew; everything was clammy and oily to the touch; it stank of lubricating oil and hydraulic fluid. Standing beside his seat he put his 'chute into the stowage and laid gloves and helmet on the seat; then he went aft down the fuselage to the navigation and W/T positions and down the tail to Phillips near the turret. "Keep your eyes open to-night," he said. "There'll be a moon; we're liable to meet a good few fighters." Phillips knew that quite as well as he did; the remark was unnecessary and in a tiny way insulting, in the light of all their operations as a crew.

Marshall looked over the more secret parts of the equipment, and made his way back through the fuselage to the cockpit. He got into his seat and pulled his helmet on, and strapped it tight and settled it upon his head, and plugged in the intercom. Then through the window at his side he shouted down into the darkness: "Sergeant Miles. Send up someone with a rag to do this windscreen. The bloody thing's still filthy."

While that was being cleaned off to his satisfaction he spoke one by one to all the members of his crew. "Hullo wireless operator. Wireless O.K. ?"

"Wireless O.K., Cap."

"Oxygen O.K. ?"

"Oxygen O.K., sir."

Satisfied with the crew, he glanced at his watch, then shouted through his window:

"O.K. for starting up ?"

"O.K. for starting up, sir."

"Stand clear. Contact starboard engine." His hand moved upon the switch."

"Contact, sir."

The starter groaned and the propeller revolved slowly; then it kicked forward as the engine coughed, choked for a moment, and began to run. Marshall started the port engine and sat while they warmed, setting his trim and making himself comfortable in his seat.

Presently he began upon his routine of running up, testing the pitch controls, the magnetos, the petrol cocks, the boost. He tried the flaps and set the compass and the gyro. Everything was in order. He signed the engine log and handed it to Gunnar, who passed it down to the sergeant fitter standing on the steps below the entrance hatch. The steps were taken away and Gunnar closed the hatch. Marshall waved the chocks away, and the Wimpey moved off slowly round the ring road towards the marshalling point at the end of the long runway, marked by small, dim lights.

The machine before them opened out and trundled down the runway, its tail light a diminishing white speck that wavered up into the night. Marshall taxied up and swung round into wind, and said down the intercom: "Stand by now to take off."

He sat staring over to the control office, thinking of Gervase with an aching heart. He knew she was not there; he had informed himself that she was on duty at Group W/T that night, three miles away at Pilsey. A green light flashed at him; he turned his head and pressed the throttles forward, and they moved. The dim lights flicked past them on each side in quickening tempo; he eased her off the ground as soon as she would take it and climbed slowly up into the night, laden with three tons of incendiaries for Mannheim.

He took her up to about nine thousand feet, passing a thin layer of cloud between three and four thousand, and put her over to the automatic pilot. The cloud below them prevented Gunnar from pin-pointing their route; he became very busy with his sextant at the astro hatch, and in computing the position at the navigating table. Marshall left his seat after a time and came and checked the course and observations with him in the light of the little shaded lamp.

"Still making these bloody sevens," he said.

In the dim, roaring confinement of the fuselage Gunnar flushed; everything that they said could be heard by the rest of the crew over the intercom. "It is only for my own work, this. When I pass the course to you I make an English seven, always."

The pilot grunted and went back to his seat in the cockpit; though they were over England still he did not care to be away too long from the controls. Behind him Gunnar Franck worked steadily at the navigation; beyond him Leech sat at the wireless reading a paper-covered Western, *Jeannie of the Golden Gulch*. Sergeant Cobbett, the flight engineer sent with them for the operation, moved between cockpit instruments and the fuel gauges, watching the engines through the little windows in the fuselage. In the rear turret Sergeant Phillips sat brooding over his guns.

Phillips did not think very quickly, nor easily adjust his mind; rather, he was patient and thorough. Through long meditation he had satisfied himself just what a Ju. 88 night fighter would look like as it came into range; he had it all set in his imagination, visualised in scale against the bars that framed the perspex of his dome. It had, in fact, looked just like that when it had come at them from behind over Rostock, and he had held his fire until it looked as he had thought it would against the framework of the perspex, and then given it the squirt. His tracer had crossed theirs as they fired simultaneously, but he had been luckier than the German pilot. The Ju.88 had reared up suddenly behind him, so that its tracer went streaming above them. For an instant he had had the belly and wing undersurface exposed, and had held himself braced at the sight, while the whole rear end of the Wimpey shook and quivered with the violence of his guns. Then it was out of range and a small point of light appeared upon it, and he ceased firing and watched tensely, and the flame grew quickly as the 88 dropped back behind until it was a flaming beacon forty-five degrees below.

He knew what it would look like, or had known until the change in his gun setting. He did not think that it would really need to look different, but he was not quite sure. He was not quite sure now whether he ought to open fire sooner or later with the new setting; if sooner, the enemy would be smaller against the framework of his dome, if later it would be larger. He did not really know what range he had fired at over Rostock, but he did know very well just how the Ju.88 had looked the instant that he opened fire, and he had shot it down. He had been quite happy previously that if he got a Ju.88 to look like that again he would shoot it down again, but now his sights were changed and it would be a bit different. He sat there brooding and a little uncertain.

They were still above the cloud when they had run out their estimated time of arrival at Dover, but before them it was growing thinner and some gaps were visible, as had been foretold at the briefing. They went on steadily; when they judged that they were over sea Marshall ordered guns to be tested. Behind him he heard the clamour from the rear-turret, transmitted mostly through the framework, dulled by the unnoticed roaring of the engines. Ahead of him he saw the barrels move as Sergeant Cobbett swung them down towards the sea, and saw the quick lines of the tracer going out ahead and to the left. They seldom used the front guns in the Wellington.

They flew on steadily, the cloud getting thinner. Marshall sat motionless at the controls, flying upon the automatic pilot, but ready to take over at the instant in emergency. He turned his gaze mechanically from side to side and up and down, within the solid angle of view that his seat permitted. He was in the region now when he might meet a night fighter to intercept them on the way, but all he saw was other aircraft now and then, Lancasters and Halifaxes and Wellingtons, all winging forward on the same course as they.

They crossed the Belgian coast; it was clear now and they could pin-point their position. A glow on the horizon showed the rising moon; presently it would turn into a bright night until the cloud behind them rolled up from the west. The glow ahead made things more difficult for Marshall; it strained his eyes, contracting the pupils as they passed across it, making it difficult to look into the secrets of the dark below.

He yawned once or twice, unusual for him; already he was growing tired. The bright light of the moon had a hypnotic influence. The steady rhythm of the engines, the fact that he had been sleeping badly, the boredom of a flight that he had done so many times before and did not want to do again, the long humiliation and unhappiness that was always in the background of his mind, all fought against his watchfulness. He found himself longing to be back in bed with a hot-water bottle, instead of flying on in this black emptiness, facing the dazzle of the moon. He was fed-up with flying bombers, fed to the teeth with Hartley, fed with everything.

He put his hand into the parachute stowage and found his bag of sweets, and began to suck an acid drop.

They had left the ground at Hartley at eight-seventeen; at ten-twelve, in the darkness far ahead of them, Marshall saw a point of yellow light, and then another close by it. He nodded absently when he saw it; Gunnar had guided them aright, and the Pathfinders had done their job; the fires that they had lit would bring the rest of the machines on to the target without effort. As he watched, a great number of searchlights sprang up in a cone above the target, thin little pencils of silvery light at that distance, pretty and innocuous.

He said down the intercom: "Captain to navigator. Target right ahead, I think. Just have a look."

Gunnar Franck came forward and stood beside him, looking out of the windscreen and the starboard window. He nodded, and went down to the bomb-aimer's position and, kneeling on the floor, uncovered the sight and began adjusting it. Presently he came back and stood by the pilot, watching the target as it grew slowly closer.

The fires grew brighter, larger, as they approached; there were more searchlights and they could see flak bursting in the cone. They were still flying at nine thousand feet. There were half a dozen flares suspended in the sky over the doomed city; no need for them to drop another for their run.

Marshall said: "Captain to crew. I'm going straight in a bit below the apex of the cone, and get this damn job over. Height will be seven thousand eight hundred. Wireless operator, drop one flare as soon as you hear 'Bombs away'; we'll leave it for the next chap. Phillips, you know the target. See if you can spot our bursts. Everybody O.K. ? All right, then let's go, and then we can get back to bed."

It was not usual for them to fly straight in without a few minutes reconnaissance of the situation at the target; Marshall was conscious of resentment in the silence of his crew, in the motionless attitude of Gunnar Franck beside him. He put out the automatic pilot and took over the control, throttled a little to lose height. Gunnar got down to the bomb-aimer's position and lay down on his stomach; his legs alone were visible to the pilot. Marshall, his eyes fixed on the target, began weaving the machine slowly from side to side. At seven thousand eight hundred he levelled off and flew in, weaving steadily.

Over the intercom Gunnar said: "Bomb-aimer to Captain. I see where the target should be, I can see the canal and the little dock. But the target itself is all smoke. There are three fires and perhaps four started there already."

Marshall said: "It doesn't matter. Put ours in the middle, as nearly as you can."

"O.K., Captain. Keep on weaving now, but turn right. More right. More. O.K., go in on that, but keep on weaving. There is a minute to go still, perhaps a little more."

The searchlights were about them now; the whole machine was lit inside with silvery light. Another Wellington passed close above them, turning for another run in. Flak was bursting close by a machine about three hundred feet above them; it was dangerously hot, but they would soon be through with it. Marshall sat making his slow, rhythmic movements with hands and feet, weaving the big machine as nearly equally on each side as he could.

Gunnar said: "Steady now, Cap, steady. Left. More left. Steady at that. Left a little. Steady. Right a little. Steady. . . ."

Beneath their feet there was a jolt and the whole structure of the aircraft sprung. "Bombs away," said Gunnar.

There was a bright yellow burst just at the port wing tip, and a twanging noise from somewhere in the wing; Marshall bore hard upon the wheel and thrust his right foot forward, and flung the aircraft round. There was another burst above them, and a third on the port bow; over the intercom they all heard Sergeant Phillips say disgustedly: "My muckin' Christ!" And then they heard Corporal Leech say: "Wireless operator to Captain. All bombs gone, sir."

Marshall said: "Get the bomb doors closed up, Sergeant Franck." The control was by his side, but he was too busy at the wheel to spare a hand for it himself. Gunnar stood up by him and pulled the lever over. Another burst came very close to them, but that was the last. The white light of the searchlights wavered and grew dim, the evolutions of the aircraft grew less violent, and they went forward on a south-east course into the friendly darkness.

Marshall said tersely: "Captain to wireless operator. Send 'Mission completed'." And then to Gunnar: "I'm going to make a wide sweep round towards the north in a few minutes. Take a point fifteen miles north-east of the target, and give me a course back from there."

He sat at the controls staring mechanically around into the darkness and the moon, feeling exhausted and drained of all energy. He knew that he had been rash in going straight in to the target in that way; however, they had got away with it. Now that the strain was over a reaction had set in; each movement, almost each thought, seemed an effort. So many sleepless nights were making themselves felt.

He began a slow turn to the north. Over the intercom Sergeant Phillips said: "Rear-gunner to Captain. There's an aircraft down below us, five or six hundred feet below. A bit behind and to port." There was a pause. "Sort of keeping station with us—Halifax, I think."

Marshall said: "All right—keep an eye on it." With so many machines in the vicinity, a collision in the darkness was a very real danger.

Presently Phillips said: "Another aircraft, Cap, a bit above us and behind." After a moment he said: "Fighter, Cap—I think!" And then: "Start jinking, he's right on top of us!"

Marshall cursed, and flung the machine round to the left; the enemy had got them silhouetted against the moon. At the same instant he felt the stammer of the rear guns transmitted through the structure, and saw bright tracer flying over his port wing from the rear forward. Star after star appeared upon the wing with sharp cracks; the port engine began to vibrate badly.

In that split-second of emergency, the rear-gunner was straining to keep his tracer on the enemy behind, exchanging stream for stream. He had hesitated as it loomed up larger, a black, unfamiliar shadow through the framework of the perspex, uncertain at what range to open fire; that hesitation gave the German pilot the chance to get the first shots off. The Wellington was already turning to the left, spoiling the aim of the attacker; his cannon fire went into the port wing for a second. Phillips was pumping fire at him from the four Brownings of the turret by that time, but deliverance came to them from the Halifax below. The mid-upper and rear-gunners of the Halifax had been vigilant, watching the aircraft above them as they closed; immediately the cannon fire disclosed the Ju.88 they opened up on him.

A stream of fire from their eight guns came up against the fighter from below and to starboard. It was too much for the German pilot; he did not seem to be seriously hit, but his fire ceased and he slipped away to port and was lost in the darkness.

All firing ceased. The whole engagement had lasted only for three or four seconds.

R for Robert was now in a bad way. They could not tell from within the aircraft how badly the port wing was damaged. Gunnar Franck climbed up by Marshall and flashed the torch through the side window along the length of the leading edge; there was damage and distortion about half-way to the tip, upon the upper surface. The D.F. aerial above the fuselage had gone and left a hole where it had been; the port engine cowling was badly torn, and Marshall had already throttled back to sixteen hundred revs. because of the vibration. Gunnar left him, and scrambled back down the fuselage to the wireless position, where there was a cellon window from which he could see the top surface of the wing. He saw great holes in it, with tattered, flapping fabric, and a white plume of petrol streaming from the trailing edge.

He plugged in the lead from his helmet hurriedly, and said: "Cap, there is petrol coming from the tanks on the port wing, a great deal of it." He heard Marshall say: "Cobbett, you got that? Get back on to the fuel system."

The flight engineer came scrambling back from the front turret to the fuel cocks in the fuselage; at all costs they must try to save the petrol from the port tanks if they were to get back home with anything to spare. Gunnar and Cobbett set to work upon the hand pump to back up the engine pumps, and Marshall put the aircraft in a sideslip right wing down to help the flow. In ominously short time they transferred what fuel was left into the right wing tanks, and Gunnar had time to look around.

In the dim light above the wireless desk he saw Leech crouching forward, his face chalk white, holding his left shoulder with his right hand; blood had come from somewhere within his Sidcot and was trickling over his right wrist. The Dane nudged the flight engineer and pointed, and went to the wireless operator. Cobbett said over the intercom: "Flight engineer to Captain. All petrol in the right tanks now, and fuel for about two and a half hours at twenty-two hundred revs. Corporal Leech has got it, sir—he's bleeding. Sergeant Franck is looking after him."

Marshall said: "If you can leave the fuel system, Cobbett, go and look after Leech and ask the navigator to give me the course."

At the wireless desk the operator raised his head. "Cap wants a course, Gunnar," he said. "I'll be all right."

The Dane left him to Cobbett. In the darkness the machine roared on, covering over three miles in each minute; whatever crisis might develop in the fuselage the navigation must go on uninterrupted. Without navigation they would soon be lost, and to be lost and short of fuel meant disaster, nothing else. Gunnar darted from side to side of the machine, peering out, seeking a landmark; in the distance on the port quarter he saw the glow of fires and searchlights at the target. He shot forward into the cockpit and read the directional gyro, and hoped it had been synchronised recently; then he went back to the chart table and pin-pointed his position on a guessed distance from the target. With pencil, map, and C.S.C. he ran the course out, noted it upon the map, and said: "Navigator to Captain—course three one five, Cap." He wrote it on his pad, tore off the sheet, and went forward and gave it to Marshall;

then he went aft again immediately to the wireless operator. Gunnar had done two and a half years in a Copenhagen medical school, and knew the rudiments of surgery better than any of them.

Marshall took the slip and stuffed it in the knee pocket of his Sidcot without looking at it, leaned forward, and set 351 upon the verge ring of the compass. He leaned back in his seat, forcing himself to an alertness that was continuous effort; he was tired to death. The machine was flying left wing down in spite of all the petrol in the right wing; she had lost a good deal of fabric on the damaged side. Another night fighter like the last, coming upon them in their crippled state, would just about finish them off. He said: "Captain to rear-gunner. Keep a good look-out. We don't want any more of that."

"Okay, Cap."

In the moonlight Marshall saw banks of cloud advancing on them from the left; this was the cloud that they had left behind them on the outwards trip rolling forward over Europe. With dulled mind Marshall wondered whether he should call Gunnar again to check the course before they entered cloud and navigation became difficult. Gunnar, he thought, was almost certainly in the middle of putting a dressing upon Leech; in any case he had taken a good pin-point from the fires at the target only a few minutes before.

Cobbett came forward and stood beside him, and they talked about the damaged engine, and the fuel. They came to the conclusion that the propeller had been hit; it made a different noise and in the white light of the torch the blur of its rotation appeared thicker at the tip. It ran smoothly at fifteen hundred revs. and it was just possible at sixteen hundred, but at that it was only developing about a quarter power. "The thing's a bloody passenger," said Marshall.

Presently they flew into the cloud at about seven thousand feet. It was a relief to do so; they had over two hundred miles to go before they reached the Channel, and at any point in that two hundred miles a fighter might come on them. It was safer for them to fly blind within the cloud.

In the rear fuselage Gunnar was making Leech comfortable upon the floor. He had found a torn, jagged wound in the right shoulder and neck, and another in the right thigh; neither was very grave, provided that the bleeding could be checked. Gunnar had bound on heavy wads of dressing upon both wounds and had given a small shot of morphia; presently he left Leech to the care of Cobbett and moved back to the navigation table. The aircraft was now flying in thick cloud, at seven thousand feet.

He said: "Navigator to Captain. Can you get her up above this for an astro fix ?"

Marshall said irritably: "And get ourselves shot up again. What time is E.T.A. the Belgian coast ?"

The Dane turned to his calculations. Presently he said: "E.T.A. the Belgian coast 11.54, Cap."

The pilot glanced at his clock; about an hour to go. In their damaged state they could not risk another encounter with a fighter; even flak would be difficult for them, with the slow rate of climb that the machine now had. Over enemy territory it was better to play safe and stay in cloud.

He said: "What airspeed did you take when you ran out the course ?"

"A hundred and ninety-five, true airspeed, Cap."

Marshall glanced at his dials; the indicated speed was a hundred and sixty at seven thousand. "That's just about right," he said. "We'll keep on as we are till E.T.A. the coast minus ten minutes—11.44. Then I'll bring her down out of this stuff and we'll get a position as we pass the coast."

They went on to discuss the fuel position. E.T.A. Hartley was about 12.31; from the gauges it appeared that they would have about twenty minutes' reserve fuel. It was going to be a near thing, but it was not too bad; there was no reason to suppose that they would have to bale out for lack of petrol.

"Give you a spell, Cap ?" said the Dane.

"I'm all right," said Marshall. "Get back and see how Leech is getting on." He would have liked a relief; he was desperately tired. It seemed to him that Gunnar Franck, with his slight medical knowledge, would be better occupied in looking after Leech than flying the machine.

He put the machine on to the automatic pilot, and they flew on in cloud in the black night.

At a quarter to twelve Gunnar came to the cockpit and stood by Marshall; the pilot throttled a little, and the machine began to lose height. They broke out of the cloud into clear air at about two thousand feet ten minutes later, opened up to fly level and stared down into the darkness. Faint, corrugated rows of white upon the black sheet below showed that they were over sea.

Marshall said: "What's your E.T.A. Dover ?"

Gunnar went back to the navigating position, made a quick calculation, and said: "E.T.A. Dover 12.09, Cap."

Marshall said: "Okay. We'll carry on." And then he said: "Captain to crew. Everybody keep a good look-out for the coast. We ought to come out somewhere near Dover in the next ten minutes."

They came down to twelve hundred feet and flew on over sea, tense and peering down into the blackness below. At 12.08 they had not seen any land at all; they were all very conscious that their fuel was running short. They now had barely forty minutes' supply left.

Marshall said: "Captain to Navigator. Get on to the wireless and see if you can get a fix. Looks as though we've drifted a bit." The coast of Kent was like a spear thrust forward to their course; if they had been set one way by the wind they would fly over sea up the Thames estuary for a long way further, if they had been set the other way they would be flying up the English Channel.

Gunnar got back and sat down at the wireless. He knew what to do, but it took him some time to do it. First he had to fumble for the light switch, and then find the card on which the stations, wave-lengths, and call signs were noted; he plugged in and, peering at the dials, set the tuning condensers. He checked everything through carefully again and then switched on, and began transmitting on the morse key their call sign and the code request for a position.

Three minutes later he was at the navigator's table with his information. It was incredible as he plotted it upon the map—in fact, he had to change maps and plot it on a new sheet altogether. He plugged in quickly and said: "Navigator to Captain. This fix say that we are out in the North Sea, one hundred and five miles east of Spurn Head at the mouth of the Humber."

Marshall said quickly: "Oh balls. That can't be right."

There was a momentary pause; the machine flew on over the black sea. Gunnar worked quickly to check his fix, and then to check the previous course from Mannheim. "There is something not right," he said quietly over the intercom. "You have been flying on 315, Cap?"

He went forward to the cockpit as Marshall bent to the compass; both scrutinised the verge ring together in the shaded light. The pilot said: "Three one five? This thing says about three fifty."

Gunnar nodded. "That is where we have been wrong. The course was three one five."

The pilot dived his hand into his knee pocket and pulled out the slip. He glanced at it, and then back at his navigator: "Sorry, Gunnar," he said quietly. "I must have set the bloody thing wrong."

He knocked out the automatic pilot and swung the aircraft round; there was no time to waste. "Give me a course to the nearest land," he said. "I'll fly on 270 meantime."

In a minute Gunnar came back on the intercom, speaking from the navigation table. "Captain to navigator. Course is 282."

"What's estimated time of arrival the coast?"

"Twelve fifty-five, Cap."

Marshall called Cobbett on the intercom for a report on the fuel, and Gunnar came forward to the cockpit and watched while the pilot set the course upon the compass verge ring to make sure he got it right this time. The fuel gauges in all tanks were nearing zero; Cobbett estimated that their fuel would be exhausted by 12.45.

Marshall said quietly: "Okay. Navigator, get back to the wireless and report our course, the landfall we expect to make, and our E.T.A. the coast. Tell them we are short of fuel, and to stand by for our position. Ask for emergency routine."

He paused a minute, and then said: "Captain to crew. Sorry, chaps, but I think we're going in the drink. Rear-gunner, you can come out of the turret. You'll be in charge of the dinghy; have a look now and see if it's all there and in order. Sergeant Cobbett, get down in the bomb-aimer's position and let me know if you see any land."

Sergeant Phillips levered himself out of the steel doors of the turret backwards into the fuselage, and reached for his parachute; he would take that forward with him and keep it to hand. He was concerned at the news that they were going in the drink, but he had too slow an imagination to be very much distressed about it. He knew that there had been some kind of a mistake between the captain and the navigator that had landed them in that position; he did not clearly understand from the conversation he had overheard upon the intercom who was to blame. In the meantime he had been given a positive job to do, to look after the dinghy and the stores for it; that was a change from sitting in the turret staring into blackness, and that itself was pleasurable.

Sergeant Cobbett, lying in the bomb-aimer's position, stared down at the sea. He had been on seven operations previously, and only one of those had been with Marshall. Before he joined up he had worked in a garage, washing motor-cars; he was still very young, developing into an intelligent and an efficient man through the responsibilities that he now had to bear. He knew this himself, and thought a little regretfully that it was a pity that it should all end now, in the black water he could see below. He could see from the run of the waves that the wind was westerly; that meant that if they should get out into the dinghy safely they would drift away from land. It was a pity; if things had gone on he might one day have been sent for training as a pilot, have been given a commission even, and become a man like Marshall in a few years' time. That was what he had set his heart upon, and every night he prayed that the war might go on long enough for him to get a commission and become the captain of his own aircraft. Now it was all to end in the black sea. He was not resentful of the captain's mistake that had landed them there; he respected Marshall too much for that. It was just a pity. He knew that there was a thirty per cent chance that they would be picked up before exposure and the bitter cold brought death to them; he knew that there was a seventy per cent chance that they wouldn't. He lay staring down at the black sea through the triplex panel, ready to shout out at the first indication of land.

Corporal Leech lay in drugged stupor on the floor of the rear fuselage, his head pillowed on somebody's parachute. Gunnar had done his work efficiently; Leech knew nothing of what was going on. Even when Phillips had to drag the dinghy pack across him, it hardly stirred his mind. When they went down into the water he would almost certainly be drowned within the fuselage; in the few moments that the escape hatch would be above water the remainder of the crew could hardly hope to get him out. He was unconscious now, wrapped in drugged slumber; in that slumber he would quietly meet his death.

Gunnar Franck sat at the wireless, painstaking, thorough, and methodical. He did not know the code groups; at each stage he had to consult the written information that he had found in the wireless operator's satchel, and this made him very slow. He transmitted slowly, too; he could not manage to send accurately at more than about seven words a minute or to receive at more than four or five. He did literally what he had been told to do, asked for emergency routine, reported their situation, and asked the stations to stand by for their last signal before they went down in the sea, in order that the rescue planes could search for them at dawn. He received the code confirmation that the written card had told him to expect, and then, surprisingly, the message went on pinging in his head-phones. His pencil moved mechanically on the pad; the message ended and he read the groups that he had written. They read: "Good luck to captain and crew."

He was very pleased at the message; almost certainly it came from Pilsey. He must tell the captain, and plugged in his intercom. He said: "Navigator to Captain. Wireless emergency routine is in force, and they are standing by for our signal. They have sent us a message, Cap, from Hartley, I think. They say: 'Good luck to captain and crew.' I think that is ver' nice to have."

Marshall said quickly: "Are you sure that came from Hartley?"

"It was Group, Cap. They gave the identification."

"Okay." He raised his voice. "You all heard that, you chaps? Hartley says 'Good luck to captain and crew.'"

He sat on at the controls, peering forward into the darkness and studying the faint lines on the sea below. He had become awake and cheerful; in that last half-hour he felt more himself than he had done for weeks. By all calculation they would be down very soon; those of them who were not killed at the impact with the water might get out into the dinghy to drift outwards from the land in the wet, freezing blackness of the sea. Many of his friends had gone that way; some had been picked up and returned to Hartley Magna in Oxfordshire, more had not. If that now had to happen to him, that was just too bad, but it had happened to better men than he. In the meantime the engines still ran, steady and even on the starboard side, like the lavatory cistern on the port. The sea beneath still seemed unreal and far away, as unreal as Mannheim.

His mind glowed at the message they had had from Group. A girl had sent that message; it was not in the words that a man would have used. And if it was a girl at Pilsey, it could only be one of two: either the operator had slipped it in upon her own, or else the W.A.A.F. officer in charge had sent it—Gervase Robertson. He was convinced as soon as he had heard

114

it that it was Gervase; she had sent the message to cheer them.

He said down the intercom: "Captain to flight engineer. Do you think that port engine's doing us any good?"

"It's helping us along, Cap."

"I think it's drinking half our bloody juice and doing no work. We're only doing a hundred and eighty. We can do that on one engine. We'd be better off to stop the port altogether and go on the starboard, wouldn't we? How much fuel is there left?"

Cobbett scrambled up to the fuel board and plugged in his intercom there. "Gauges say about twenty-five gallons, Cap."

"Well, that's the thick end of half an hour for one engine. Stop the port engine—switch it off and let it stop. Then I'm going to throttle back the starboard until we're doing a hundred and thirty. Navigator, give me a new course at speed hundred and thirty."

The port engine died and came to rest; the note of the starboard engine dropped slowly as Marshall eased the throttle back. A new sensation as of silence broke upon them; their ears were so attuned to the roar that the lessened level of the noise came as quiet to them. When they spoke now the intercom, set at the previous volume, seemed to bellow in their ears.

Gunnar said: "New course is 279." He came through to the cockpit and set it on the verge ring himself.

"Where does that bring us over land?"

"Just north of Spurn Head, Cap."

"Okay. Get through to Group and ask for another fix to check up." He paused, and then said: "Captain to crew. If we get over land we'll bale out, so be ready for that because we haven't got much height. Rear-gunner, got your dinghy ready?"

"All ready, Cap."

"Well, now clip on Leech's parachute and tie that cod-line to the ring. If we bale out, we'll drop him out first." They would make the line fast at the machine before they dropped him; as he fell away the line would pull the ring and the parachute would open as he fell. Unconscious and inert he would land heavily, but it was the best that they could do for him if it came to baling out.

They flew on in the darkness, peering forward and down. Their slow speed now seemed to mock them; it needed intellect and mental effort to appreciate that they would get a few more miles by creeping along like this. Cobbett lay on the floor and peered down through the bomb-aimer's hatch. Gunnar Franck moved rapidly between the navigator's table and the wireless. Phillips worked over Leech, and pulled and lifted him nearer to the escape-hatch.

Marshall sat on in the cockpit, quiet and resigned. If now they went into the drink it was too bad; he had done everything possible. Gervase had sent him a message; that meant she was still interested. He knew it was a very tiny thing, but after the trouble of the last few weeks it came to him as balm, as a little faint voice whispering that things would be all right. Immediately it had reacted on his work; he had started to take an interest in R for Robert once again, and had shut off the damaged engine.

At 12.52 Gunnar got a third fix, plotted it, and pondered for a moment. It showed them to be about fourteen miles from land. He said: "E.T.A. the coast seven minutes, Cap."

"Okay. What's the petrol looking like?" But the needle of the gauge was jumping at the zero stop, and might have been two gallons or ten.

They sat tense and motionless as the minutes crept by. Each of them had found his own position from which to watch the sea: Cobbett through the triplex of the bomb-aimer's window, Gunnar from the starboard window of the cockpit, Phillips from a cellon panel under the rear fuselage. Each strained his eyes down to the black, ruffled sea below them; each had his ears tuned to the beat of the engines, ready at the first falter to get up and stand by for their captain's orders.

Cobbett said: "Flight engineer to Captain. Breakers, Cap— on a beach. We're coming over land."

Marshall peered down into the darkness. "Okay—I see. Navigator—put on our navigation lights. What's the gauge showing?"

Gunnar switched on the wing-tip and tail lights and turned to the fuel board; Cobbett got up and stood beside him. The needle stood steady and uncompromising at zero, without even a flicker. "All fuel gauges zero, Cap."

They were over land, anyway. Marshall said: "Okay. Bring Leech along here to the hatch, and drop him out, quick as you can. Everybody stand by to bale out."

He pulled the nose of the machine up a little, hoping to gain more height for their jump. Beside him there was heaving and struggling as they pulled the heavy, unconscious body of the wireless operator to the hatch, and a sharp blast of cold air as the floor hatch opened.

Suddenly Marshall said: "Hold everything!" He leaned over and grabbed Gunnar by the shoulder, and pointed forward. Before them stretched the dim, twin lines of light that showed a runway, barely three miles ahead. "What's that ?"

The Dane said: "There is here a station, Whitsand. That must be Whitsand.

They stood fixed for a minute, staring ahead at the lights, listening to the engine. "Okay," said Marshall. "We can make it now." He paused for an instant, and then said: "Shut that hatch, Cobbett."

The flight engineer stooped to the open hatch to close it. Something unusual in the blackness of the space beneath them drew his attention; he stooped to the cold rush of air and jumped back in horror. He thrust his plug into the intercom. "Climb, Cap," he said urgently. "There's another kite exactly underneath us!"

Marshall looked quickly down through his side window, but could see nothing. Gunnar shouldered Cobbett back and knelt down at the hatch. "Lancaster, Cap," he said, "about a hundred feet below, on the same course, going in to land. Better go round again."

Marshall thought quickly. They had no fuel to go round again; to try that could only mean disaster. Better to put his trust in the captain of the Lancaster to land according to the book, and to hope that the far end of the runway was soft. He said: "Okay, Gunnar. Put out navigation lights, Cobbett. Gunnar, stay at the hatch and tell me how we go. I'm going to land over him, and chance it."

Cobbett screwed himself round to the instrument board and put out the lights. Marshall said: "Gunnar, tell me how we go. I want to keep fifty feet above him, and land in front of him."

With a dry mouth the Dane said: "Okay, Cap. He is now going ahead of us, and sixty or seventy feet below. You should now see his wing from your window." And then urgently: "He has throttled; he is falling away below us now."

"Okay," said Marshall quietly. "I see him."

He throttled back the one engine that was running and sank after the Lancaster towards the landing lights. "Cobbett!" he said urgently. "Quarter flaps down."

He sat motionless at the controls, his face turned to the open window at his side, watching the Lancaster intently. If the big machine ahead became aware of them and took fright, and put on power to go round again, Marshall was ready to slip quickly out to starboard, away from its probable turn. If it went on to make a normal landing they would be all right, provided that the captain of the Lancaster kept his head.

For a moment he considered landing in the black, unknown terrain beside the runway. It would probably be quite all right provided that the ground was hard, but on a strange aerodrome in April would the ground be hard ? He felt that of the dangers that lay round about them he preferred the danger of collision with the Lancaster upon the ground.

He said: "Sergeant Phillips. Get back to the turret and plug in the intercom. I'm landing ahead of this Lanc. When we're down on the runway, tell me how we go, so that I can keep ahead of it, in case it butts us up the arse."

He heard the sergeant laugh, and say: "Okay, Cap."

They were very low now, and the lights were near. The pilot ordered half flap; they sank down with the Lancaster towards the ground at something over a hundred miles an hour in the dim blackness of the night. There was a faint glow upon the wing-tip of the Lancaster reflecting the red navigation light that showed Marshall the machine below him; that faint red glow, and the dim yellow lights that marked the runway, were the only clues to safety and disaster that the pilot had.

Gunnar had moved to the bomb-aimer's window. He said: "Cap, he is down."

"Okay," said Marshall. He drawled the word out absently.

His hand moved on the throttle; the note of the one engine rose in a slow burst and slowly died again. They levelled and swept over the big machine as it ran down the runway and sank down ahead of it. Marshall said: "Navigation lights now, Cobbett—quick. Rear-gunner—how do we go ?"

Phillips said: "Well ahead of him." The wheels touched on the ground; the machine bounced, sank, and touched again. Marshall steadied her on the dim lights still ahead of them as they ran on tail-up. Phillips said suddenly: "Keep going, Cap—he's closing up on us."

Marshall moved his hand upon the throttle very slightly; they ran on tail-up. The dim lights flashed past them one by one; they were very near the end of the runway. Without more ado he closed the throttle firmly; if the Lanc ran this far they would all pile up into the hedge together. The tail sank to the ground and the last light loomed up to them; he pulled the wheel hard back and pressed the brakes on to the utmost that he dared. The drums squealed, the tail bounced light upon the ground, and the Wellington ran on past the last light, down a little hill, and on to grass. Sergeant Cobbett switched off the engine and turned off the petrol; they ran on, slowly now, until the port wing hit a post and felled it, slewing them round to port with a tangle of telephone wires across the fuselage. So R for Robert came to rest, somewhere in England, after bombing Mannheim.

CHAPTER FIVE

Oh what can ail thee, knight-at-arms,
    Alone and palely loitering?
The sedge has withered from the lake,
    And no birds sing.

I met a lady in the meads,
    Full beautiful—a faery's child,
Her hair was long, her foot was light,
    And her eyes were wild. . . .

                            JOHN KEATS, 1818

Marshall travelled back to Hartley in the train next day by
way of London and Oxford. He travelled with his crew in a
third-class compartment; the fact that they might not travel
in first-class comfort with him added its quota to his black
mood.

They were all short of sleep. They had, in fact, spent the
night battling with trouble ever since they had put down at
Whitsand. They had dropped out of the fuselage hatch down
on to the ground in the black darkness, landing one by one into
a bed of stinging-nettles; getting to their feet most of them had
fallen again over the telephone lines that lay draped over R for
Robert, and the remains of the little short telegraph-pole that
they had felled. Stumbling back to the runway to find somebody to fetch an ambulance for Leech, they had come upon
the sergeant pilot of the Lancaster, now stopped upon the ring
runway a short way behind them. The sergeant pilot was considerably shaken and told Marshall all that lay upon his mind;
he did not know that he was speaking to an officer and would
not have altered one word if he had known. In the end
Marshall had to appeal to the crew of the Lancaster, now
gathering in the darkness. "For Christ's sake put a sock in it,"
he had said. "Which of you is the radio operator? You? Well,
get back in your machine and call up your control, and tell
them I want an ambulance down here at once for my own
operator. And look sharp, or I'll put you on a charge."

The ambulance came presently, and with it lights and a
young medical officer; they got Leech carefully out of the

machine and saw him carried off. A truck materialised out of the night and took them to the control office; Marshall, reporting to the control officer, was received with some coldness and was informed that by his act and deed he had cut off the station from all contact with the outside world except by radio. His comment on a station that was served by overhead lines at the runway's end did not help the matter.

The three sergeants were taken to the sergeants' mess, where they were given a meal and camp-beds hastily arranged; Marshall had to wait till four in the morning before traffic on the W/T permitted him to send his message to Hartley stating very briefly what had happened to R for Robert. He had then slept for a few hours on the bed in the control office.

Morning found them gathered at R for Robert, sourly inspecting the damage. The port wing was clearly for the scrapheap: the geodetic torn and buckled over nearly a third of the surface, the tanks ripped and pierced by cannon-fire. The port cowling and exhaust manifold were obviously U/S; the port propeller had one tip bent forward and ripped fantastically. Until the cowlings were stripped off for inspection it was difficult to say what other damage she had suffered, but clearly the aircraft was in no condition to fly back to Oxfordshire. Marshall went back to the Headquarters office, made his apologies to the Group Captain, and asked for air transport. The weather was poor, so they gave him a railway guide.

All afternoon and evening they sat together in a crowded third-class carriage in a packed train, dozing and shifting restlessly. A mood of the blackest depression had descended on the pilot. After so many operations it was an acute personal grief to him that he had pranged his Wimpey. It was clearly in his mind, far too clearly, that the cause of their misfortune was an error of his own, a gross and unpardonable mistake in navigation. But for the grace of God, he thought, they'd all have been cold meat; a fit and proper end for the incompetent, but bad luck on the chaps that had to crew for him. The fact that they had been so decent to him, with never a word of reproach, only made it worse. Now he would have to tell the Wing Commander all about it, but what to tell, or how to explain their trouble, left him utterly defeated. Moreover, to top everything, they had to travel for ten hours in a slow railway train to get to Oxford just before midnight, and that was eleven miles from Hartley Magna. If he had any sense at all, he thought, he'd go into the lavatory and cut his throat

They crossed London in a taxi in the black-out, had a slender meal at the Paddington buffet, and took the train for Oxford. There was transport there to meet them, and they got back to the station shortly after midnight. Marshall got down from the truck and, carrying his parachute and harness, went into the mess.

In the ante-room the lights were on still; he stuck his head in at the door, and there was Pat Johnson sitting by the fire. Mr. Johnson raised his head. "Evening," he said. "There's some beer and sandwiches here if you want it."

Marshall hesitated, a little touched at the thought, and went forward into the room. "Bloody trains," he said awkwardly. And then he said in explanation: "I had to leave Robert up there."

Mr. Johnson nodded. "We guessed you would. Bring the boys back with you?"

"All but Leech. Got him into hospital."

"Bad?"

"Not very."

He turned to the side table and took a sandwich and poured himself a glass of beer. Pat Johnson said: "What sort of a place is Whitsand?"

"Bloody."

"Sounds like something out of a limerick. 'There was a young lady of Whitsand' . . ." Mr. Johnson mused for a minute, a coarse rhyme on the threshold of his mind, but it escaped him. "How did you come to get up there?"

They had been friends for a year, and there was no one else in the room. Marshall said bluntly: "I put the wrong course on the mucking compass."

"Many a better man than you has done that, laddie," said his comforter. "All be the same in a hundred years."

"I don't know what in hell I'm going to tell Winco."

"I know what I should tell him."

"What?"

"Tell him you put the wrong course on the mucking compass. So what?" Pat Johnson got up from his chair and yawned. "I'm going up to bed."

Marshall took a couple of the sandwiches in his hand. "I'm coming too. Did everybody else get back all right?"

Mr. Johnson nodded. "You were the only mutt. It was 'Where is my wandering boy to-night?' until we got your signal. Your young woman got into a proper state, she did."

Marshall stared at him. "My young woman?"

"The black-haired one, the one you gave the pike to. Fair blubbering her eyes out, she was. I had to muscle in and do a bit of comforting, old boy—as between friends, I mean, I thought you wouldn't mind." He dodged hastily and made off upstairs before Marshall, cumbered with his flying-suit and parachute, could come up with him.

There was an element of truth in what he said. At the Group W/T station three miles from the aerodrome Gervase had watched the girls working the bearing upon R for Robert during all three fixes that they had asked for, had seen them transmit to the leading station. She had marked down the first fix on the plot that they kept and had stared at it in dismay; thereafter all her work became a nightmare. She had slipped in the little message of good cheer to them quite irregularly; that was all that she could do. After that she had to go on with her work as if nothing was happening; in her misery her training gave her strength. All the other machines asking for fixes were asking for her help; she did not fail them.

By one in the morning her work at Group W/T was over; she could close down for the night. She rang through to the control at Hartley to enquire for Robert, but no news had come through. She was told that the air/sea rescue routine was being put in hand for them; at dawn the Lysanders and the Walruses would go out flying low over the grey, dirty sea, questing and searching on the line of drift. It was uncertain, she was told, what the chances were; the only station in the vicinity that they might possibly have reached was not taking any signals.

She had gone back to Hartley with the girls in the station transport in the black night. She could not bear to go back to her quarters; she went to the control upon the aerodrome to see if, during the short time that she had been upon the road, there had not been some message. Section Officer Ferguson was still there with a telephonist, trying to make contact with this dumb place, Whitsand. And two of the pilots were there, still in their Sidcot suits, Flight Lieutenants Lines and Johnson.

She had been a little embarrassed, even in her unhappiness. She said: "I just looked in to see if anything had come through about Robert."

Lines said: "Not yet. I don't think he's in the drink.

He'd have sent us his position before going in."

Mr. Johnson said: "He may have baled out over land, or he may be at this bloody place that won't answer. I don't think he's in the drink." He offered her a packet. "Cigarette?"

She took one gratefully and sat on with them in silence, waiting, in the bare office with the blackboard, the big shuttered windows, the four telephones. In the next room they heard the intermittent complaints of the telephonist to various exchanges up and down the country, Service and post office, as she tried for Whitsand by way of Hull and Scarborough, Grimsby and Market Weighton. They heard the girls in the next room talking to the lighthouse at Spurn Head, and to the air-raid wardens at a post at Hornsea. They sat on, weary and anxious and cold as the time crawled by.

Once Johnson had said kindly to her: "I should go to bed. We'll send a message over to you if anything comes through."

She said: "I can't. I shouldn't go to sleep, anyway."

Lines had gone through into the other room. Mr. Johnson said quietly: "It's like that, is it?"

Gervase looked up quickly; he was grinning at her. "What do you mean by saying it's like that?" she asked indignantly. "It's like nothing of the sort."

Mr. Johnson wagged his head. "He gave you a bit of fish."

"I know he did. It was a very nice bit of fish," she said, colouring. "He gave you a bit, too."

"Nice bit of fish my foot. It was a bloody awful bit of fish." He shook his head. "I always said no good would come of that fish."

She moved away into the telephone-room, anxious to break off the discussion. In the end, at four in the morning, the brief message came through relayed from the Command that Robert was down at Whitsand and damaged; that the radio operator had been removed to hospital. Gervase went back to her quarters sick with relief and utterly exhausted. She took three aspirins, but it was dawn before sleep came.

At eleven o'clock next morning Marshall went into the Wing Commander's office. Dobbie looked up from his desk. "Morning, Marshall, " he said. "Have a cigarette?" He offered his case. "What's Robert like?"

The pilot said: "I don't think she's too bad, sir. The port wing got shot up, and then I hit it with a stump or something and finished it off." He sat on the edge of the chair that Dobbie had given him, recounting the damage to the aircraft.

He spoke nervously and with lack of self-assurance. He smoked very quickly as he spoke.

The Wing Commander helped him now and then with a question. Dobbie was thirty-two years old, a regular officer of the R.A.F. who had done two tours of Bomber Command in the early days of the war, followed by a year at Coastal; at Hartley he still flew occasionally on an operation, though he never served as captain of the aircraft. His work was now executive upon the ground. He had to run the station and control the crews; it was natural that the crews should be his first concern. They fluctuated in number between twenty and thirty-five, a hundred or a hundred and fifty flying personnel all told. He knew them all by name, and a great deal about each one of them; he did not know the ground staff nearly so well.

He had among his crews a few old stagers that formed a solid backbone of experience at Hartley. However many raw and callow young men came to him, so long as he had Lines and Johnson and Marshall and Davy, and Sergeant Pilot Nutter and Sergeant Pilot Cope, he felt that the Wing could play its part; the youngsters would learn from these men and absorb their knowledge imperceptibly. The casualties were all among the newcomers from the operational training schools. Nothing, it seemed, could really help these raw young men but to rub shoulders every day with the seasoned veterans of many raids. The loss of one such veteran crew was a very serious matter indeed to Wing Commander Dobbie, to be prevented at all costs. Those men were worth their weight in gold to him.

He heard about the damage to R for Robert. "Doesn't sound too bad," he said. "Morrison is speaking to them this morning; they should have finished the inspection by now."

Marshall said: "I should think she'd take a week or ten days to repair."

"That means three weeks." The Wing Commander blew out a long cloud of smoke. "How did you come to land up at Whitsand, anyway?"

Marshall said miserably: "I had a bit of a balls-up with my navigator, sir, and the wrong course got on to the compass. I did it—it was my fault."

"I did that once," said Dobbie. "Bloody, isn't it?"

"I can't think how I came to do a thing like that," said Marshall wearily.

"Tell me what happened from the start," said Dobbie. "What time was it when you reached the target?"

Marshall told him the story of the flight, speaking in little bitter sentences. He took no pride in the fact that he had extricated the machine from a most difficult position over the North Sea and brought it safely back and landed more or less in one piece; his black depression was too great for him to recognise virtue in anything that he had done that night. The Wing Commander had to penetrate the veil of bitterness with which the pilot cloaked his account to see the fine airmanship that had got Robert down at all.

In the end Dobbie laughed. "I bet the pilot of that Lancaster had a fright," he said boyishly.

"He was bloody rude," said Marshall. "He was a sergeant."

"I bet he was bloody rude," said Dobbie. "I can't think of anything much worse than to see another aircraft plump down on the runway right in front of you at night."

There was a pause. "I suppose I'd have been mad if somebody had done that to me," the pilot said at last.

There was another pause. The Wing Commander broke it. "I think you might as well get off on a spot of leave," he said, "all the lot of you. A fortnight. It'll be quite that before you can go up to Whitsand for Robert." He glanced at the calendar. "Get off as soon as you like and come back on the nineteenth—Monday fortnight. You might pass the word to your crew, and tell them to come up for their passes."

Marshall got to his feet. "Thanks, sir," he said quietly. "I think that'd be a good thing. It's been just one thing after another lately."

Dobbie glanced at him. "In what way?"

The pilot said bitterly: "Everything I touch seems to go wrong these days."

The Wing Commander felt as if a veil had been partially drawn aside revealing a familiar scene, a scene he did not care to look at very closely. He said: "I suppose that means you've had a spot of bother of some sort."

"I suppose it does," said Marshall. "I'd rather like to get away from here for a bit."

"Okay," said Dobbie casually. "See you again on Monday fortnight."

The pilot went out of the office. Dobbie leaned back in his chair, staring thoughtfully at the calendar. It was a good calendar, adorned with a beautiful picture of a nude young woman, kneeling and attractive; in some obscure manner she was there as advertising for TAUTWING AERO DOPES. The Wing Commander muttered to himself: "I bet that's it."

He got up from his chair and opened the door communicating with the Administration office. Squadron Leader Chesterton was not in the room, but his secretary was there, a grey-haired and efficient W.A.A.F. sergeant. He said to her: "Sergeant Pilot Franck and Sergeant Cobbett and Sergeant Phillips will be coming in for leave warrants and ration cards. Make them out to the nineteenth. When they come, bring them in to me. I want to see each of that crew before they go on leave—not all together, one by one."

He saw Sergeant Cobbett first, within half an hour. "Morning, Cobbett," said the Wing Commander. "Sit down for a minute." The sergeant sat a little nervously on the chair. "I'm sending you all off on leave for a fortnight. It'll take quite that time to fix up your machine at Whitsand."

Dobbie flipped over the pages of a little book he kept upon his desk. "I see this was your eighth operational flight—and you've been with Sergeant Pilot Dennison, and now for the last two with Flight Lieutenant Marshall." He put down the book and looked over to the young man before him. "I may have to re-arrange the crews a bit while you're away," he said. "Is there anybody that you'd like to be with particularly?"

The flight engineer said: "I don't know, sir. Couldn't I stay with Flight Lieutenant Marshall?"

The Wing Commander said, as if reluctantly: "Yes, I suppose I could arrange that if you particularly want to stay with him. Would you rather do that?"

"I would, sir."

"Why?"

The young man smiled awkwardly. "Well, sir—I always feel safe with Mr. Marshall. And I think that makes a difference, because you do your work better."

"I wouldn't say that you were any of you so safe last time," said Dobbie dryly. "It's a long way from here to Whitsand."

The sergeant protested: "But that was just a muck-up with the navigation, sir. What I mean is, Mr. Marshall knows how to nurse his motors, and he knows how to fly. I tell you, sir, you should have been with us at that landing up at Whitsand. He put her down a treat."

"All right," said Dobbie. "If you want to stay with Mr.

Marshall I'll see if we can fix it. You hit it off with him all right?"

The sergeant hesitated. "I like being with Mr. Marshall because he knows his job, sir. I wouldn't say but that he's been sharp with all of us lately, like as if he was worried or something. The others, they noticed it more because they've been with him longer. But I don't want to change."

Dobbie said: "All right, Cobbett—I'll see if I can arrange things so that you stay with him. Now you can get off on your leave. Got your pass? All right. Have a good time."

The sergeant went out and the Wing Commander sat thoughtfully at his desk for a few minutes. Presently he drew a sheet of notepaper towards him, got out his fountain-pen, and began to write a note to Corporal Leech.

It was his habit, whenever any of his flying personnel went into hospital whether for accident or casualty, to write a letter in his own handwriting. It was one of the little things that made him a good officer, one of the tiny cares that built up a good record of operational flights from Hartley Magna. He wrote rather illegibly, in an irregular, boyish hand:

My dear Leech,

I was sorry to hear about your bad luck over Mannheim, and I hope you aren't having too much trouble, and that you will be back with us before long. I have sent the rest of your crew off for a fortnight's leave, and it may be three weeks or a month before they go out again. I will send a temporary operator with them till you come back if you want to go on with that crew, but if you specially want to be with some other captain, will you let me know? As you know, we do not like to make more changes than we can help, but this is an opportunity if you want a change.

If there is any difficulty over anything while you are in hospital, or if you want anything sent up from your quarters, let me know and I will do what I can.

Yours sincerely,

J. C. Dobbie, Wg. Cdr.

He sealed the letter and addressed it. The W.A.A.F. sergeant put her head in at the door as he tossed it into the OUT basket. "Sergeant Phillips is here, sir," she said.

"All right—send him in."

He turned to the door. "Morning, Phillips," he said.

"You've seen Flight Lieutenant Marshall? We decided this morning that you'd all better get in a fortnight's leave while your aircraft is put right."

"Thank you, sir."

The Wing Commander sat down at his desk and made the rear-gunner sit down. He turned to his little book and frowned. "You seem to have been with Mr. Marshall a long time," he said. "Were you with him in his first tour?"

The gunner said: "That's right, sir. I did eighteen operations with Mr. Marshall in his first turn; before that I did fourteen with Pilot Officer Hocking. You remember, sir—him that hit the gasometer."

Dobbie remembered very well, and did not want to be reminded of that crash. "And then you went on with Mr. Marshall on his second tour, and you've done twenty-four more."

"That's right, sir. Fifty-six in all."

"Quite a lot of operational flying," said Dobbie. "Beginning to feel you'd like to stay on the ground?"

Phillips shook his head. "No, sir." He enjoyed the relatively easy work of a rear-gunner, and he still felt a certain glamour in the job.

The Wing Commander said: "We shall have to make a change or two now. You'll have to have a new wireless operator, for one thing. In fact, I may have to do a good bit of shuffling the crews around in the next week or two. Do you feel you've been with one captain long enough? Would you like a change?"

The rear-gunner stared at him. "No, sir. I don't want any change."

"You're quite happy as you are, with Mr. Marshall?"

"Yes, sir. We've been together a long time. I wouldn't want to start with anybody new."

"You get on well together? I'm glad to hear it."

Sergeant Phillips hesitated. "We have our little troubles now and then," he said. "Like quarrels in a family, if you take me. But nothing to signify."

The Wing Commander grinned. "I see. Been having one recently?"

"Well—you might say so. You know the way we register the graticule sight with the guns." He launched into an involved technical explanation of the focus of his four Brownings. "The Armament Officer, Mr. Higgs, he said I could have it my way, sir, but then Flight Lieutenant Marshall come along and said it had to be like in the book, and got real nasty about it. Not that that troubled me," he added quickly.

"I see," said Dobbie. "That sounds rather unreasonable, on the face of it. Is he often like that?"

"No, sir. It's just that he's been worried recently, I think."

"Do you know what he's been worried about?"

Sergeant Phillips was not a very quick thinker, but he knew well enough when he was treading on thin ice. He said carefully: "I think somebody shot him down, sir."

Involuntarily the Wing Commander glanced at TAUT-WING AERO DOPES; his first guess had been a good one. "Somebody on the station?"

"I wouldn't know that, sir."

"I bet you do," said Dobbie.

He had a duty in this matter to perform. One of his best and most reliable crews had suddenly deteriorated and had put up an extremely poor performance after Mannheim. It was his duty to try and get them back into their original state of efficiency, because the example of the old hands influenced the raw young crews that came to him from operational training. He had so few of the old stagers left, the men who knew all the angles, who had great experience. If one of them went wrong, it was his duty to do everything within his power to get the matter right.

"Do you know who it is?" he asked directly.

"No, sir, I don't. I know who it might be."

"Who?"

The sergeant hesitated, feeling most uncomfortable. "He asked once if I could find out the name of one of the section officers," he said.

"Which one?"

"The one with black hair that does signals."

"You mean Section Officer Robertson?"

"That's right, sir."

The Wing Commander glanced at the sergeant; he sensed resentment, and knew that Phillips felt these questions to be unfair. "A very nice girl," he said quietly. "I'm sorry if she shot him down."

He got to his feet; the sergeant got up in relief. "All right, Phillips," he said. "Get off on your leave, and have a good time. I'll try and fix it so that you stay with Mr. Marshall if you want to."

"Thank you, sir. I wouldn't want to start with anybody new."

He went out; immediately the W.A.A.F. sergeant came in. "Sergeant Pilot Franck is waiting to see you, sir."

"All right, show him in." This was the last of them, this foreigner. He turned again to his little book, and was studying it when Gunnar Franck came in. The way this crew had stuck together!

He said to the big, red-faced young man: "Morning, Franck. I suppose Flight Lieutenant Marshall has told you that you've got a fortnight's leave?"

The Dane said: "Yes, sir."

"Sit down a minute." Gunnar sat down on the chair. "I wanted to see you for a minute just to tell you that I know it wasn't your fault your machine went off its course. I've had the whole thing from Mr. Marshall. He tells me that you passed him the correct course in writing, but that he set it on the compass wrong."

The sergeant said: "I have thought that I am ver' much to blame, sir. Always I look to see if the course is right upon the compass when there is a little time free. This time I did not look."

"Why didn't you look?"

There was a pause. Gunnar said at last: "I thought it might make Mr. Marshall angry if I look to see that he has done his work all right."

"I see." The Wing Commander thought for a minute. "I know that there has been some friction in your crew," he said at last. He turned to the book before him. "You've been with Mr. Marshall a very long time," he said. "You did most of your last tour of ops together and all this one. Do you feel that's long enough? Would you like to go with some other captain for a change?"

The Dane said: "If Mr. Marshall wants me to stay in his crew, I would like to stay."

Dobbie said: "Don't think Marshall wants to get rid of you. This was my idea. I thought that if things had become difficult you might like a change yourself."

Gunnar said: "I would like to stay with Mr. Marshall, sir."

Dobbie stared at the red-faced young man before him thoughtfully. He knew Franck to be an intelligent, educated man, a medical student in his own country. He had a shrewd idea that this foreigner was really the backbone of the crew, the hard core of solid competence.

He leaned forward a little. "Look, Franck," he said. "I know that you and Marshall have been together a long time, and you've done wonderfully well together. Now, as far as I can make it out, some friction has arisen and you don't get on so well together as you used to. Well, that's nothing new, you know—it happens now and then, and I deal with it by shifting people round a bit. What I don't quite understand is why you don't want to be shifted."

The young man said: "If Mr. Marshall wants me, I would like to stay with him. I do not think that it would be good for you to fuss him with a new navigator just now."

The Wing Commander nodded; this was getting somewhere. "He's worried over something, isn't he?"

"For three weeks now, sir, he has been ver' worried. I think it is that which has made him angry over little things that do not matter."

"What sort of little things?"

The Dane smiled ruefully. "Always I make the figure seven with a cross, as we do at home. I cannot help it, sir—I try to make the English seven, and then I forget. Now for the first time Mr. Marshall has been angry that I make them so, and he goes on and on about my sevens, and I have been angry with him in turn. Last week I was coming to ask if I might become posted to another station, and then I did not."

Dobbie said gravely: "I see. But why are you so set on staying with him now?"

"I think it is not the right time to go. When things are not so good, then one should stay and help to get them right again."

The Wing Commander sat in silence for a moment. His first feeling was confirmed; here was the backbone of the crew. This foreigner meant that he was quite prepared to go out again as navigator to a pilot who had insulted him and had made at least one technical mistake that had put them all in danger. Old comradeship still held these men together.

He said: "What's Marshall worried about?"

"I do not know, sir."

Dobbie said: "Do you know Section Officer Robertson?"

Their eyes met. "I know Section Officer ver' well," said Gunnar. "I think she is a good young lady, but I think she has behaved ver' silly."

Dobbie thought of the wrecked aeroplane at Whitsand, of

Leech in hospital, of the hour that he had spent that morning in unravelling the matter. "I couldn't agree with you more!" he said explosively.

He got to his feet, a little ashamed of that remark. "All right, Franck," he said. "I shall remember what you've said. I want you chaps to stay together if you can; it makes a big difference to the other crews. But I do realise that you can't if things become unpleasant. Leave it with me."

Gunnar Franck got up and went towards the door. "He is a ver' good captain, sir," he said. He looked up, smiling boyishly. "It is perhaps the spring. I think that you must lose a lot of aircraft in the spring."

The Wing Commander said: "Get on with you! Have you got somewhere to go for your leave, Franck?"

"Yes, sir, thank you. I have ver' good friends from my country living at Blackheath."

"All right. Have a good time."

Dobbie dropped back into his chair and sat deep in thought, staring at the nude. It was tricky, this—too tricky to be handled in a hurry. By giving them a fortnight's leave he had given himself time to think. When he had thought about it for a day or two he would have a word with Chesterton, and they would decide together what was to be done; he had a great respect for his Squadron Leader (Admin.), old enough to be his father. Perhaps, too, he would talk it over with his wife. Dobbie had married during his first tour of bombing ops in 1940; he well remembered the distraction from his work. But his had been a straightforward affair; he had asked Joan to marry him and she had said yes, and they had been married—just like that. She had not kept him in suspense, but even so he had found courtship in the intervals of night raids over Germany to be a severe nervous strain. He had a joke with Joan about "the happy couple"; they had proved by their experience that no one could be happy while they were engaged. Now they had a baby fifteen months' old, and had just embarked upon another one. Peace of mind did not come till you were married, once the trouble started. The surest shield that any bomber pilot could possess was peace of mind.

He sat there for ten minutes, deep in thought.

Gervase met Marshall in the ante-room before lunch. He came into the room, hesitated, and then crossed over to her. "Morning," he said. "I'm going off on leave this afternoon. I did want to ask you one thing before I go."

134

She said: "What's that?"

"Someone slipped a message to us on the W/T, when we were in a spot. Did you do it?"

"Yes. I'm glad you got it."

"I'm glad you sent it."

There was a pause; neither knew how to break it; they stood awkwardly together in the crowd, not caring whether anyone was looking at them or not. "Where are you going for your leave?" she asked.

"Just home, to Northwood."

She said awkwardly: "I do hope you have nice weather." And as she said it she thought despairingly, "This is absurd. Last time we spoke to each other it was about getting married, and now this stupid talk."

They moved away, both miserable.

Gervase went through her afternoon routine restless and troubled. She went back to the mess for tea, and, passing the letter rack and looking for her post, she found a sealed envelope with her name, unstamped. She opened it and saw it was from Marshall, and thrust it in her pocket unread. She had tea quickly and went back to her quarters to read it in peace, unreasonably excited.

It said:

> As from, Crossways,
> Oakleigh Road,
> Northwood.

Dear Gervase,

I'm not sure that I shall be coming back to Hartley. I've not been doing so well lately, and I think perhaps it's time I had a change. But what I want to say is this, I'm sorry I didn't thank you better for that message you sent with the fix. I made about six different mistakes that night, which wasn't quite so hot. Up till the time I got your message I did every bloody thing wrong. After that I did every bloody thing right.

This doesn't need any answer, but I just wanted you to know.

> Yrs.
>
> PETER MARSHALL.

She sat on her bed staring at this letter with a lump so high up in her throat that she could hardly swallow. The tone of it was so unlike the Peter Marshall that she knew, the brisk young man who went out catching pike and shooting pigeons. Gunnar had told her bitterly that Marshall had been different in the last few weeks; the letter told her he was different indeed. All the self-confidence was gone. The superman who had brought his crew through fifty-four or fifty-five raids over Germany and Italy hadn't been doing so well lately.

She sat staring at the carpet at her feet, sick with a new feeling of responsibility. She had done her best to put it to him nicely in the wood that day; she had done everything she could to avoid hurting him. But she had hurt him; she knew that, inevitably. She now knew that she had hurt him far more than she realised. He had grown sharp and bitter with his crew; she knew that from Gunnar. He had grown casual and ineffective in his work; he had told her so. Unhappily she realised that she now knew what had happened to R for Robert.

She got up presently and put on her cap before the glass; she felt that she must get out and get some air. She went out in the evening light to walk round the ring runway; it was nearly three miles round the aerodrome past the dispersed bombers; she could cover it in fifty minutes. She went striding out of the camp into the quiet stillness of the field. There was no flying going on that night; the Wellingtons stood gaunt and spectral and deserted on their concrete rounds, their great wheels shrouded with the canvas drip covers.

She walked on, hard and earnestly. The quick exercise eased her mind, preventing concentration; reason was dulled, but instinct was alive. She entered the last reach of the broad tarmac track forty-five minutes later feeling that action from her was required. Matters in R for Robert had gone desperately wrong. Unknowing, she had started up the trouble; it was for her to put it right. The next move lay with her.

As luck would have it she ran into Sergeant Phillips as she walked back into the camp. In the last light of evening Sergeant Phillips was mowing a little bit of lawn outside the control office with a motor mower. He enjoyed mowing with the motor mower; it was gentle exercise and pleasantly mechanical; the putter of the little motor pleased him, and the smell of new cut grass. He had hung about idle all the afternoon, cursing the close season that prevented fishing, till he had remembered the motor mower and the spring grass that had been growing up where they had had the lawn the year before. For an hour and a half he had been happy. Now it was time to pack up; it was getting too dark to see. But that

would do till he got back off leave; he could have another go
at it then.

Gervase walked past him, hesitated, and turned back. She
said a little diffidently: "Aren't you Sergeant Phillips?"

He straightened up, surprised. "That's right," he said.

"I thought you were all going off on leave. You're in
Robert, aren't you?"

He nodded. "I got further to go. There's only one train in
the day goes from Oxford to York, where I come from. I can't
go before to-morrow morning. They won't let me go through
London on the pass—and it wouldn't be no quicker, anyway."

She said: "I was sorry to hear you had that trouble after
Mannheim. Tell me, what happened?"

He had been all through this in the sergeants' mess, several
times. He grinned. "Seems like the captain and the navigator
added in the date when they was working out the course," he
said. "I was back in the turret, so I didn't see nothing of it.
But we weren't going the right way at all."

Gervase said: "I thought you didn't do that sort of thing in
R for Robert."

"We didn't used to," said the sergeant dryly.

There was a time, she felt, for plain talk to be used and this
was one of them. She had a Yorkshire background, and she
was talking to a Yorkshireman; spade called to spade, although
they did not realise it. "I had a word with Sergeant Franck
the other day," she said. "He had a moan about Flight
Lieutenant Marshall. He said that you were all getting fed-up
with him. Is that right?"

"We ain't fed-up with him," the sergeant said. "Best captain I ever been with, up till recently. Then he got a bit
awkward, but we all do that. We'll be all okeydoke when we
get back off leave. I said so to the Wing Commander—I don't
want no shift, I said."

"I see," said Gervase thoughtfully. So Wing Commander
Dobbie was in on this.

Sergeant Phillips leaned against the handles of the mower,
confidential in the half-light. "'Course," he said, "this is
a bad time of year, when you don't know what to do, and
that don't make things easier. Up till March there was the
fishing, 'n that made a lot of difference, because we was all
keen on that, 'n we used to go down to the river and do it all
together, captain and all. It was when the fishing finished
things seemed to go wrong. I know I hadn't got nothing to

do with myself, afternoons, and Leech neither, nor Gunnar Franck. And I guess the captain, he was same as all the rest of us and he hadn't got nothing to do either. It's weary when you don't know what to do."

She said, wondering: "I never thought of that."

The rear-gunner said: "Well, it makes a difference when you have a bit of fun together, all together, like."

She felt that she had to know everything now. It was nearly dark, and darkness gave her confidence. She said: "Is that all that's been wrong with Marshall? It doesn't sound much."

Phillips said: "I was talking to Gunnar. Seems like he had a bit of a dust-up with one of his girl friends, and she gave him the works. That's what we thought."

Gervase said: "You're right there. That was me."

The sergeant laughed, suddenly and boyishly, relieving the tension. "Better not tell Gunnar Franck that, or he'll wring your neck."

She said indignantly: "I didn't mean all this to happen!"

There was a long pause; there was no more to be said. The sergeant stooped and fiddled with the Bowden at the carburettor; Gervase stood awkward for a few minutes, not knowing what to do. "Well," she said at last, "I must be getting on. Thank you for telling me what you did."

"Okay," the sergeant said. He hesitated, and then said: "If I can do anything, any time, just say."

The girl nodded. "I'll let you know. I hope you have a good leave."

She walked up to her quarters, and up to her little room. She pulled the chair up to the table and sat down to write a letter; it seemed to her to be very urgent that she should do so. In spite of that she sat for a long time before beginning, trying to sort out her feelings into concrete terms. In the end she wrote:

> R.A.F. Station,
> Hartley Magna,
> Oxfordshire.

Dear Peter,

I got your letter and it was nice of you to write. Before you do anything about leaving Hartley I think we ought to talk it over, if you think it's anything to do with me, because it seems a frightful pity to break up your crew and not so good for the war. I'll meet you anywhere you say if you'd like to talk things over, if you give me a ring. But anyway, don't do anything in a hurry; things may seem different when you've had a holiday. They do, you know,

Yours sincerely,

GERVASE.

It was nearly time for supper when she had finished this, and sealed it in an envelope, and stamped it. The last post had left the station, but there was a collection at the post office in Hartley Magna at eight o'clock if she went quickly. She put on her raincoat and got out her bicycle and rode down to the village and posted her letter; she rode back with a mind that was at ease. Supper was over when she got back to her quarters; all she got was a small slice of Spam with luke-warm potatoes, and some bread and cheese. But she had her chocolate ration, and her letter was on its way, and she was happy.

Her letter travelled quickly, too quickly for her to have rehearsed her part sufficiently. She was called to the telephone during lunch next day; squeezing into the stuffy little box and shutting the door carefully behind her, she wondered what on earth she was to say. She lifted the receiver and said: "Section Officer Robertson speaking."

"Peter Marshall here. Hullo, Gervase."

She said: "Oh—hullo."

"I got your letter."

"Oh—fine." And then she said idiotically: "It's been frightfully quick."

He disregarded that. "Look, would you like to have tea with me in Oxford one day, Gervase? We could meet at Fuller's in the Cornmarket, where we went before."

She said: "Isn't it a frightful bore for you coming all that way?"

"No, it's not. What about to-morrow afternoon?"

She said: "That's all right for me if I'm allowed out. You know what I mean." Before an operation the station was hermetically closed, without notice.

He said: "I'll take chance on that. If you don't turn up I'll ring up again and we'll have another shot."

"All right. Half-past four?"

"I'll be there."

There was little doubt about that, she reflected. She said: "All right. Good-bye, Peter. See you then."

"Good-bye, Gervase."

She travelled into Oxford by the bus next afternoon, reaching the confectioner's at exactly half-past four. She found him at a table in an alcove, a table flanked by tall oak screens designed to prevent eavesdropping, designed to hinder a young woman from getting away before she had listened to what a young man had to tell her. She viewed it with misgiving as she crossed the room, thinking that he must have got there in the middle of the afternoon to have secured that table.

She said shyly: "Hullo, Peter."

"Hullo, Gervase." She slipped into the seat beside him and took off her cap. "What are we going to eat?"

She asked for tea and cakes and waited while he ordered them, and till the girl had gone away. Then they turned and looked at each other.

He said: "This is frightfully awkward, isn't it?"

She laughed nervously. "You don't know what I've been feeling like on the way in."

"I do. I've had further to come."

They laughed together, and the tension was reduced. She said: "Have you done anything about a transfer yet?"

"Not yet. I was going to write about it in a day or two."

"I do think it'd be an awful pity to break up your crew."

He smiled faintly. "That's what you said in your letter. I don't think that matters a bit; as a crew we aren't so hot just now. And you said something about the dear old war, too. I don't care two hoots about the bloody war."

She stared across the room, feeling that he wasn't in a very easy mood. It occurred to her that possibly he had a point of view that she had not appreciated, that she did not completely understand. She said:

"If you put in for a transfer, what would you do?"

"I'd ask to be put back on Coastal. I was there to start with, so I know the work."

"Would they let you do that?"

"I think so. I've done a good long spell in Bomber Command, and with a lousy show behind me like this last one I could say my nerve had gone. I think they'd let me go."

There was a pause.

Gervase said: "We should miss you frightfully at Hartley."

"Who do you mean by 'we'?"

She turned to him: "Everybody, Peter. I don't mean me

140

especially. We'll talk about that later, if you want to. I mean everybody else upon the station. Everybody would miss you terribly—I mean, all the flying crews."

He stared at her. "Why would they miss me? There are lots of other pilots."

"But, Peter, not with your experience." She struggled to express herself. "I mean, all these raw young men who come in, when they're too young to know what it's all about, before they've got real confidence in themselves, all pimples and pink cheeks. They see people like you and Pat Johnson, and half a dozen others who have been on scores of raids, and they hear the way you talk amongst yourselves. You don't know what it means to them. It gives them confidence."

He thought about it for a minute. "That might be an argument for keeping me in Bomber Command," he said at last. "But it's no reason why I should stay on at Hartley."

"Your own crew would be lost without you, Peter."

He said bitterly: "My own crew would be glad to see my back."

She said hotly: "That's not true, and you know it."

He grinned, and pushed forward a plate of highly-coloured pastries. "Have a bun."

She stared at him, laughed and relaxed. She chose a pale éclair, and transferred it to her plate. She said: "Do you want to leave Hartley, Peter? Is that it?"

He hesitated. "I don't know," he said, irresolute. "I used to like it there, but it's gone ropey in the last few weeks."

She said in a low tone: "Is that because of us?"

He nodded without speaking.

"I am sorry, Peter. I've given you a lousy time."

"It's not your fault," he said. "It's just the way things have happened. But I think a change might be a good thing, in a way."

She took a mouthful of her éclair, and stared across the room, avoiding his eyes. "I feel I've been frightfully clumsy over this," she said. "I didn't mean to make you miserable, Peter, when I said we oughtn't to meet any more. If I'd known that it was going to do all this to your work I—I'd have thought of something different, perhaps."

"Because of the dear old war?" he said gently.

The suggestion confused her. "Not altogether," she said uncertainly.

"I'd like to think it was because of the dear old me," he said.

"I know you would," she replied. "But you mustn't."

"All right," he said quietly.

She turned to him. "When I said we oughtn't to meet at all, I thought it was the best thing for you, Peter. Honestly, that's what I was thinking. It's not that I don't like coming out with you—I do. But I thought it would be better for you if we didn't."

"Pat Johnson says," he remarked, "that all maidens are mutts or they wouldn't be maidens."

"I didn't come here to listen to what Pat Johnson says."

"No. But I've told you what I think. I think we ought to try it for a bit and see how we get on."

"You mean, try going about and doing things together?"

He nodded. "See how we get on."

"I don't want to keep you dangling on a string, Peter."

He said gently: "I wish to God you'd stop worrying about me. I like a dangle now and then. I'll drop off if I get fed-up with it—you see."

There was a little pause. At last she said: "My way hasn't panned out quite so well. If you really want it, Peter, we'll try yours for a bit. But you do realise I'm not in love with you?"

He grinned. "I wouldn't know about a thing like that. Pat Johnson says you are."

She checked an angry impulse to say what she thought of Mr. Johnson. "Well, I say I'm not."

"All right, you're not. Have another bun."

"No, thanks."

They sat in awkward silence for a minute or two, each wondering what to say next; the tension mounted till it grew unbearable.

At last he said: "Look, I'll tell you what I'll do. If you'll try it my way for a month we'll know by then whether there's anything in it for us, or not. I won't bother you longer than that if it's not going to work, Gervase. But if we chuck it then, I think I really had better go away. We don't want this all over again."

She smiled faintly. "I agree with that."

He said: "You want me to come back to Hartley because of the dear old war, which you think can't get on without me. I want to come back to Hartley because I want to be with you, to see you, and to hear you talk.

He paused. She did not speak.

"When I come back," he said, "I'll try and work things so

that if I have a leave after the month my crew will settle down with someone else and be as good with him as they have been with me. I'll try and work it so that there's a first-class chap to take them over when I go. But if we find it doesn't work out, and we have to chuck it, I shall want to go."

She said: "All right, Peter." She was growing exhausted by the tension of their scene; she was shocked at the depth of feeling she had roused, the things that she had done to this young man. She was a factor in his life, whether she liked it or not; her whim could turn the entire current of his work. She was unhappily aware of the responsibility of an attractive woman, for the first time in her life.

Marshall sat up briskly and bit into a doughnut. "Okay," he said. "Now we've got to work fast." He glanced at her, and poured her out another cup of tea; she took it from him mechanically. "Will you come to the pictures with me?"

"Now?"

"Now. We've only got a month."

She smiled. "What's on?"

"I don't know. We'll walk round and see."

"All right."

"Will you come up to Town and do a show with me on Saturday, and go on to the Savoy and dance?"

She sipped her tea; it was then Tuesday. "I suppose I could put in for week-end leave," she said. "I'd have to stay with Aunt Ethel at Hampstead."

"If you're going to put in for week-end leave," he said, "you could get off on Friday night and come up to London, and we could do something on Saturday morning."

"I'm not going to work as hard as that," she said. "I'll come up on Saturday morning and have lunch with you."

"All right. But don't think you aren't going to work hard. When I get home I'm going to write you a nice letter—you'll get it on Thursday morning. Will you answer it?"

She protested: "But, Peter, I shall be seeing you on Saturday."

"I'm thinking about Friday, when I'm going to get an answer to my letter in the morning post—if you've written it. Will you?"

She hesitated. She had promised to try it for a month in his way and she felt that she must stick to her promise, but she had not visualised all this. "All right," she said at last. "Don't make the pace too hot."

He glanced down at her, suddenly compunctuous. "Would you like to be let off that one?" he asked gently.

"No—I'll answer it." She put down her cup of tea.

He grinned at her. "Okay. Let's put a sock in the emotion now and get on to the pictures. Want to powder your nose?"

She said: "Er—yes, perhaps I'd better."

"Okay. I'll meet you downstairs at the cash desk."

They walked out presently into the crowded street; in the throng of people on the pavements he took her arm and piloted her through the crowd. In the warm darkness of the Regal, in the middle of the Gaumont News, hand crept experimentally into hand; it was dark, Gervase reflected, and nobody could see. In any case, everybody else seemed to be doing it. His hand pleased her; it was firm, but gentle, and warm, and comforting.

The afternoon had tired her; she was new to that sort of strain. She lay back in her seat leaning a little towards him, letting him caress her hand. She was content with the decision they had made, content to let things rip for a month. At the end of that time there might be more trouble for them, but that would not be her fault. She could do no more to help him than to do what he wanted; if in the end trouble came to them, well, trouble came to everybody in the world.

He took her to the George restaurant for dinner, before putting her upon the bus to go back to Hartley. Over the meal they talked about the arrangements for their week-end; they decided that it would be nice to go and see "Arsenic and Old Lace." She said: "You'd like me to bring a dance frock, Peter?"

He nodded. "I've never seen you out of uniform."

She said: "All right, I'll bring one up. That means you'll have to let me go back to Hampstead to change, during the afternoon." She was not quite sure in her own mind that this dance frock was a very good idea. The fire, she thought, was hot enough already without fanning it; she felt no urge to drag out feminine allure. The severe, business-like lines of uniform gave her confidence. But if he was taking her to the Savoy to dance, she couldn't go in uniform as if it was a N.A.A.F.I. dance. Dance frock it would have to be—the pastel blue one with the silver slippers.

They sat for a time over coffee; then they left the restaurant. In the black streets he took her arm and piloted her to the bus station in the market; they stopped by a wall in the darkness to say good-bye.

She said: "Are you happier about things now, Peter?"

He was holding both her hands. "Of course I am," he said. "Are you?"

She said slowly: "I know you're going to be frightfully nice to me, Peter, and that we'll have a lovely month. But I'm afraid I'm going to hurt you terribly when it's all over."

"We'll worry about that when the time comes. In the meantime we'll have the lovely month."

She wondered if he was going to kiss her; she would have let him if he had demanded it. But he was put off by her last words and did not press that one, and presently they said good night, and he put her in the bus.

Gervase travelled back to Hartley tired to death, but not unhappy. She felt queerly that things were on the right track now, that she had managed to undo some of the damage she had done. She was quite sure in her reason that a mass of trouble lay ahead of them that they would run into sooner or later; she was too tired to bother about that. She went to bed immediately she got back to the station, and slept for ten hours solidly in a deep, dreamless slumber.

Marshall went down to the railway station, walking upon air. He waited an hour and three-quarters for a train to London, arriving at Paddington a little after three in the morning. At four-thirty he got into an empty train for Northwood, and walked into his father's house at half-past five, as the grey dawn was just beginning to show above the trees. He went to bed and drifted off to sleep, utterly content.

That morning Wing Commander Dobbie got an answer to the letter he had written to Corporal Leech in hospital. It ran:

R.A.F. Emergency Hospital,
Yorks.

Dear sir,

I got your letter it was very nice to get it and it was very nice that you found time to write. Thank you. I do not want anything because it is very nice here and they say I shall only be a fortnight and then out. I am hastening to write to tell you that I would not like to change my crew please because we all get on all right together and it is very nice. I like being with Mr. Marshall although he can be sharp sometimes but we don't mind that. Please try and keep a place for me back in that crew.

I hope you are quite well.

Yrs. obediently,
ALBERT LEECH.

Wing Commander Dobbie glanced this over thoughtfully; it did not help him in his problem. Still holding it in his hand he went through into the next office. He said to Chesterton: "You might come in when you're free."

The Adjutant came in a few minutes later and found Dobbie sitting at his desk, the letter still in his hand. Dobbie said:

"Shut the door behind you. Have a chair." And when that was done he said: "I say, what am I going to do about Marshall's crew—R for Robert?"

The older man said: "They're all fighting, aren't they?"

"Not exactly," said the Wing Commander. "There's some friction, but it all seems to come from Marshall. He's riding them too hard, but at the same time he's got slack and casual himself. You know."

"Is that why they went roaring off to Whitsand?"

The Wing Commander nodded. "Marshall set the wrong course on the compass, and his navigator was afraid to go and check it. He's been pretty rough with them. He's got a good navigator, too—that Dane."

"Gunnar Franck—the one who was a sergeant pilot?"

"That's the one."

The older man said: "You'll have to split them up. Once they start quarrelling like that they hardly ever get back as a team again. It's too bad to let them go on?"

"I think it is. Well, look at last time."

Chesterton took out a cigarette, tapped it upon his thumbnail, and lit up. "It's a great pity," he said slowly. "A great pity to break up a crew like that."

"What's more," said Dobbie dryly, "it's not so easy. I had them all in one by one before they went on leave and asked them if they'd like a change. They all said that they wanted to stay where they were."

"They did?"

"Every one of them—Gunnar Franck and all. Even the radio-operator that got shot up wants to stay in that crew." He flipped the letter across to Chesterton.

The Squadron Leader read it carefully. "What's behind it?" he enquired at last.

"I don't think anything's behind it. I think they just like him."

"But still you don't think they can go on?"

"No, I don't," said Dobbie. "If we let it slide I think they'll all be killed in some damn silly way. I think we've got to do something."

The Squadron Leader read the letter through again. "What's the matter with Marshall?" he enquired. "I always thought him quite a pleasant chap."

"He is," said Dobbie. "I like Marshall. It's the usual, of course. He got mixed up with a young woman and she gave him a bump."

"Somebody on the station?"

"Yes."

"Who is it—do you know?"

"Section Officer Robertson."

"Oh." The old Squadron Leader sat turning the letter idly over in his hand. It was tricky when W.A.A.F. officers were involved. He had had similar episodes once or twice before and it was always troublesome; it meant dealing with very senior W.A.A.F.s whose point of view was alien to him. He never understood their mental processes in such matters; they were kind where he would have been stern, brutal where he would have been lenient. Queer people to deal with; when you started anything with them you never quite knew what would happen.

"She's all right, isn't she?" he said at last.

"I think so," said Dobbie. "I think it's all quite above board. The rear-gunner says she shot him down. I suppose that means he wanted to marry her."

Chesterton nodded. "I should think that's it. They're the marrying sort—both of them."

"If that's the way of it," said Dobbie irritably, "why the hell doesn't she marry him?"

"She's very young," said Chesterton. He had two daughters himself, both older than this girl, and neither was married.

"The great adventure on this station isn't bombing Germany," said Dobbie bitterly. "They don't think anything of that. Falling in love is the big business here."

"What else do you expect, considering the age we take them in?"

147

"I don't know. Anyway, what are we going to do about Marshall?"

Experience was here to help them; it was not the first time that they had had similar incidents at Hartley Magna. "You'll have to shift one or other of them," said Chesterton. "The sooner the better. If what you say is right, Marshall will never settle down. You'd better get the girl shifted."

"Return her to store, and get another one?"

"That's it. She can go back to Group."

"I suppose that's the right thing to do," said Dobbie doubtfully.

"I think it is," said Chesterton. "Look at it from Marshall's point of view. He wants to marry this girl. She's not having any. But yet they've got to rub shoulders in the mess every day in front of all the rest of us. It's not fair on any man, that —especially a vigorous man like Marshall. I'm not surprised he's getting bad-tempered. I should be."

Dobbie said: "I'm rather surprised he hasn't asked for a transfer."

"That's the old business of the moth and the candle. But he will ask for a transfer. That'll be the next thing. If you want to keep him here, you'd better shift the girl."

Dobbie picked up Corporal Leech's letter from the desk and glanced it over again. "I'd like to have a crack at keeping him," he said. "I believe this crew might get on to its feet again. They all want to stay with him—every one of them. If we shift the girl he may settle down. I think it's worth trying. But it's bad luck on the girl."

"She'll be all right," said Chesterton. "She'll be just as well off as signals officer at Wittington or Charwick as she is here. She'll be doing the same job."

He paused. "I tell you what I'll do. I'll slip over and see that Wing Officer at Group—Mrs. Harding—and fix it up. I'll tell her we've got nothing against the girl."

"You can tell her a bit more than that," said Dobbie. "The girl's good at her job. She's intelligent, and she's quick, and she's hardworking. The only thing we've got against her is that she doesn't want to marry one of my pilots, who I don't want married anyway."

"I'll tell Mrs. Harding all that," said Chesterton. "I think she'll understand. They're very good, you know."

Dobbie lit a cigarette, and blew out a long cloud of smoke. He sat silent for a minute, deep in thought. "I don't like it," he said uneasily at last. "You never know how they'll take these things. She's a good girl, and they've been very discreet. She may get a bad mark against her if we send her back to store over a thing like this. And if we crack her up and tell the Queen W.A.A.F. what a wizard girl she is, she'll get a worse one."

Chesterton smiled. "Well," he said, "we don't want to pile it on too thick. You'd better stay out of this and let me handle it. You're too young. The Queen W.A.A.F. will think that my grey hairs make me pretty safe."

"She doesn't know you," said the Wing Commander.

There was a silence in the office for a minute. In the end Dobbie sat up briskly. "I'm sorry," he said incisively, "but I don't like that way of handling it a bit. We've got to shift the girl, but I think she ought to ask for a transfer herself. She can go to her Wing Officer and ask to be moved to Charwick or Wittington. If they ask her why, she can say that she's been bothered by one of the officers here, which happens to be true."

"I see your point," the Squadron Leader said thoughtfully. "That couldn't possibly make any trouble. And we can back her up in that, and say that we think she's behaved very well."

Wing Commander Dobbie pushed back his chair. "Well, that's the way we'll take it," he said. "You have a talk with her and get her to put in to be transferred. Make it effective before Marshall comes back off leave, if you can."

"Me have a talk with her?" said the Squadron Leader, in dismay.

Dobbie laughed. "It's your job," he said. "It's administration. Besides you've got daughters as old as Robertson, or older."

"I know I have," said Chesterton. "But I never muck about in things like this—I let them go their own way. What am I to say to Robertson?"

The Wing Commander said: "Just tell her the truth. Tell her that Vickers don't put much armour on the Wimpies because of the weight. Tell her that the crews who go and come without incident have secret armour. Tell her that the crews that come back safely are the crews without personal troubles, who sleep sound at nights and have fun in the daytime." He paused, considering his long experience.

"The secret armour of a quiet mind," he said. "Tell her about that."

"You tell her," said Chesterton hopefully. "You know the lines."

"I'm too young," said the Wing Commander. "You just said so. You wanted to handle this. Well, go ahead and do it."

"All right." The Squadron Leader thought for a moment. "She's just put in for week-end leave," he said. "I think I'll wait till Friday and put it to her just before she goes. Then she can get in touch with her Wing Officer next week."

"Do it any time you like," said Dobbie, "so long as she's off the station before Marshall comes back."

Chesterton went back into his office thoughtfully. If there was one job that he thoroughly disliked and dreaded it was anything to do with the disciplining of W.A.A.F. officers. He got very little practice at it, for one thing; they had their own organisation and seldom came before him in that way. Only once before during four years of total war had he been compelled to ask a young woman questions about her behaviour; on that occasion it had been a nice point which of them had been more frightened.

He brooded over his problem for the next two days, rehearsing various openings, considering all the angles. When Friday came he was still unprepared, but set himself grimly to his task. He went up to Gervase in the ante-room before lunch. "Come along to my office this afternoon, will you?" he said. "I've got one or two things to talk over. About three?"

Gervase said: "Yes, sir," and wondered what signals had to do with Chesterton, and whether something frightful had happened over one of her girls. She presented herself at his office at three o'clock with some misgivings. He greeted her with forced heartiness, made her sit down, and gave her a cigarette.

He plunged straight into the matter without beating about the bush; it was better, he thought, to get it over quickly. "We've had a long talk about one of the crews," he said, "Wing Commander Dobbie and I. We're a bit worried about R for Robert. They used to be a very good, reliable crew. But last time they went out they got lost and landed up at Whitsand, just like a pack of boys straight in from the training school."

Gervase sat motionless, her heart right up in the middle of her throat. This wasn't something frightful about one of her girls. This was something frightful about herself.

The Squadron Leader went on: "When a crew goes off

colour in that way, Wing Commander Dobbie always tries to find out what's the matter, so that we can put it right if possible. In this case we found that there had been some friction, and there didn't seem to be much reason for it. The crew all seem to like their captain, Flight Lieutenant Marshall."

Gervase raised her eyes. "I think they do," she said. "I was talking to the rear-gunner about it the other night."

Chesterton smiled; the way seemed easier. "I thought perhaps you might be able to help us," he said. "I don't really know what this trouble is about, but, so far as I can see, the captain is to blame for most of it." He paused, expectantly.

A man of fifty is seldom a match for a young girl. He had talked too much and too slowly, and thereby made a tactical mistake. He had given Gervase ample time to recover her self-possession after the first shock of realising that she herself was on the carpet. Now she was ready to parry any thrust.

She smiled at him with innocent candour. "It is funny, isn't it?" she said. "We were all talking about it in our mess the other night. We couldn't understand why such an experienced crew should start making mistakes. But then I met the rear-gunner and heard all about it. I don't think you need worry about them now. I think they'll be all right when they go out next time."

There was a momentary pause. "What makes you think that?" he asked gravely.

She said: "I've got them some fishing."

CHAPTER SIX

Beyond this place of wrath and tears
   Looms but the Horror of the shade;
And yet the menace of the years
   Finds, and shall find, me unafraid.

                W. E. HENLEY

The old Squadron Leader blinked in surprise, trying to focus his mind upon this new aspect of the matter. "I beg your pardon?" he enquired.

Gervase looked up at him in starry-eyed innocence. "The rear-gunner told me," she said. "You see, they're all such keen fishermen in that crew, and they used to do it all together. But after the coarse-fishing season ended in the middle of March things started to go wrong, and they got on each other's nerves a bit, because they were all so bored with having nothing to do. I know it sounds silly, sir, but that's what he said."

She paused. "So I got permission for them to go fishing in a lake near here. It's nothing to do with me, of course, but I thought it might help. I hope I've not done wrong."

"But if the fishing season is over, how can they go fishing?" he asked in perplexity. It sounded to him to be a fishy sort of story altogether.

Gervase smiled tolerantly at him. "Trout-fishing starts in March, when the coarse-fishing ends," she said. "I got them some trout-fishing."

Chesterton thought of the flat country around Hartley, and the slow, muddy streams. "I didn't know there was any round here," he said. "Tell me, how did you get hold of it?"

She had lain awake in bed for half an hour on the Wednesday morning, after a long night's sleep. She lay staring at the ceiling in a dream, thinking of Peter Marshall and of the warm pressure of his hand on hers, thinking of all the problems of their relationship, thinking with scared delight of the weekend which was going to plunge her deeper into trouble. From that she came to think about the crew and Sergeant Phillips, and their fishing, and his phrase: "It's weary when you don't know what to do."

And suddenly she thought: "This is ridiculous." Trout-fishing at that time of year was in full swing, and there were trout in Kingslake Woods; she had seen them herself and poked at them with a stick. She had no idea who they belonged to, but that she could find out. Fired with the enthusiasm of youth she got up and had a bath.

She rang up Mr. Ellison at the tractor depot in the middle of the morning. She said: "This is Section Officer Robertson speaking, from the aerodrome. Do you remember me, Mr. Ellison? I came to your pigeon-shoot with Wing Commander Dobbie in the Jeep."

He said: "I remember. Miss Robertson, is it?"

"That's right. Mr. Ellison, you know everybody round here. Who lives in Kingslake House, over by Chipping Hinton?"

"Blowed if I know. I could find out for you."

"Could you? I want to know this morning, if I can." She hesitated. "I'll tell you what it's about. There's a lake there, with a lot of trout in it. Some of us were wondering if the owner of the house would let us go fishing there."

"I get you," he said. "Give you a ring back in half an hour."

She went on with her work; he came through on the telephone later in the morning. "About those trout you want to fish," he said. "You haven't got a hope. Nobody's allowed near them."

She said: "Who does the house belong to?"

"Well, there's a Brigadier Carter-Hayes, who lives there with his mother, Mrs. Carter-Hayes. They're county people, all frightfully toffee-nosed and Poona. Brigadier Carter-Hayes is away, out somewhere in the Middle East. There's only the old lady there now, and she won't let anybody near those fish. Seems like they're a sacred trust she's keeping for him."

It did not sound too promising. "She must be pretty old if she's got a son who's a brigadier," said Gervase.

"Getting on for eighty. Runs the house with three maids, all over sixty. The tweeny is a child of sixty-three."

Gervase thanked him, and rang off, and sat for a time slightly damped. Her beautiful idea now did not seem so good; at least, it would be difficult to realise. And then she thought that nothing would be lost by trying; if she went out to visit this old lady and to ask for permission for the crew of Robert to go fishing in the lake, the worst that could occur would be a smart rebuff, which wouldn't hurt for long.

She rode out that afternoon upon her bicycle. She rode on

past the point where they had gone into the woods to find the badger, crossed a little stream that was the outlet from the lake up in the woods, and so came to the drive that led up to the house.

It was a long drive, leading through a park studded with beech trees. There were a few sheep grazing, and some of them had lambs; she turned her head to watch them as she rode. She would have liked to have got off and sit upon the fence to study them for a little; it was sunny and bright, and pretty in the wooded park. But she had business to attend to; she had not come out there to look at lambs.

She rode on, and came out in front of the house. It was sheltered and peaceful, surrounded in the front with beech trees and a wide mown lawn, and many rhododendron bushes. There was prunus in bloom, and currant; the house lay quiet in the sun in an atmosphere of old security.

Gervase leaned her bicycle against the wall, went up to the front door and rang the bell. The oak door opened presently, and she saw a grey-haired maid, very neat in servant's costume of the last century, black dress, starched apron, and starched cap on the grey hair.

Gervase said: "Good afternoon. Can I see Mrs. Carter-Hayes?"

The old maid said deferentially: "I am sorry, madam. Mrs. Carter-Hayes is not at home."

The girl stared nonplussed. "I don't want to be a nuisance," she said. "But I've come a long way. Is Mrs. Carter-Hayes away?"

The maid said severely: "Mrs. Carter-Hayes is not at home to anybody to-day, madam."

Gervase said: "Please, don't you think she could see me just for a moment? I've bicycled seven miles from Hartley Magna because I wanted to see her, and if I can't I'll have to ride back and come out another day, and it's fourteen miles each time."

The old maid said: "Oh madam, that is a long way."

"It is," said Gervase feelingly. "Couldn't you ask her if she'd see me just for a minute?"

"Mrs. Carter-Hayes is not very well to-day. I could ask her, madam, seeing that you have come so far. May I have the card?"

Gervase said: "I'm sorry, but I haven't got a card. Would you tell her that Miss Robertson would like to see her for a moment ? I won't stay."

"Does she know you, madam ?"

"No she doesn't, I'm afraid."

"Would you step inside, madam ?" Gervase went forward into the hall, and the old maid closed the door carefully. "The wind is still cold, isn't it ?" she said. She beamed at Gervase like a mother. "Now if you would wait for just one minute, madam, I will see if Mrs. Carter-Hayes will see you, seeing that you've come all that way." She bustled off down the hall.

Gervase stood looking around. There was a great smell of camphor and floor polish and old leather, the smell of an old country house maintained in the old manner. There was a silver salver on a table with a couple of cards on it; beside it three brass polished candlesticks with candles and match-boxes ready for use. There was a very large Burmese gong upon a stand, brilliantly polished; there was a bright fire burning in the hearth. Upon the walls were a few old, faded sporting prints; upon a bracket there was a little glass case containing a round shot half-buried in an ancient piece of timber. Gervase knew houses of that sort fairly well; there were many of them in the North Riding near her home.

The old maid reappeared. "Would you kindly step this way, madam ?"

She went forward with the maid, and was shown into a long drawing-room. Through the window at the far end of the room she saw a wide mown lawn; beyond that there were the woods and the little lake that she had visited with Peter, the first day of all. The sight of it gave her courage.

She looked for her hostess. She saw a formidable old lady sitting very upright in a chair before the fire, gazing towards her; she wore a black dress unadorned except with a little white frill at the collar. Her thin grey hair was parted in the middle and drawn straight and severely back over her head; she had rather bushy black eyebrows and a white face.

The door closed quietly behind Gervase. She said shyly: "Mrs. Carter-Hayes ? My name is Robertson. It's awfully good of you to see me."

The old lady said testily: "Well, come on in, child, and don't stand over by the door. What's your other name ?"

"Gervase—Gervase Laura." She moved forward to the fire.

"I suppose your mother had been reading Tennyson. Bless me, what sort of costume have you got on ? Is that a uniform ?"

"Yes—it's Royal Air Force uniform. I'm a section officer."

"Well, turn round and let me see the back of it."

Gervase rotated slowly, hoping that by doing so she was achieving trout-fishing. "I think it's very ugly and un-womanly," said the old lady decidedly, "but you look quite pretty in it. I suppose you must be a good-looking girl in decent clothes. You must be very young."

"I'm, twenty-one, Mrs. Carter-Hayes."

"Do you have to polish all those buttons yourself every day?"

"No—the batwoman does that for me. I used to have to when I was an airwoman."

"What's an airwoman?"

"Like a private soldier. You have to start off in the ranks."

"But you're a lady. Do you mean that you have to live with a lot of factory girls?"

"Everybody has to start like that," said Gervase. "It's rather a good thing."

"It sounds to me to be a very bad thing, and most unsuitable for a young girl like you. I suppose you learned all sorts of language. And now do you have to look after the factory girls and try and stop them having babies?"

Gervase said: "I'm not on the welfare side. I'm a signals officer. That means I look after the girls who work the wireless station and the radio telephone and the ordinary telephones. Somebody else takes care of their welfare, but of course I have to help them all I can."

"Dale told me that you had bicycled from Hartley Magna. Is that where all the aeroplanes come from, that keep flying over in the middle of the night?"

"Probably—or they may come from the aerodrome at Charwick. I think the Charwick ones may be the ones you hear. They'd pass right over here on their way out to the Ruhr."

"You don't go with them?"

"No—I stay on the ground and run the wireless."

"Well, what is it you wanted to see me about?"

Gervase hesitated, wondering how to put the matter of the trout-fishing to this formidable old woman.

"Well, sit down if it's going to take you a long time. Sit down there. Will you stay and have a cup of tea with me?"

Startled, Gervase said: "I'd like to awfully." And then she turned to the old lady. "It is going to take me a long time," she said. "It's such a funny thing to ask."

"Ring that bell beside you." Gervase got up and rotated the old handle; a wire scraped in the wall and a bell sounded faintly in the house. "Well, tell me what it is."

Gervase said: "It's about one of our bomber crews. The men who fly one of the bombers over Germany. They're all keen fishermen in that crew, and they've been all at sixes and sevens since the coarse-fishing season stopped. I was wondering perhaps if they could come and fish in your lake when they're off duty."

The door opened behind her quietly. The old lady said: "Dale, bring some tea for this young lady."

The door closed softly. She turned to Gervase. "My son had that lake stocked with little trout two years ago, before he went overseas, in order that there might be good fishing when he came home," she said severely. "I have never allowed it to be fished, for that reason."

Gervase thought, that was that. It was just as Ellison had told her; she might have saved her journey. But the old lady's case was reasonable according to her standards; Gervase felt that she might talk all night, and do no good.

"I'm so sorry," she said. "I didn't know it was like that. This crew need fishing very badly, and I thought perhaps this might be an opportunity."

The old lady said: "My dear, you keep on talking about a crew, and I don't know in the least what you mean. Is it the crew of a ship?"

Gervase said patiently: "No, it's the crew of an aeroplane. We call the men who go in the bombers the crew. There are five in these aeroplanes."

"Five men?"

"Yes."

"And do they fly the bomber over the Ruhr, and drop the bombs? Are those the men you call the crew?"

"Yes."

"They must be very brave men to fly all that way over Germany at night."

The thought was a new one to Gervase. She had been so intimately associated with them that she had never seen them in that light. "I think they are," she said slowly. "I think they're very brave men."

"And this bomber crew that you say are all at sixes and sevens. What do you mean by that?"

Gervase said: "It's a frightful strain on them, going out like that night after night." The door opened quietly behind her, and the old maid pushed in a rubber-tyred trolley with a silver teapot, delicate china, cake and bread and butter; she arranged this quietly between them as they talked. "Each night, some of them don't come back; they just get—killed. But some of them go on, night after night and month after month. And the crews who do that are usually all great friends who know each other very well, because then they get to work together as a team."

The old lady nodded. "My son always says that a good polo team is best made up of friends," she said. "That is what you mean?"

Gervase knew nothing about polo whatsoever, but she thought it safe to say: "That's it."

"Well? What's all this got to do with fishing? Do you take sugar with your tea?"

"Please." She thought for a moment, and then said: "They all used to go fishing together until the coarse-fishing season ended in March. It was their one big interest, and they all did it. Then when the season ended they hadn't got anything to do, and they began sort of snapping at each other. It's a frightful strain." She paused. "And then they began to make mistakes, and last time they were very nearly killed."

The old lady gazed at her quizzically. "And so you thought if they could come and fish my lake they might get together again."

Gervase turned to her, surprised at so much understanding. "That's exactly what I did think."

"Who are these men? Has the crew got a captain?"

The girl nodded. "Flight Lieutenant Marshall. All the rest are sergeants, except the wireless operator, who is a corporal."

"But do you mean to tell me that they all go out fishing together? The officer with the sergeants and the corporal?"

"Yes."

"How very odd," said the old lady shortly.

There was a pause while she poured out tea with a very shaky hand, and gave the girl a slice of bread and butter. Gervase noticed that she took only very weak tea without milk or sugar herself, and a thin wafer biscuit.

"And which one is it that you are in love with?"

Gervase very nearly dropped her cup. This was worse than Pat Johnson. "I'm not in love with any of them," she said warmly.

"Well, which one is in love with you?"

Gervase was silent for a moment. She did not want to tell lies to this unpleasantly direct old lady; moreover, she was by no means sure that she would get away with it if she tried. "Peter Marshall," she said weakly.

"He is the officer—the captain?"

"Yes."

"Are you going to marry him?"

"I don't know." This was terrible.

"Well, make up your mind quickly and don't keep him waiting too long. You can't afford to dilly and dally in times like these."

Deep down in her heart Gervase felt that it had been worth riding fourteen miles upon her bicycle to hear that said. But she was suddenly inarticulate and filled her mouth with bread and butter to avoid having to reply, colouring a little.

Very slowly and painfully the old lady raised herself from her chair and reached for an ebony stick. "My son thinks very highly of the Air Force," she said. "I am going to show you a letter that arrived from him only last week, the last letter we have had."

She moved very slowly across the room to a walnut escretoire, selected a key from a bunch that she took from a pocket at her girdle, and unlocked a drawer. From the same pocket she extracted a spectacle-case, and put them on. She picked a letter from the drawer, took it from the field service envelope, and stood reading it. "This is the one," she said slowly, "all about a carpet. Such a funny word to use."

She moved back to her chair before the fire and sat down again. She examined the three pages of the letter carefully, selected the middle page, and handed it to Gervase. "That is the part, I think," she said. "Read that, child."

Gervase took the sheet. It was written unevenly in black Italian ink, as if by a hand unused to writing recently, forced to use as desk the tail-board of a truck or a petrol-can. It said:

"The Air Force have been magnificent all through. We should never have got through the wadis except for their help. They laid what Tedder calls a carpet for us; all day, over and over again they came down to ground level ahead of us, shooting up everything they saw resisting the advance, and bombing all the anti-tank positions. It was magnificent, but it was very costly to them because the Germans have

NEALE

plenty of light flak. Over and over again in the last few days we have found crashed Hurricanes and Kittihawks in our advance, scores of them, some with the body of the pilot still in the seat. The Germans are resisting desperately; if we get through to Tunis it will be because of what these Air Force boys are doing to prepare the ground ahead of us and their self-sacrifice."

Gervase handed back the letter gravely. "Thank you for showing me," she said.

The old lady took the sheet and placed it in the envelope with the others and laid it carefully upon the table at her side. "I am sure if my son were here he would want to help you," she said gently. "If fishing in the lake will really be some good to your crew, I do not think he would want me to refuse it. After all, the lake can always be re-stocked when you have taken all the fish out of it."

Gervase said: "That's terribly kind of you, Mrs. Carter-Hayes. We'd pay for the re-stocking."

The old lady sat up. "Mind you, I am not going to have the whole Air Force tramping through my garden and upsetting everything. Write down the names of these men, the crew, and I will write a little note to invite them." She passed a pad and pencil to Gervase.

The girl wrote down all the names and the addresses; the old lady took the sheet and studied it. "Sergeant Pilot Franck," she said. "What an odd name. Is he English?"

Gervase said: "He's a young Dane. A medical student before the war. He is the navigator—the most senior of them, next to Flight Lieutenant Marshall."

"How odd."

There was a short silence; Gervase began to think about going. But presently the thin old lady said:

"Have all these sergeants and corporals got rods for fly-fishing?"

Gervase said: "I don't suppose so, because they're only used to coarse fishing. But don't worry about that—they'll get them fast enough. They aren't badly paid."

"Somebody was telling me that it is very difficult to buy fishing tackle of any sort now. Are you going to fish with them?"

Gervase smiled. "I've only tried once or twice, and then the line was always getting caught up. I'd like to try again, if I might."

The old lady reached slowly for her stick and struggled to her feet. "Let us go and see in the gun-room," she said. "I know there are several rods there."

She moved very slowly from the room out into the hall; Gervase following behind her step by step. She moved down the passage to a closed door, which she unlocked with a key from her reticule. They went forward into a little room, dim with a drawn blind; the old lady moved forward to the window and snapped the blind up, flooding the room with light. Gervase looked around.

On one side of the room were drawers and cupboards, covered with a thin film of dust. In the middle was a deal kitchen table. On the other side of the room there was a small iron fireplace, flanked on the one side by a glass case containing half a dozen guns, on the other side by a row of hooks from which eight or ten rods in their fabric bags hung suspended. The old lady moved over to these and began handling them.

"This is a trout rod," she said slowly, "and this one. This—no, this must be a spinning rod, and those two are for salmon. This is another trout rod, I think." She laid the trout rods one by one upon the table. "And the reels and the lines used to be in this drawer. Here they are."

Gervase said: "It's awfully good of you to take so much trouble, Mrs. Carter-Hayes."

"If your friends have any difficulty in buying their own tackle they may borrow any of these things, my dear. Only they must keep them here and not take them away."

"Of course," said Gervase. "Are you sure your son won't mind them being used?"

"Oh no—these are the rods he keeps here for his friends to use when they come and stay." She bent painfully and opened a cupboard and pulled out a little leather case about four feet long and opened it upon the table. Inside upon a bed of red fabric there was a beautiful little rod with its reel. "This is the rod my son always uses," she said. "If you want to fish yourself you may use this one. It's very light. But I would rather that nobody else used it, except you." She took up the butt joint in her gnarled old hand. "I used to fish with a little rod like this," she said, "when I was a girl your age. A great many years ago."

Gervase said: "Are you sure your son won't mind me using it?"

"Oh no. It will do it good to be used."

She turned to the drawers and began opening them one by one. "There are a lot of flies here somewhere, I know," she said. "Not those—those are salmon flies. I think these must be the ones—oh yes, and here are the casts." She turned to Gervase. "Everything is here in these drawers," she said. "You may use anything you like. I will tell Dale, and she will let your friends in here when they come, and then they can go and fish as often as they like."

She moved from the room out into the passage. "Now I am going to turn you out," she said. "At my age one gets tired very soon. Thank you for coming to see me, my dear."

Gervase said: "It's terribly kind of you to do all this for us, Mrs. Carter-Hayes."

"Not at all. If you decide to marry that young man, bring him in for me to have a look at."

Gervase laughed awkwardly, and left, and rode back to Hartley very pleased with herself. She went first to her office at Headquarters; on her table there was a message scribbled on a message pad asking her to ring up Mr. Ellison.

She sat down and called his number. He said: "Oh, look, Miss Robertson. I've been hearing a bit more about that Kingslake House. I wouldn't go out there, if I were you."

"Why not?"

"Leave it a bit. You know I said there was a son who was a brigadier in the Army? Well, he's been killed out in Tunisia. The old lady only got the news yesterday."

CHAPTER SEVEN

And it's, buy a bunch of violets for the lady
  (*It's lilac time in London; it's lilac time in London!*)
Buy a bunch of violets for the lady
  While the sky burns blue above:

On the other side the street you'll find it shady
  (*It's lilac time in London; it's lilac time in London!*)
But buy a bunch of violets for the lady,
  And tell her she's your own true love.

ALFRED NOYES

Squadron Leader Chesterton went into the Wing Commander's office. "I've been talking to that girl Robertson," he said.

"Put the hard word to her?"

"It's not quite so easy as we thought. She's much more mixed up in the Robert business than I knew."

"Mixed up in it?"

"That's right. She says that crew will be all right from now on, because she's got them some fishing."

Dobbie stared at the older man. "That's a new one," he said slowly. "Let's have the gen on that."

Chesterton told him briefly what he had heard from Gervase; in the end he laughed a little ruefully. "So after that I piped down and let her go off on her week-end," he said. "I thought you'd want to think about it a bit more."

"You didn't tell her that we wanted her to ask to be shifted away?"

"No, I didn't. I wasn't sure if it was still a good idea."

Dobbie sat for a moment deep in thought. Whoever ran an air station successfully in time of war inevitably became an amateur psychologist; the Wing Commander was very well aware of the power of occupations and hobbies to keep his young men happy. It was perfectly true that Marshall and all his crew were keen fishermen; if this girl had got them fishing in the neighbourhood it might well be a real factor in the revival of their efficiency, which he ought not to disregard.

"I suppose the girl's right in on this?" he asked. "No girl, no fishing?"

"Well, she's the one who's raced around and got it for them."

There was a silence in the office. Dobbie sat staring out of the window at the wide reaches of the aerodrome, thoughtful. "She's got us foxed," he said at last. "If we push her back to Group they'll lose this fishing, and they'll all get bloody-minded about that."

"I think she's got us foxed all right," said Chesterton. "If you're going to try this fishing scheme of hers, you'll have to let her stay."

The Wing Commander lit a cigarette. "Where is this trout-fishing?" he asked. "If I let her get away with this, I'm going to have a smack at her trout."

"Chipping Hinton," said the Adjutant. "But look, what about Marshall? What are you going to do about him?"

"If she stays here she's got to play fair with Marshall," said Dobbie. "I'm not going to have him mooning round the mess like a sick cow."

"That's probably what's in the wind," said Chesterton. "She's probably made up her mind she wants to marry him. That's why she's taken so much trouble about this fishing."

The Wing Commander sat up suddenly. "If she's going to marry him, I wish to hell she'd get on with it," he said irritably. "I'm fed-up with her. If young women would just stop and think before they shoot the boy friend down, we'd have a lot more pilots."

The old Squadron Leader nodded. "Girls have to be very wise these days," he said.

"So do Commanding Officers," said Dobbie. "I'm going to get a job as Aunt Ethel in *Betty's Weekly* when the war's over."

There was a pregnant silence.

"What are you going to do, then?" asked the Adjutant. "Let things take their course a bit?"

"I know what I'd like to do," said Dobbie viciously. "I'd take them both and lock them up together in a bedroom for a week, and feed them rations through the ventilator. I'm fed-up with this damned nonsense."

"I'm afraid we might have trouble with the Queen W.A.A.F. if we did that."

"Pity."

In the end they decided to do nothing at all.

Gervase travelled up to London next morning, and got to Paddington before lunch. Marshall was waiting at the barrier to meet her; she greeted him rather shyly as he took her case.

"Hullo, Peter."

"Hullo, Gervase. I got your letter. Look, what would you like to do ? Would you like to go and have lunch at the Zoo ?"

Her face lit up. "Oh, that'd be fun!" She had been apprehensive about this week-end, fearing that she was going to have to spend most of it fending off passion. This suggestion of the Zoo put matters on a different plane; if there was passion in the offing, at any rate there was a bit of fun attached to it.

"Okay. Look, shall we park your bag in the cloak-room and pick it up later on ?"

She agreed, and they left her suitcase, and secured a taxi with some difficulty. It was bright and sunny and warm; the top of the taxi was down and they drove through the streets to Regent's Park sitting fairly close together, but not touching. By the time they got there they were very happy.

They lunched in the restaurant by a window looking out over the gardens, Gervase a little thoughtful. She had to tell Marshall some time during the afternoon about the fishing; now that the time had come she was unsure, afraid that he would be angry with her for having meddled in his trouble with his crew. The more she thought of it the more difficult it seemed; constraint descended on them as the meal went on, and one or two long silences came which neither quite knew how to deal with.

It was a relief when the meal was over and they could get out to the animals. The elephant house did not seem to Gervase to be very suitable for finesse, nor did the atmosphere of the lion house engender confidences. The monkey house was fun but quite unsuitable for her purpose, and though the reptile house was quiet and dim, it was a little sinister. But then he took her into the Aquarium, and she took courage from the fish. This was the place, she thought, if anywhere.

In the semi-darkness they paused by a green translucent window of trout. Gervase felt that she would never get a better opening than this; she turned to Marshall. "I've got something to tell you about trout, Peter."

He glanced down and met her eyes, and thought again how lovely she was. "About trout ?"

She hesitated for a moment. "I was talking to Sergeant Phillips the other night," she said. "He told me how bored he'd been when the fishing season stopped, and Gunnar Franck and Leech, too, hanging about the camp with nothing to do. And I remembered where we saw the trout that day in Kingslake Woods, and I went and asked the old lady in the house if she would mind if your crew went and fished for them."

"What did she say?"

"She said they might. She's got a lot of rods and things there, too, that they can use."

"Am I in on this?"

"If you want to be." There was a little pause; she raised her eyes to his. "You aren't angry because I did that?"

Impulsively he reached down for her hand and captured it. "Of course not," he said. "Whatever made you think I should be angry?"

She was relieved, both by his words and by the pressure of his hand, warm and friendly. "I thought you might be cross because I'd been meddling," she said. "We could have talked it over if you'd been at Hartley."

He had raised her hand to waist level, and now held it in captivity with both of his. "Did you really think that I'd be angry with you for meddling in my business?" he said. "Seems to me you haven't got the right idea at all."

She glanced up, and saw that he was laughing, and the tension was relaxed, and she laughed too. "It was only this once," she said. "I'm not going to go on meddling in your affairs as a regular thing."

He said gravely: "Of course not." She looked up again and saw that he was laughing at her now, and she coloured a little and tried to remove her hand. But he had got it.

"Let me have a look at this," he said. "I've never examined it before." He looked down at her hand, slim and white and tapering in his own. "You don't use nail-polish, do you?" he asked.

"No. I just rub them over with the little pad thing."

"You don't need varnish and stuff on them."

"I just can't be bothered with all that."

"What's this little scar?"

They bent over her hand together. "That's where I cut it, cutting ham for mother. It bled all over the ham."

"Made it a bit more tasty, I suppose."

"Don't be foul."

"All right." They stood together by the golden-green window; he was still holding her hand and she was content to let him do so. "Let me have a good look at you," he said.

Gervase raised her eyes to his. "All right."

He drew back a little, but still held her hand. She stood there looking up at him, feeling his gaze playing over her, noticing the firm line of his chin, the brown muscles at his neck. "You cut yourself shaving," she said.

"I was all of a doo-dah this morning," he said. He grinned down at her. "You've got just a little lipstick on, haven't you?" he said. "Just a touch?"

She nodded.

"But nothing on your cheeks—no rouge or anything?"

"I seem to get by all right without it," Gervase said. "All I use is powder." She coloured a little, thinking how very peculiar it was that she didn't mind being stared at in this way, that she was answering such personal questions. And thinking so, she decided that it was time to bring this to a close and go on looking at the fish, and so she glanced at the trout, and said: "Have you seen all you want to?"

Marshall said: "Oh—er, yes." She looked up at him curiously and saw that the corners of his mouth were twitching, and that he was trying not to laugh. She wondered for a moment, and then laughed with him. "I think you're a pig," she said. "You know I didn't mean . . ." She turned, still laughing with him, and embarrassed. "Come on, let's look at some more fish."

They paused before the pike in genuine interest. "That's what you ate a bit of," said the pilot. "Remember?" Gervase remembered very well; it was dim in the hall before the pike-tank, and there was nobody much about, and it seemed a pity to lose touch altogether by letting go hands. And so they wandered on from tank to tank in the dim light, talking about the fish and unobtrusively holding fingers linked down by their side.

And presently they went out into the sunlight of the gardens, and the first thing that they saw was a captain in the Tank Corps walking hand-in-hand with a corporal in the A.T.S.

"Look at that," said Marshall quietly. "It's what you have to do here. Custom of the country." Five minutes later the Tank Corps captain coming out the Pets' Corner saw Gervase and Marshall standing hand-in-hand and laughing at the penguins and said the same thing to his corporal, and so everyone was happy.

They spent a quarter of an hour with the penguins, and then

they left the gardens and went back in a taxi to the station to collect her suitcase, and then back in the same taxi to the aunt at Hampstead, where she was to stay the night. And when the meter of the taxi clicked up to nine shillings, Gervase said: "Peter, we can't go on running up taxis at this rate. We'll be ruined."

"All right. Let's."

"Anyway, I'm going to pay half."

"Over my dead body."

She turned to him as they went past Swiss Cottage. "No, honestly, I must pay half."

He grinned at her. "You've got me some nice fishing. I owe you for that, anyway. If you'd feel safer paying half and half, Gervase, I'll take your money even if it breaks me heart. But I'd much rather not."

"I don't feel like that, Peter," she said slowly. "But I always have paid half and half when I've been out with people."

"I've got eleven pounds," he said. "If we get through that I'll come down on you."

She was shocked. "But, Peter, we can't go spending money like that!"

He said: "You see." The taxi drew up at the block of flats that was Aunt Mary's residence, and they abandoned the discussion.

Aunt Mary was a spinster about fifty years of age, who worked at the Red Cross. She was only partially effectual; her interests chiefly were in the Universal Language and in the League of Health and Beauty; she held strong views on vivisection, and disliked the Nazis. She welcomed Gervase cordially and was interested and polite to the young man that Gervase had brought with her. Half-way through tea Aunt Mary woke up to the realisation that she had never seen Gervase looking so pretty; that she was positively radiant. Aunt Mary decided that she would have to write a little note to her sister, Gervase's mother.

Gervase went to change in her bedroom, and Marshall went into the bathroom for a wash, and then sat on talking to Aunt Mary until Gervase was ready. He found Aunt Mary troublesome. Her work was concerned with the despatch of Red Cross parcels to prisoners of war, and she was anxious to find out all she could about the recipients. After nearly eighteen months in Bomber Command, Marshall knew a good deal about prisoners of war; much of what he knew was secret and all of it was distasteful to him. It seemed to him to be unhealthy to spend your time in speculating what would happen to you after you had been shot down, as unhealthy as the business man who displays keen curiosity about the procedure in bankruptcy. He answered her many questions politely but reluctantly, and was relieved when Gervase came to set him free.

She was in her pastel blue dance frock, with the silver slippers. Her mother had chosen it for her, so it was simple; she wore no jewellery because she only had a couple of lockets and a brooch or two. There was nothing, really, to make Peter Marshall feel that he had just picked up a thousand-pound bank-note—only Gervase in a civilian frock with rather more Gervase and rather less frock than he was accustomed to seeing. He thought she was most ravishingly beautiful.

Aunt Mary lent her a fur coat as a cloak and gave her the latch-key; then they were ready to go. As they went down the stairs arm-in-arm Marshall said: "Got your money with you?"

She glanced at him. "Only a few shillings, Peter. I'm not going to let you spend eleven pounds, or anything like it."

"It wasn't that that I was thinking of," he said. "I was thinking that you'd better pay half and half after all. You want all the safety you can get in that frock."

She laughed, and they went forward happily together, and found a taxi and drove to the Piccadilly and had a dry Martini before going to the theatre. And while they were drinking this the pilot said: "What are we going to do to-morrow?"

Gervase glanced at him. "I hadn't thought about to-morrow. I ought to stay and see something of Aunt Mary."

"When have you got to be back at Hartley?"

"I've got to be back there to-morrow night. That means the four o'clock train from Paddington."

"I thought it would be nice to get some sandwiches and have the day in Kew Gardens." He paused. "All the spring flowers will be out now."

Gervase said innocently: "We could take Aunt Mary with us." He looked up and saw that she was laughing at him, and he said: "You can see all you want to of Aunt Mary next month. I told you I was going to work you hard this month."

Gervase thought for a moment. Spring flowers sounded lovely; she had never been to the Botanical Gardens at Kew, and she wanted to go. Curiously the memory of the old lady in Kingslake House came to her mind, and her words: "Make up your mind quickly, and don't keep him waiting too long. You can't afford to dilly and dally in times like these." She knew that that advice was right. A month should be time enough for her to make her mind up whether she wanted to spend her life married with Peter Marshall; in any case, that was all the time she had. It would be unfair to him to keep the matter dragging on longer than that, she felt; a girl of any character should know her mind within a month. But here they were with nearly a week of that month already gone, and in that week they had met twice and written once each. When he got back to Hartley things would be constrained and difficult at their meetings in the mess. Time was denied to them, and opportunities were rare; she must not be silly over the ones they had, in fairness to themselves.

She smiled at him. "All right," she said. "I'll work. I don't know what Aunt Mary will think."

"I do," he said.

"So do I," said Gervase. "But it isn't true."

"Of course not," he said gravely. They caught each other's eye and burst out laughing, and got up and went off to the theatre.

They came out some hours later, weak with laughter, having held hands throughout each dim-lit act and moved decorously apart during each interval. They did not know their way about the Savoy, and that made their entrance into a pleasant adventure; presently they found themselves at the table that Marshall had reserved on the edge of the dance floor.

They started off with a smart argument about the drink. "We've not got to champagne yet," said Gervase firmly, "and for all I know we never will. And, anyway, we can't afford it."

"This night of all nights," said Marshall.

"This night of all nights," said Gervase, "I've evidently got to keep my wits about me. I'll have ginger-ale." She compromised to the extent of having gin in it; the wine waiter departed very much annoyed with her.

They dined well because they were very hungry, and they danced well enough to satisfy each other, which was all that mattered to them. They laughed at the cabaret and danced again, and suddenly it was midnight and everything was packing up. The car that Marshall had ordered was waiting for them, and they drove back to Hampstead, sitting very close together and arm-in-arm.

At the flats Marshall told the car to wait, and took Gervase in and up the stairs. In the dim passage she said: "I've had a lovely, lovely day, Peter. Thank you for being so nice to me."

They paused together. "Better than you thought it would be?" he enquired.

She hesitated. "Yes, it has been," she said. "I wasn't sure if I really wanted to come, but I'm glad I did."

He smiled. "I know. You were afraid I'd breathe hot love all over you and make a rude suggestion in the taxi."

She laughed awkwardly; it was exactly what she had been afraid of. "I wasn't," she declared. "You aren't that sort of person."

"Don't you believe it," said the pilot. "I'll make a rude suggestion quick enough as soon as I think you want to hear it." He took her hand. "But I don't think you do."

She shook her head; it was an odd sort of conversation, she thought, but she was not annoyed. "No, I don't." Standing with him in the dim hallway, hand-in-hand, the queer thought came to her that no suggestion he might make could ever be rude because he wanted to marry her, and that seemed to cover everything. She said: "After all, you made your rude suggestion weeks ago in asking me to marry you."

"I did that," said Marshall. "And I'll make it again if you give me half a chance."

He had both her hands by this time. "Would it spoil things if I kissed you?" he asked gently.

She did not answer; ten seconds later she could not have answered if she had wanted to. He was a comprehensive kisser, she decided breathlessly; she said: "Peter, I don't want to be eaten alive."

Holding her in his arms, he said: "Then you oughtn't to smell so nice. You'd better go to the chemist and get something for it."

She laughed softly and stood there in his arms, feeling comforted, secure, and infinitely alive. And, standing so, they talked in low tones about their arrangements for the next day, how he would call for her at about eleven, having gathered up some sandwiches somehow or other. And presently they kissed again more gently, and she slid out of his arms and vanished into Aunt Mary's flat. Marshall went down to the waiting car and was driven back to his hotel, tired and content.

Morning found Marshall sitting on his bed in the Cumberland Hotel polishing his buttons to go out with Gervase, and found Gervase sitting on her bed in Aunt Mary's flat polishing her buttons to go out with Marshall. Eleven o'clock found them simulating regret at parting with Aunt Mary, whom they had treated very badly, and walking out into the Hampstead street carrying Gervase's suitcase and a large packet of sandwiches.

They found a taxi presently and went to Paddington to park the suitcase. And there it seemed to them that it was getting on for lunch-time, and it was a pity to rush things, and the six-forty-five was quite a good train, after all. So they crammed the sandwiches into a suitcase and went by Underground to Piccadilly, and up into the sunlight again. And as they walked around looking for somewhere to have lunch it seemed prudent to them to go hand-in-hand in case they might get separated and waste time looking for each other, and that was quite all right because everybody else seemed to be doing the same thing.

They lunched at a little place in Jermyn Street, which set them back the thick end of two pounds, and came out pleasantly full and very pleased with themselves. And having investigated the state of the exchequer and discovered that they still had two pounds fifteen left before Gervase took over the expenditure, they took a taxi to Kew Gardens at considerable expense. They had the top down for the sun, and soon discovered that that made it draughty, so there was no point in sitting at opposite ends of the seat. Indeed, by the time they crossed Kew Bridge they were getting along so well that Marshall suggested they had better tell the driver to turn round and go back to Piccadilly.

Gervase detached her arm, sat upright, and adjusted her cap before the mirror. "I won't do anything of the sort," she said. "I want to see Kew."

"Pity," said Marshall. "I was just going to bring out my rude suggestion. I'd got it out and sort of dusted it, all ready."

She laughed. "Never mind. I'll let you spring it on me some day as a great surprise."

He said anxiously: "Promise you'll be shocked?"

Gervase said: "Of course I'll be shocked, Peter. I'll say: 'Oh, Mr. Marshall, whatever made you think I was that sort of girl!'"

"That'll do," he said, a little grudgingly, "but you'll have to get more feeling into it. Burst into tears and say something about your mother."

"I'll remember," said Gervase obediently.

They paid off the taxi and went into the gardens hand-in-hand, because you never quite knew what you might not meet in a Botanical Garden, as Marshall pointed out. It was, perhaps, as well they did not meet the W.A.A.F. Police.

It was beautiful in the gardens. It was the middle of April, but after the open winter everything was a month early, and the lilac was in bloom, and the laburnum, and magnolias. The whole place was a riot of colour in the sunlight; every glade was full of blossoming trees. The pilot and the section officer walked over the short grass silent with wonder; it was so beautiful that they could hardly speak about it. Once Gervase stopped, somewhere near the Pagoda, and said quietly: "I've never seen anything so lovely in my life. Peter, did you know that it would be like this?"

He shook his head. "I knew it would be good, but not like this."

They sat down presently and talked and talked and talked. They told each other all about their homes, about their parents, about their brothers and sisters, about their schools, their interests, their lives. And in a flash the time slipped by till it was after five, and they must be beginning to get back to Paddington if Gervase was to catch her train.

"It seems a shame to have to go," said Gervase. "It's so lovely here."

"I'll be back at Hartley next week," said Marshall. "We'll go out and have a crack at your fishing."

She smiled. "That'll be fun."

He hesitated. "You know I've only got five more operational flights to do?" he said quietly. "Before I've done my second tour?"

She stared at him. "Oh, Peter, I never thought of that. Does that mean you'll be leaving Hartley?"

He nodded. "After five more trips."

"How long for?"

He said: "I was grounded for three months after the first one; they sent me to Stamford. But I don't think I'll be coming back to Hartley at all." He was fingering her hand. "They don't make us go on for a third tour in Bomber Command, unless we volunteer," he said. "I'm not so keen on Germany as that. I want to get back to Coastal for a change, and fly a

Liberator in daylight."

She said: "So you'll be leaving altogether."

He nodded. "After five more trips."

"You could get through those in a fortnight," Gervase said. "Then you'd be going."

"I know." He glanced at her, and they were now both deadly serious. "The one thing we haven't got is time. I wanted you to know that—in case it might make a difference."

She said: "I'll remember that, Peter. Thank you for telling me."

"I was wondering about next Sunday," he said. "If I came back to the camp on Saturday, could you arrange to get Sunday off, all day, so that we could try the fishing before the crew come back?"

"I could if there isn't an operation on," she said. She smiled at him. "People will pull your leg if you get back before your leave is up."

He laughed. "I can wear it. Will they pull yours?"

She said: "It's different with us. We get asked if our intentions are strictly honourable."

They laughed together, and presently they got up, and he took her back to Paddington by bus and train.

In the station they retrieved her bag from the cloak-room. And then, because the train was likely to be full of Air Force going back to Hartley or the Group off week-end leave, they went nosing round the outskirts of the station for a quiet corner, and presently found one, dim-lit, between a deserted mail-van and a pile of fish-boxes, with nobody about. And here they put the suitcase down and he kissed her, and they stood quietly together for a while, enjoying the last minutes.

"I've had a lovely time," Gervase said softly. "Thank you for everything, Peter."

He kissed her again, and presently they broke it up and she went off alone to catch the Oxford train. He stood among the fish-boxes and watched her through the crowd till she was out of sight.

Gervase got back to Hartley four hours later, happy enough, but tired to death. She went straight up to bed without waiting to have supper; as she undressed she ate a few of the sandwiches that they had put into her suitcase earlier in the day. She was so sleepy that she went to bed with a half-eaten sandwich still in her hand.

In the few minutes before sleep came to her she thought of

Marshall and his work. She was very glad his time in bombers was drawing to a close; he was a good bomber pilot, but she knew he would be happier in Coastal. No man, she thought, could really be happy in the risks and hazards of night bombing; you could be used to it and do it as a function of the war, but it was as unpleasant as riding in a tank. When he had done his second tour he would deserve to have a job that was fun; he wanted to fly a Liberator in Scotland, and he deserved to get what he wanted. She wondered, half asleep, if she would like Scotland. But that, she reflected, was quite premature, because she hadn't made up her mind if she even liked Peter Marshall. Not nearly yet. She was smiling as she drifted into sleep.

She got a letter from him punctually by the first post on Tuesday morning, and read it in the privacy of her room. She answered it on Tuesday afternoon, when she was supposed to be resting for the coming operation, which was Dusseldorf. She spent the night on duty out at the Group W/T station. That night twenty-two machines left Hartley Magna. Sixteen came back, one landed in Essex, the crew of one baled out near Guildford, and four failed to return altogether.

She got another letter from him on Thursday, and on Thursday night the Wing went to Essen. Twenty-six machines took off, one of which hit a tree a mile away and crashed in a great sheet of flame that lit up the whole aerodrome. Twenty-one landed back at Hartley, one put down in Kent, and three failed to return. In the short space of two days the Wing had lost eight machines.

At Group Headquarters the next day Wing Commander Dobbie had a long talk with the Air Commodore. Dobbie was looking drawn and tired; he had flown all night in L for London with Sergeant Pilot Hogg, but instead of sleeping he had come to Group to talk about his casualties. "There's no reason to make any change," he said. "It's just the luck of the game— two months ago we did six ops right off and never lost a machine. We've just had bad luck on these two. There was nothing in last night's show that was at all unusual."

The Air Commodore nodded. "I think that's right. Charwick lost nobody at all last night. Wittington lost one. How are your crews taking it?"

The Wing Commander made a slight grimace. "Not quite so good," he said. "They're all so young. . . . I was going to ask if you could rest us for a week, and let me get them up on the top line before the next one."

"I'll try."

"Another thing, sir. I've got very few old stagers with me now. Johnson and Davy, Marshall and Lines, Nutter . . . really, you can count them on one hand. I wish you'd remember that in the drafting. It makes a big difference."

"I know it does. I'll see what I can do." There was a pause. "You've got an E.N.S.A. concert to-morrow night, haven't you ?"

"Yes, sir. That'll help—if it's a good one."

"It's quite a good show," said Air Commodore Baxter. "I saw it the night before last at Wittington. I laughed a lot."

Dobbie thought for a moment. "I shan't do anything to-night," he said. "It's too soon. They'll have the E.N.S.A. show to-morrow, and then on Sunday I'll give them a surprise and we'll have a dance. Can you square the Padre to let us have a dance on Sunday, sir."

"I'll fix him."

"A surprise dance always goes down well," said Dobbie. He paused for a minute, thoughtful. "It makes a lot of difference having all these W.A.A.F.s upon the station, when the crews are a bit down," he said. "They recover much quicker."

"I know. They talk it over with the girls and get it off their minds."

Dobbie went back to Hartley, worked in his office for an hour, and then went back to his house for lunch, and to spend the afternoon in sleep. He was on the telephone at tea time mustering all his ground officers with a summons to dine in the mess that night, and to Flight Officer Stevens inviting the W.A.A.F. officers. He made similar arrangements for the sergeants' mess; by six o'clock he was playing billiards in the lounge himself with Flight Lieutenant Davy and a couple of moody pilot officers.

Section Officer Robertson came in while he was playing, and stood watching the game for a minute. Dobbie ordered her a gin and Italian. "I wanted to see you," he said. "This concert to-morrow night. What was the name of that tractor chap that we said we'd invite ?"

"Ellison, sir."

"I remember. And there was the farmer, too—Jack Barton. I want to ask them both to come and dine in the mess to-morrow night before the concert. Can you get hold of them ?"

"I think so, sir."

"Pity Marshall isn't here," said Dobbie. "He knows them both."

Gervase said: "Flight Lieutenant Marshall will be back to-morrow night." Immediately she wished she hadn't said that.

"His leave isn't up till Monday," said the Wing Commander. He glanced at her, and a slow smile spread over his face. "Okay," he said. "If he's going to be here he can help entertain them."

Everybody dined together in the mess that night, brightly cheerful, and afterwards they played snooker and darts and shove-halfpenny and poker and bridge. They made a great deal of noise and everybody very nearly had a marvellous time, and only two or three young men went creeping quietly to their rooms because they couldn't bear it any longer.

Marshall arrived back in time for tea next day, to find the Wing Commander taking tea in the ante-room; at times like that Mrs. Dobbie saw little of her husband. Dobbie noticed him with satisfaction; he wanted all the old stagers on the station for the next few days to steady the young men. He said: "You're back early."

"The trains aren't very good on Sunday," said the pilot lamely. He had not expected to meet Dobbie before Monday. "Besides, I wanted to be here for the E.N.S.A. concert."

There was a brazen quality about that statement that won Dobbie's respect; a man who could say that he had come back early from his leave to listen to an E.N.S.A. concert was a man to be reckoned with. "Look," he said quietly, "do what you can to make the party go to-night. I dare say you've heard about our luck."

Marshall nodded. "I heard. You're having the W.A.A.F.s in for dinner again?"

The Wing Commander nodded. "I asked your pal Ellison and Jack Barton. I'll have Barton at the end table with me. You take Ellison down among the boys and get one or two of the W.A.A.F.s to help you whoop it up a bit."

"Okay," said Marshall.

"We'll see if we can get Jack Barton to stage a rabbit hunt, or something, one afternoon next week," said Dobbie. He went off to meet the E.N.S.A. party, who were fixing up their stage in the canteen, and to prime them with local jokes.

Marshall met Gervase in the lounge before dinner. He re-introduced her to Mr. Ellison, and they collected Section

179

Officer Ford, and Pat Johnson, and a dry little man in civilian clothes who was something to do with the E.N.S.A. party and whom they discovered later in the evening, to their cost, to be the chief comedian. They dined at the far end of the room from Winco and managed to drag into their party most of the table, driving back the shadows for a while. Three pilot officers, newly arrived that afternoon from operational training, quietly enquired about the two flight lieutenants, and were impressed to hear that one of them had fifty-four operations to his credit and the other fifty-five. Their first impression was that Hartley was a place where pilots lived long and had fun.

They moved on to the concert, Gervase sitting close by Marshall, with Ellison on her other side. There was a trick cyclist, and a lady with a piano-accordian, and a burlesque or two. And then their dinner guest came on and in long, rambling monologue told them about a flight lieutenant at a station he was visiting last week who went out fishing—"very fond of fishing, he was, and all his crew"—and caught an awful, ugly fish—"fair give you the cold shivers to look at that fish"—and brought it back upon his handle-bars. He spun it out for a good ten minutes and had the hall in fits of laughter all the time, which seemed to Marshall to be in poor taste. But after that a middle-aged young woman came on and sang about a nightingale in Berkeley Square, a song that both Gervase and Marshall admired very much. They contrived to rub knees while she was singing it without anybody noticing.

As they were leaving the hall in the crowd after the show they managed to exchange a few words in the privacy of the unheeding crowd. "All right for to-morrow?" Marshall said.

She nodded. "What time?"

"Shall we meet out there?"

"No, let's ride out together. It doesn't matter." His heart warmed to her. "Half-past ten, outside Headquarters."

"Okay," he said. "I'll get Mollie to cut some sandwiches."

Marshall lay awake in bed for some time that night, reading *The Fisherman's Vade Mecum,* and thinking about Gervase. He had achieved a good deal of purely theoretical knowledge of wet fly fishing by intensive study during the week, though not so much as might have been the case if his mind had not been occupied with his young woman.

It was sunny and bright next morning; they met outside Headquarters with their bicycles and rode out of the camp together. They reached Kingslake an hour later, rode up to the front door and rang the bell. Gervase said: "Is Mrs. Carter-Hayes at home. We've come about the fishing."

The maid said: "Mrs. Carter-Hayes is in her room, madam. But that will be quite all right." She took them through the hall and opened the gun-room and left them to it.

Gervase and Marshall spent the next half-hour poking about among the fishing tackle. They found one cast already made up with three flies, and made up another with March Brown, Peter Ross, and Butcher. They found lines and wound them on the reels; presently they left the house and went down to the lake carrying rods, tackle, and a landing-net.

They fished for an hour; occasionally their flies were in the water, more often in a tree or bush. Even the unsophisticated trout in the little private lake shrank back from the resounding splash that their lines made in falling on the water; by lunch-time they were looking at each other ruefully. "Let's have a sandwich and look at the book," said Marshall.

"It's difficult," said Gervase. "It was like this when I used to try before."

The pilot said: "It must be good fun when you can do it, though."

They began to eat their sandwiches, sitting very close together by the lake and reading the same part of the book. "Well, that's just what I've been doing," said Gervase. Sitting as she was, sandwich in her left hand, she picked up the rod with her right, with a rod length of line hanging down. "It says you come back smartly, pause to let the line straighten out behind, and then cast forward."

She suited the action to her words idly, sitting as she was. The line, carried by a puff of wind from behind, went forward and fell lightly on the water; they watched it ruefully. "Why can't it do that when I'm trying properly?" she said.

There was a sudden boil at the tail fly, a pluck, and a little scream from the reel. She dropped her sandwich and grasped the butt of the rod with both hands; the little rod was bent like a bow and the taut line was still running from the reel. She said: "Oh, Peter!"

He scrambled to his feet urgently. "You've got a fish," he said. "Keep the butt upright—that's what it says in the book."

She laughed, excited and triumphant. "You and your book! I know what to do now—I've seen my uncle doing it."

She let the fish run, reeled him in a little, and let him run again. The rod that she was using was very light; it took her ten minutes to wear him out. Finally she drew him to the bank exhausted; he made one more run when he saw the net, then Marshall slipped the net under him and they got him on shore. He was a nice big trout, about a pound and a quarter.

They killed him with a smart blow, and knelt down together to examine what they had got. The full lines of the fish, the red spots, and the golden belly pleased them tremendously; it was the first fish Gervase had ever caught, and she was very excited about it. They left their sandwiches and began fishing in earnest.

In the course of the afternoon Gervase caught another and Marshall caught three; they discovered the benefit of wind in carrying the line out gently. Even so, they would not have done so well but for the fact that the little lake had not been fished for two years; the trout were unsophisticated and took any-thing that came their way. Instead of catching five they might well have gone home with fifteen, but that their interest in the trout was short-lived in comparison with their interest in each other. They sat together for a long time on the grass at the head of the lake, talking, and eating their sandwiches, and holding hands, and admiring their little row of fish laid out neatly in the shade.

In the evening, their sandwiches long finished, hunger drove them back to camp. "We'll bring out some more food next time," said Gervase. They walked up to the house and put their rods and tackle carefully away in the gun-room. They left a message of thanks with the old maid, put their fish into their bicycle-baskets, and rode back to camp.

Exultation over their catch quite swamped their ordinary discretion. They rode in past the guard together, and went together into the mess, carrying a bicycle-basket full of fish. They went to Mollie in the kitchen and got a dish and laid the fish out on it. The W.A.A.F. kitchen-maids came crowding around Gervase. "My, ma'am, aren't they lovely! Did Mr. Marshall catch them?"

"Miss Robertson caught two," said Marshall.

"*You* caught them, ma'am?" said Mollie. "Fancy that!"

They had a little discussion over when they should have them and how they should be cooked, then, bursting with pride, they carried them into the dining-room and put them on the table to admire. For the first time, in the kitchen, they heard that there was to be a dance that night.

They found Pat Johnson and Lines in the lounge. Marshall said: "Come and see our fish."

"Not another like the last one, laddie?"

Lines said: "What do you mean, *our* fish?"

"I caught two," said Gervase. "He got three."

The two flight lieutenants followed them into the dining-room, and two or three young pilot officers followed. "They're quite nice-looking fish," said Mr. Johnson in surprise. "You're coming on, laddie." He turned and bowed to Gervase. "And lassie."

One of the pilot officers said: "Where did you get them, sir?"

Marshall grinned. "I'm not letting that one out."

"Last time he went fishing he brought back something that he caught in the main sewer," said Mr. Johnson. He turned to Gervase. "I suppose he didn't like to take you fishing there."

The girl wrinkled up her nose. "I think you're a pig. If you mean that pike, it was a very nice fish."

"Nice fish my foot," said Mr. Johnson. "It made a lot of trouble, that pike did. I'm not sure that we've heard the last of it, either."

A young man behind them, seeing trout for the first time in his life, asked: "What are they?" They became thronged with interested young men; Dobbie, entering the vestibule, saw them pressing into the dining-room, and went in behind to see what was going on. He saw three of his best pilots and one of the W.A.A.F. officers laughing and talking over a plate of fish, surrounded by a crowd of unsure, pimply young men. He pressed forward through the crowd, thankful for the new diversion. "Who got these?" he asked.

Lines said: "Those two got them, sir. They won't say where."

Dobbie laughed and said to Marshall: "Be a sport."

"I'm not a sport," said Marshall, "and I'm not telling anybody. I'm keeping this fishing for my crew." He grinned. "Of course if you like to come with us next Op, sir, you might qualify."

Dobbie said: "Well, damn it, I will." He scrutinised the fish. "Have you weighed them?"

"Five and a half pounds," said Marshall. "Miss Robertson got two of them."

"What did you get them on?"

"Butcher and Peter Ross."

They talked fishing for a while with the young men round them; then Dobbie went off to the billiard-table to play snooker with whomever he could find. He was pleased, although he knew that he would get no fishing in the way he had suggested. On the next operation he would fly to Germany with some diffident, enthusiastic, and unsafe young man, who would be impressed and honoured at having the Wing Commander in the aircraft with him, and who would be steadied by the experience. He saw no point in flying with a good pilot.

Later that evening he stood with Chesterton in the canteen watching the dance. The atmosphere was noticeably lighter than it had been a few days before; the crews were more spontaneous, there was more healthy noise, more laughter. Chesterton said presently: "See Marshall?"

Dobbie nodded. "They were out all day together, fishing."

The Squadron Leader said: "And now they're dancing all night." He laughed. "More trouble. You'll have to find another signals officer."

The Wing Commander said: "I don't mind about that. He can get every section officer in camp in trouble for all I care. The camp's a different place with that chap in it."

CHAPTER EIGHT

Dear! of all happy in the hour, most blest
    He who has found our hid security,
Assured in the dark tides of the world that rest,
    And heard our word, 'Who is so safe as we?'
We have found safety with all things undying,
    The winds, and morning, tears of men and mirth,
The deep night, and birds singing, and clouds flying,
    And sleep, and freedom, and the autumnal earth.
We have built a house that is not for Time's throwing.
    We have gained a peace unshaken by pain for ever.
War knows no power. Safe shall be my going,
    Secretly armed against all death's endeavour;
Safe though all safety's lost; safe where men fall;
And if these poor limbs die, safest of all.

RUPERT BROOKE, 1915

Gunnar Franck did not get many letters, and the ones he got were seldom from old ladies. He had great difficulty in deciphering the words of the letter that he found waiting for him when he returned from leave, and more difficulty still with the meaning. It read:

Kingslake Hall,
Oxon.

Mrs. Carter-Hayes presents her compliments to Sergeant Pilot Franck and would be pleased if he would care to use her lake for fishing. Miss Robertson can make the arrangements.

He turned it over and over, his big red face wrinkled in perplexity. He understood that it was about fishing, and that was all he did understand. He took it to Sergeant Phillips to interpret, only to find that the rear-gunner had received one just like it.

"I dunno," said Phillips. He scratched his head. "The only Miss Robertson I know of is that Section Officer of the Cap's. Do you know any other?"

Gunnar said: "One of the girls in the airmen's mess is Robertson."

"You mean the fat one with a face like a cow? She's Mrs.

Roberts." He paused. "I dunno any other Robertson but that Section Officer."

Gunnar folded up the letter and put it in his wallet. "I will ask her. She is a nice young lady, and she will say if I am wrong."

"It must be her." There was a pause, and then the rear-gunner said slowly: "Come to think, we was talking about fishing just before I went on leave. I wonder if the Cap's had one like this?"

"Do you think that the Section Officer is now friends with the Cap?"

"I dunno—looks rather like it. If so, we'll all be a bloody sight safer."

They laughed together, and later in the day Gunnar Franck went into the signals office diffidently. "Please," he said, "I have here a letter that I do not understand. I think perhaps it is to do with you?"

Gervase took the note and glanced at it. "That's right, Gunnar," she said. She explained to him the arrangement she had made about the fishing. "Flight Lieutenant Marshall knows where all the things are kept—he can show you. We went out there yesterday and got five lovely ones."

He took back the letter. "It is ver' kind of this old lady," he said. He hesitated. "You are friends now with the Cap?" he enquired, grinning.

She laughed. "Yes, we're friends again for the time being."

The Dane said: "He is ver' good man. Over a year I have been flying with him, and I know."

There was a little pause. "Thank you, Gunnar," Gervase said at last. "I know that, but it's nice to be told."

He had to wait for his introduction to fly-fishing, because next day they flew to Whitsand to collect R for Robert, now repaired and in flying condition with a new wing and a new port engine and propeller. They flew up as passengers in S for Sammy, piloted by Flight Lieutenant Johnson, taking off with the first light of dawn and arriving in time for breakfast in the mess. They did a flight test of Robert in the forenoon and found it satisfactory, and flew back in company with Sammy after lunch.

Before taking off they received a final word of advice. "Don't go and stick the wrong course on the compass this time, laddie," said Mr. Johnson. "There's no future in that." But he laughs longest who laughs last; Mr. Johnson, exercising his rear-gunner at the navigator's table, made a deviation on the way home due to the reciprocal of wind, and landed back at Hartley twenty minutes after Robert.

At the dispersal point the ground crew received Robert critically, unwilling to believe that a good job could have been carried out upon a Wellington at any Lancaster station. The air crew gathered with the ground crew to examine the repair; the machine was flying left wing down, the port engine was running rich, and the rear turret and the D/F set were still unserviceable. "We'll have a crack at her to-morrow morning," said the pilot. "If we can clear off the port engine and the ailerons with a flight test, we can go fishing in the afternoon while the armourers get busy with the turret."

He turned to his crew. "We've got some trout fishing offered to us," he said. "Rods and all thrown in."

Sergeant Phillips said: "We all got letters about it, Cap. Where is it, anyway?"

"Out by Chipping Hinton. I'll show you, if you're interested."

The rear-gunner rubbed his chin. "I never fished with fly. I'd not know how."

Sergeant Cobbett said unexpectedly: "I have. I'll put you in the way of it."

They turned to him in surprise. "Where did you pick that up, Flight?"

He said: "My mother's people got a farm in Wales. I got a rod and all back home."

Sergeant Phillips said, still doubtful: "Maybe I'll bring some gentles, anyway."

"Okay," said Marshall. He was no purist, and they weren't his fish.

He took them out next afternoon; Gervase was on duty and could not come. He caught one fish and saw Gunnar Franck catch another, but his mind was not upon the job, and presently he left them to ride back to Hartley for tea in the mess, where he would find Gervase.

In the evening light he took her for a walk around the country lanes; with no more than a fortnight of their month left to go, they deemed a day wasted if they did not meet. As they went they talked about the work. "We're all ready to go again now," said Marshall. "They passed the turret out this afternoon. That was the last thing."

Gervase said: "I believe the station has been give a week's

rest—if so, that's up to-morrow night. Charwick and Wittinton were out on Saturday, and again last night." She glanced up at him. "How are you feeling now, Peter?"

He glanced down at her. "I feel fine," he said. "I'd rather like to do another one."

They turned aside presently behind a spinney and exchanged a token of mutual goodwill; presently they came out again a little dishevelled and sat upon a stile and smoked a cigarette together before turning back to camp. They were sitting on the stile when the crew found them, Gunnar and Phillips and Cobbett all riding back to camp upon their bicycles from Kingslake House.

Marshall slipped down from the stile and stopped them; the sergeants got off and Gervase came up to them. "Do any good?" asked Marshall.

Sergeant Cobbett said: "We got seven beauties—the one Gunnar caught while you was there and then six others. They come on fine just after you left, sir."

They gathered round, examining the fish and talking about flies. Phillips had caught one on a gentle and had then been shamed by Gunnar Franck to the use of fly, and had caught another on a Butcher. Cobbett, who was unexpectedly expert, had caught four; Gunnar had caught one.

"Pity old Leech wasn't with us," said the gunner. "He wouldn't half have had some fun."

"He'll be back before long," said Marshall. "He's leaving hospital and going off on leave to-morrow."

"It won't seem right," said Phillips, "going with a stranger in the crew."

That day was Wednesday. They did their next operation upon Friday night to Cassel, loaded with incendiaries. It went without incident in R for Robert; the long hours of watchful peering through the darkness from the pilot's seat passed pleasantly enough for Marshall because he had arranged to take Gervase to the pictures the following afternoon to see a film with Dorothy Lamour in it, and he liked Dorothy Lamour, and he liked Gervase better, and altogether it was something to look forward to while swinging his head mechanically from side to side, looking for trouble, from the port engine, over the twin pencils of the forward guns, to the starboard. They landed back a little before dawn, and he slept quietly and happily and well till lunch time.

Gervase did not do so well. She spent the night in the

control office, a night of secret worry and anxiety until the "Mission completed" signal came from Robert. For the next two and a half hours she went through her duties mechanically, still anxious, till the machines began to arrive back, and there was the little light that was in Robert winking in the sky over to the south-west, signalling for permission to land. She went out to the balcony and watched the aircraft land and taxi to dispersal, then she went back to her work sick with relief. She did not see any of them that night. A couple of hours later she went to bed, but she had been too strained and anxious for the last few hours to sleep very well. This operation made fifty-six. There were only four more to be done before he would be safe.

They went fishing on Sunday afternoon, and on Monday night the Wing went in full strength to Dortmund, losing two machines by collision over the target. Marshall by that time was at the top of his form; he felt that he had got the whole job buttoned up, that his crew were behind him better than ever before. He was sleeping well and eating well. Gervase was sleeping poorly and was too anxious to be happy. Fifty-seven. Only three more to go.

The evenings were growing long by that time; it was early May. By agreement they slept on into the afternoon the day after Dortmund, and met after a large meal of tea and fried eggs at five o'clock, to go fishing for the evening rise. They had packets of sandwiches with them; they did not propose to get back before dark.

They got to Kingslake at about six o'clock and fished for a couple of hours and caught three fish. Then they sat down by the water's edge to eat their sandwiches, waiting for the rise of fish that the book told them would come with the last half-hour of daylight.

Marshall glanced up at the house. "What's she like?" he asked, nodding at it.

Gervase said: "She's nice, Peter. Very outspoken, but quite nice all the same. I promised her I'd take you up and introduce you one day." She did not say in what circumstances.

The pilot said: "I'd like to do that. It's been bloody good of her to let us have this fishing. It's made a lot of difference to the boys."

"I was talking to Gunnar yesterday," said Gervase. "He told me he's been up to have tea with her twice."

"Gunnar has? How did he work that?"

189

"The first time he went up to say 'Thank you' for them all when they were fishing here, and she gave him some tea. The second time she saw him from the window and sent her old maid down to ask him if he'd like to take tea with her." Gervase paused. "I dare say they'd hit it off together pretty well," she said thoughtfully. "They've probably got a good deal in common."

Marshall stared at her. "What have they got in common?"

She said: "They're both lonely, aren't they? I know she is."

The pilot considered for a minute. "I suppose you're right. I suppose he *is* lonely."

"He never goes out with a girl, does he?"

"He does just now and then," said Marshall. "Not often with the same one. I think he's got a girl of his own back in Denmark."

Gervase said: "Poor old Gunnar . . ."

"Poor old Gunnar my foot," said Marshall. "If she's in Denmark and he's here, he can't have a scene with her. If she was here he'd be in anguish all the time, not knowing if she was going to marry him or shoot him down again."

He met her eyes and they smiled together. "Are you in anguish all the time, Peter?" she asked.

He did not answer for a moment. He was looking at the soft line of her throat where it passed below her collar. "I'd like to know as soon as you can tell me," he said quietly. "I'm not in anguish, because you've given me a square deal, and that's all I wanted. If you decide that you'd be miserable if you married me, I shan't agree with you. I shall be frightfully sorry, and I'll want to go away, but I shan't cut my throat."

She stared out over the lake. "I wouldn't be miserable," she said slowly. "I think you'd be nice to me."

He took her hand and slid his own hand up her arm to the elbow. "You wouldn't like to decide now, would you?" he said huskily.

She looked at him gravely. "No, I wouldn't," she said quietly. "I don't want to be a beast, Peter, but I want my month. There's only ten more days to go." She sensed the disappointment in his touch. "If I had to give you an answer now, it would be yes, I think. But I don't want to give you an answer now."

"All right," he said gently.

She turned to him. "Being married is for all your life, and you must be quite sure. I didn't want to marry anyone till I was much older—and it hurries things so much to marry when you're in the W.A.A.F.s." He did not understand her, but he did not interrupt. "I wouldn't want to marry you unless we could be together like a proper married couple, Peter."

He smiled at her. "Ten days more?"

She nodded. "Only ten days, Peter."

They sat together in silence and warm contact as the shadows lengthened; fish began rising in the lake, but their rods lay unheeded on the bank. They did not fish again. They sat on for an hour, deeply in love. Presently they disentangled and got up and took the rods back to the gun-room. In the warm twilight they rode back to Hartley, almost silent, infinitely happy.

Two days later the aerodrome was closed as usual before an operation; at the briefing in the evening the target was disclosed as Hamburg. Marshall and Gunnar Franck had been to Hamburg several times before; they had the outline of the town and the dock area well in mind already. It was familiar to them as a town is familiar that one has passed by in a train on several occasions, but never stopped in; they knew the lay-out of the streets and squares and railway stations well enough, though they had never set foot in the place, nor ever would.

They had as wireless operator that night a Corporal Forbes, a dark lad from Chester; he was painstaking and thorough, and he was deferential to their experience. He was not interested in catching fish, and that weighed against him slightly, but he was only there as a temporary measure till Leech returned to them.

Robert was scheduled to take off at 10.34, by which time it would be very nearly dark. The crew met in the crew-room at about a quarter to ten, and began dressing for the night's work. Marshall was happy; for him everything seemed to be moving in the right direction. He had seen Gervase at lunch time in the mess and talked to her for a little; he had not seen her since. He had slept quietly and well for a great part of the afternoon, resting with an easy mind.

Gervase had also rested nominally. She had lain down on her bed with the blind drawn, but she had hardly slept at all. Her duty that night was in the control office on the aerodrome, supervising the signallers and keeping track of the machines as the reports came in, marking them up upon the blackboard for the duty control officer to see, searching the country by telephone for the missing. She would see R for Robert taking off, she would wait hours for the "Mission completed" signal made over the target, and she would wait again. All her work now seemed to be composed of waiting and anxiety and fear. Over her loomed the shadow of disaster, terrifying, monstrous, and incredible. She slept very little.

In Robert the crew were in good spirits as they started up the engines and settled into their places. The moon, a thin crescent, was dying in the west; the night promised to be clear and starry most of the way. They began upon their normal routine of testing the equipment of the aircraft and running up the engines. Once Marshall left his seat and thrust his way down the fuselage, clumsy in his flying-suit and harness and Mae West, to the new wireless operator. He grinned at the corporal. "All okeydoke?"

The boy smiled back at him. "Everything quite all right, sir."

"Got your card?" The pilot went through the routine with him shortly, and saw that he had spare valves and aerial properly stowed, and talked to him for a minute or two. In the end he said: "Okay. We'll be moving off pretty soon now," and went back to his seat and made ready for flight.

He waved the chocks away at 10.25 and moved his hand on the throttles; Robert stirred and moved forward, and turned on to the ring road, falling into line behind the other aircraft moving to the runway to take off. At the marshalling point they waited on the ring road, watching Sergeant Pilot Ferguson in A for Apple move away and go spinning down the track in the dim light, then they moved forward and turned into wind.

"Captain to wireless operator," said Marshall. "Flash our letter." He sat staring over in the direction of the control. In there, he thought, Gervase would be sitting at her little desk in the corner beside the door that led into the communications office. Perhaps she was standing at the window watching his flash. He smiled, and as he did so his own letter was flashed back at him in green.

He turned to the work in hand. "There's the green," he said. "Captain to crew—stand by now for take off. Okay, boys, here we go."

He pressed the throttles forward and then moved his right hand back to the wheel; by his side he knew that Gunnar Franck had put his own hand to the throttles as soon as

Marshall had left them, in case they should vibrate back during the take off. He smiled again as he watched the runway streaming up to him; good old Gunnar, he thought, careful as ever. He held the heavily loaded machine down longer than was necessary, slowly raising the tail, letting her gain speed upon the ground; with three hundred yards or so to go he lifted her off. By his side he knew that Gunnar was in readiness. "Undercart up," he said, and as he spoke the lever moved and the vibration of the hydraulic motors made a new note in the rhythm. He sat with his eyes glued to the dim scene ahead; it was still light enough to see the trees. At a hundred feet he said: "Flaps up." By his side Gunnar folded up the second pilot's seat, moved back to the navigator's table. Marshall put the Wimpey into a slow turn to port; presently he straightened out upon the first leg of his course, climbing slowly.

He levelled out at ten thousand feet, and put the control over to automatic. They had been flying for forty minutes, and were approaching the Suffolk coast; Marshall left his seat and moved back into the fuselage. He stood with Gunnar at the navigator's table for a while, studying the course, while Sergeant Cobbett stood up at the windscreen, keeping watch for him; in the cockpit the wheel and pedals stirred from time to time, moved by an invisible influence to keep the aircraft on its chosen path. The course that they were steering was to take them most of the way over the North Sea, clear of the fighter cover over Germany; presently they would turn in and come down on Hamburg from the north.

Gunnar said: "It is ver' clear night. I think we will get good astro fixes over the sea."

"Want to try one now?"

The navigator said "Presently. It will be less bumpy over sea."

The pilot said: "Okay. Give me a shout when you're ready and I'll try and hold her still."

He moved on aft to Forbes. "Everything okay?"

"Lot of German R/T," said the boy. "I reckon they've got fighters up."

"Is it strong?"

"About Force 5." The pilot plugged in to the set to listen. In the dim tunnel of the fuselage they crouched together; a spot of light from the hooded lamp illumined the pilot's hand as he slowly turned the dial. He paused for a time listening to one German voice repeating monotonously words that he could not understand over and over again. His hand moved and he paused again upon another station. Then he plugged back to the intercom. "There's nothing much in that," he said. "I think it's pretty normal. They've probably got fighters up, but then they always have."

He moved back to the cockpit and seated himself at the controls again. He plugged in to the intercom. "Captain to rear and front gunners. We're just crossing the coast now. Test guns as soon as you can see the sea."

Presently the twin guns ahead of him stuttered, and he saw the bright tracer flying out ahead; behind him, through the structure, he felt the vibration of the rear guns firing. Over the intercom he heard Cobbett say: "Front gunner, sir. Front guns functioning correctly." He replied: "Okay, front gunner. Stay where you are." He heard: "Rear-gunner reporting guns okay, Cap." The pilot said: "Okay, rear-gunner."

He sat quiet at the controls as they moved out over the dark sea, flying in automatic, watching the instruments from time to time to check their course, watchfully peering from side to side. Gunnar Franck came up beside him and let down the second pilot's seat and sat by him watching to starboard; they flew on in silence into the starry night.

They were not alone in the air; there were other aircraft all around them. Flying at their set height and with all aircraft winging out to the same target, the danger of collision was small. At that time the Wellington was growing obsolete for operations, being superseded by the larger and more powerful Lancasters and Halifaxes; for this reason they had started ahead of the faster bombers, though they were scheduled to arrive at Hamburg when the defences were already heavily engaged. The big machines were overtaking them; from time to time Phillips would report: "Rear-gunner here, Cap. Aircraft coming up on us, same course, port quarter, above." Pause. "It's a Lanc, Cap." "Okay, rear-gunner." Presently the big machine would draw in sight above them and become foreshortened as it vanished into the black sky ahead.

Marshall sat at the controls at peace. He loved the sense of these great starry, quiet nights, when flying was easy and the world serene. On cloudy nights, or on nights of bright moonlight, or on nights when there was icing of the wings—on ninety-five per cent of the nights, that is to say—he suffered from anxiety or fear; he could not tell the difference. You were unhappy on those nights; you reached the target drawn and with a sense of strain. Usually he was able to relax on the way home however bad the weather might be, when the end meant cocoa and buns and bed with a hot-water bottle. It was the outward journey that he usually found most difficult.

On these serene nights, winging steadily under the bright stars, it did not seem that anything could ever happen that would bring you ill. Sitting there at the controls or in the gunner's cupola a man was forced to contemplation, to the study of beauty for a quiet hour. The knights of the Arthurian legend before battle spent a night of vigil at the altar; it was hardly different in the Wellington on nights like these. You reached the target in a calm serenity, ready for anything that might befall.

At half-past eleven Gunnar left the cockpit and went back to the navigator's table; he appeared a minute later, sextant in hand, and nodded to Marshall. The pilot took the controls from automatic, fixed his gaze upon the stars ahead, and concentrated upon keeping the machine steady. Standing in the astrodrome the Dane brought Procyon to the bubble, averaged quickly, and noted time and altitude. He swung round and worked upon Arcturus; then he dropped down to the table and began computing the position. In the cockpit Marshall put the automatic in again, and they went on in the still, starry night.

At half-past twelve they saw flak rising up ahead of them, thrown from a coast they could not see. Marshall called Cobbett back from the front cockpit to check the petrol in the tanks, and sent him back again to man the front guns. They crossed the coast, weaving a little to defeat the flak, and then altered course towards the south. Already they had seen a glow of fires at the horizon, fifty miles away; the fires were in two groups, one spreading and extensive, and one, over to the west of the other, mere pin-points of light. As they flew on, the little set of fires grew in magnitude, dwarfing the one that had seemed larger at the first. The Germans had not got away with their decoy.

Now they could see the searchlights, hundreds of them, grouped in six or seven cones around the burning city, with flak bursting in great clusters of bright stars at the apex of each cone. Marshall sat studying the searchlights and the flak as they drew near; by his side the Dane was standing, peering forward at the target through the windscreen. "Putting up a lot of barrage to-night," said the pilot. "See it all coming up in bursts ? You'd think they'd run out of ammo, going on like that."

The Dane studied the situation. "I think it is at two heights, Cap, the barrage. See—that I think is higher than us; perhaps it is twelve thousand. And that one to the left is lower, and the searchlights are lower also. I think the fuses are set for the barrage at about twelve thousand feet and at about seven thousand. It may not be easy that they change them quick."

"Go in about nine thousand ?"

The navigator nodded.

"I think so, too." The pilot raised his voice. "Captain to crew. We're going in at about nine thousand, chaps. I'm going to stooge around a little longer and work round it to the south. Looks as if there's a bit of a gap down there. I shall be turning in about five minutes from now; if we can spot the target we'll only do the one run. Got that, rear-gunner ?"

"Rear-gunner here. Okay, Cap."

"Rear and front gunners, keep on your toes for fighters. There must be a lot of them up to-night."

"All I seen is Lancs and Halifaxes so far."

"You won't see fighters over the target. Watch out as we're going away."

They were still ten miles from the city, but the glow of fires lit up the machine; accustomed as their eyes were to the darkness, the faint yellow light seemed bright to them. They were in the region of the outer defences; a few searchlights waved about their path questing for them or other aircraft near them; a little burst of flak showed up near some machine ahead. Marshall put the nose down, throttling a trifle, and increased his speed; he began weaving rhythmically from side to side of his mean path.

Beside him and below, Gunnar Franck was kneeling at the bomb-sight setting the height and speed and course and wind upon the bars. They went on for a little longer, till the pilot said:

"Turning in now, chaps. Bomb-aimer, height nine thousand two hundred. Bomb doors open."

"Height nine thousand two hundred. Halifax just below us and to starboard."

"Okay. I see him. Can you see the target yet ?"

"Not yet. I have seen the river. Five degrees to port, Cap, but keep weaving."

"Okay."

This was the tense moment of the flight. Beneath them the shocking furnace stood revealed. Great columns of black smoke were eddying up to their height, shrouding the leaping fires; between the smoke and fires they could see the streets. Suddenly they became caught and held in a white, blinding light; other beams swept and focused on them; they were held fast in the cone.

Marshall said: "How much longer, bomb-aimer ?"

"Two minutes, Cap."

"Okay."

There was nothing to be done about the searchlights but to keep slipping and weaving, and to hope that down below the gunners would have trouble with the fuses. Over the inter-com Sergeant Cobbett said: "Front gunner, Cap. What's happened to all the flak ?"

His eyes fixed on the gyro to maintain his mean course while he weaved, Marshall had had no time to study what was hap-pening outside. He raised his eyes and glanced round quickly, and saw nothing bursting in the sky. "Christ!" he said. "Front and rear gunners, keep a damn good look-out now. They've probably got fighters up."

The intercom said: "Wireless operator to Captain. A lot of German going on the R/T, Cap. Strong, too—about Force 9."

"Okay, wireless operator. Keep your eyes skinned, gun-ners. Bomb-aimer, how do we go ?"

"Okay, Cap—I can see the target. Stop weaving now. Now left a little, left. Steady."

The white, brilliant lighting was intolerable; they were held pinned upon the blackboard of the night, and yet no flak came to them. With a dry mouth Marshall said:

"How long to go ?"

"Thirty seconds. Right a little. Steady."

They sat tense, strained, hardly breathing. Exposed as they were, it seemed impossible that they could escape the enemy.

It was impossible. Over the intercom a shout came: "Rear-gunner, Cap! Fighters coming down on us, one each side. I'll take the starboard. Try and get the port one, Cob!"

The pilot heaved upon the wheel and put his whole weight on the pedal, throwing the big machine around to port to bring the forward guns to bear. He felt a jolt in the structure and heard Gunnar Franck say: "Bombs away." He dropped his hand to close the bomb doors and gain speed, and as he did so he felt through the fuselage the stammer of the four rear guns. A stream of tracer, pure bright yellow in the white light of the outer world, shot over him from behind and dropped towards the cockpit. There was a hammer blow upon the armour plate behind his head and two more at his back; ahead of him the windscreen starred and the double revolution counter sprang from the instrument board and disintegrated.

The twin front guns began stuttering ahead of him, firing out to port against an assailant that he could not see. A stream of tracer came from the port side, but that was now above the pilot's head because he had the aircraft on one wing-tip in a tight turn to port. It ceased suddenly, and Marshall flung his weight back on the wheel to right the aircraft and come back on a straight course. It was imperative, he felt, to fly straight, at whatever risk, to get away from the target, to escape this blinding light that showed up every movement that they made. To keep on turning in the searchlight cone meant certain death.

Over the intercom there was a sobbing, and then: "Rear-gunner, Cap. The sod's got me in the legs." By his side Gunnar was struggling to regain his feet; as the acceleration eased he stood up. Marshall said: "Bomb-aimer, get back to the rear-gunner and take his place."

"Rear-gunner, Cap. The sods are coming down on us again. I'll take the starboard one again, but the mucking turret's leaking."

He flung the machine round in another violent turn to port. Behind he felt the clamour of the guns again, and then: "I got him, Cap!" He raised his head with difficulty in the violence of his turn and looked up and to port, and a great mass swept into his view at the wing-tip. It hit their wing and the wheel was snatched from his hands and spun round madly, and the Wellington flicked to a steeper bank, throwing him down to port. A bullet shattered the perspex above his head.

In that instant the pilot saw a dreadful sight. A great part of his port wing was wrecked and locked with it was what had been a single-engined fighter, Me.109. It was on fire on his wing-tip; fire was spurting up from the torn engine cowl and glowing in the cockpit. The pilot, a young man with a fat, white face, had both hands up above his head, struggling to undo the sliding cockpit cover, which seemed to have jammed. His starboard wing was tight locked with their own port wing, and they were falling locked together in a violent side-slip, turning to a dive. Already fire was streaming up the ruins of the wing from the wrecked fighter.

Marshall said: "Okay, chaps, we'll shake this mugger off," and flung himself on the controls. He was now lying on his side upon the arm-rest of his seat; the wind noise at the cockpit rose to a shrill scream. He heaved the wheel to him with all his strength and thrust it from him violently in fierce, rhythmic time, and he said: "Bomb-aimer. Come and help me shake this mugger free."

Over the intercom he heard: "Christ, Cap—you'll have the bloody tail off!" and he said fiercely: "If we don't shift this mugger we won't need a bloody tail."

He could not do it. He stopped heaving on the stick and trod hard on bottom rudder, and pressed forward on the stick, and thrust both throttles forward through to the full boost. The Me. had hit them from behind; if they dived hard enough he might come free. The scream of air rose to a shriller note, the brilliance of the light grew less intense, more rose-coloured from the flames of the burning town below. He dared dive no longer; he must try and pull out now or dive into the ground. He pulled the wheel to him with all his strength against top rudder and top aileron.

There was a great, rending crack from the port wing. He flashed a glance back and along it; the Me. was no longer there, but his wing ended now in jagged wreckage ten or twelve feet out from the port engine. He eased the pressure on the stick and worked with his wrists to bring the port wing up; the aileron control was inoperative and locked. He jerked it violently; it moved, grated, and came free, and the machine came level. He found himself in a straight dive at about forty-five degrees and very low.

He eased the stick back gently and glanced at the altimeter. They were at fifteen hundred feet, still diving hard. Ahead of him a stream of yellow tracer shot up at them from the ground. At anything below six thousand feet they were a sitting target for the ground defences; he could not hope to climb to a safe height over the guns of Hamburg. But there was light to help them, searchlights blazing out in half a dozen cones above their heads. He cried: "Captain to crew. We're all right now, chaps. I'm going down to zero altitude, and we'll hedge-hop out of this."

He shot a glance at the gyro; it showed 140; they were heading south-east into Germany. He said: "Navigator, course is one four oh. Give me the height of ground."

"Just a minute, Cap."

There was a factory ahead of him, a tall building in square blocks; from the roof guns were firing at him, missing behind. He swept low over it, and there were railway lines and a canal and little houses; then he was down to roof-top height, his Wimpey travelling as she had never gone before. He said: "Front gunner, get aft and see what's happened to Phillips. Relieve him if he's wounded and man the rear turret yourself. Wireless operator, get aft and help get Phillips out of the turret."

Over the intercom he heard: "I got both legs broken, Cap, I think. The sod's put a cannon-shell in here with me." The voice was trembling and hysterical.

"Get you fixed up in a minute now," the pilot said. There was a church ahead, sticking up above the roofs and streets; he lifted the machine up over it and down again. Trees now, they were getting out to the country, and the white light reflected from the sky was growing faint. He shot across a water-works and got an ineffective burst of tracer from it; he was too close and too fast for the guns to follow him. Over a river bend and a railway; then there were fields ahead, dotted with tall trees.

"Wireless operator here, sir. I won't be half a minute, just while I do my hand." The voice was trembling and shaken. "I think the receiver is U/S—it's got some bullets through it. Shall I try if I can send 'Mission completed'?"

"No—don't send anything. We're getting too far off the target—they'll D.F. us." Another fighter directed on to them by radio from the ground would find them easy meat. "What is the matter with your hand?"

"I got something right through the middle of it." There was a high, hysterical laugh. "It don't half look a mess. But I can fix it."

"Sergeant Cobbett's coming aft. Get him to help you, and then see if you can help Phillips." He could still see the trees. He swept across the fields no more than thirty feet up, pulling up as he came to obstacles and putting down again. The machine was flying heavily port wing low; it needed all the power of his wrists to hold her level. But the engines were apparently untouched and pulling loyally; they could still fly fast and climb. It did not occur to him just then that there might be some difficulty in flying low.

"Navigator to Captain. The height of the ground level is two hundred feet, just below. That is the highest round about."

In the strain and pressure of events, with eyes glued to dim grey fields and woods racing upon him, he could not calculate. "What height should the Kollsman show to clear trees a hundred feet up, Gunnar?" It would soon be too dim to see anything, but he must, must keep low.

"One hundred and forty feet, Cap."

"Okay." He snatched a glance at it; that seemed about right. "Have a look at the tanks, Gunnar, and start pumping. I want all fuel in the starboard wing. Tell me how much we've got left."

A little hill with a church on it leaped out at him, right in his path. With aching wrists he lifted the machine over it, and down again into darkness among dim forms of trees. It was crazy going on like this with practically no light at nearly two hundred and fifty miles an hour, but it would be crazier to go higher till they could climb up to a decent altitude. He had told Gervase once that the boys didn't care for flying through the woods at night; this time they would take it and like it. He must find the sea; over the sea he could climb up to quiet and starlit flight in safety. Course about 330, he thought, should take him to the coast. He began edging round to north as opportunity offered.

"Sergeant Cobbett here, sir, at the wireless. You want to take it easy, Cap. There's a lot of damage back here."

"What?"

"You know about the port wing, sir? It sort of comes to an end about half-way out, just where the aileron should be."

"You're telling me!"

"We've had several hits in the rear fuselage—quite big holes, Cap—holes you could climb out through. I wouldn't chuck her about too much—some of it looks pretty weak to me."

"Okay." The structure would have to take its chance, but he would bear it in his mind—one factor in the many dangers that he had to weigh. "Is Forbes bad?"

"Not bad, Cap. He put a dressing on his hand himself, and it seems to have stopped bleeding. He's got the set in pieces now, but it's U/S."

"Get on aft and see what you can do for Phillips, Cobbett. I'll send Gunnar Franck to help immediately I can spare him. Get the turret manned soon as you can."

He swept low over the roof-tops of a village, and on, working round to north, tense, concentrating upon keeping low and missing things. He passed through north, and he saw far ahead of him, faint in the distance, three silvery pyramids of light that were searchlight clusters. His heart lightened when he saw them, believing that they stood upon the coast; moreover, they showed obstacles in his path in silhouette if he went straight for them. Once past those he would be over sea, and this nightmare, suicidal dash through trees would be behind, and he could climb.

"Sergeant Franck here, Cap. Port outer tank is empty and I am pumping from port inner to the starboard. Starboard tanks, I think, are not leaking. We now have two hundred and eighty gallons, or a little more, I think."

"Fine." That was plenty to get them home. "Fill the starboard outer right up full, and try and trim her for me."

"Is she ver' difficult to hold?"

"Bloody awful. Makes your wrists ache."

"I will come and fly for you as soon as I have pumped the fuel."

"I'm all right for a bit, Gunnar. When you've done the fuel have a look and see if you can find out where we are, and let me have a course. Then get aft and see what you can do to fix up Phillips. You'll do that better than I could."

Ahead of him the searchlight pencils stood and swung in cones with little points of flak-bursts upon high. He would crash through them at a hundred feet and take his chance of the machine-guns and the forty-millimetre stuff, jinking and weaving, hoping for the best. Beyond that lay the sea and the calm quiet of the starry night, a great peace into which one could climb up and be safe, and relax a little on the way home. And Gervase would be there.

*   *   *

In the control-room Gervase sat at her telephone; behind her the W.A.A.F. corporal wrote upon the blackboard at her instigation a large M for Mission Completed. She said: "D for Donald."

The corporal wrote M in the precise manner of a schoolmistress, which, in fact, she was. "That only leaves London and Robert now," she said brightly.

Gervase nodded shortly. This was what training was for, she thought. This was what discipline was for, to enable you to pigeon-hole your feelings and carry on and do the job you had to do. Discipline, she thought sadly, meant the difference between a grown-up and a child. A child would cry.

Wing-Commander Dobbie came into the office, having been over to the mess for a few minutes. He stood in cap and overcoat looking at the board. "London and Robert still to report?" he said thoughtfully.

The control officer, a grounded squadron leader, said: "That's right, sir."

On the desk before Gervase the telephone buzzed quietly. She lifted the receiver, listened, and replaced. She turned to the W.A.A.F. corporal. "M for London," she said. The corporal wrote it up.

Dobbie stood scrutinising the board. It was one-fifteen; Robert had been airborne at 10.34. Immediately before, Apple had taken off at 10.31, but Apple had reported "Mission completed" at 12.53. Sammy, airborne directly after Robert, had made his signal at 12.59. Whichever way you looked at it, Robert was twenty minutes late.

He turned aside and went out through the light trap on to the balcony in front of the control office. Too bad about Robert, he thought; he would not get "Mission completed" from them now. He stood there staring out over the starlit aerodrome; in another hour he would have the runway glows put on for the first aircraft to come home.

He stood there for ten minutes in the great peace of the night. He knew all the crews up to a point, because that was his job. He tried not to get to know any of them more than that because of equity, and because it only made things more painful later on. It was bad enough to have watched throughout the war the passing of most of his old friends from Cranwell and the peace-time R.A.F.; there was no need to add to it by making friends with these young men who came and went so soon. But sometimes it was difficult to dodge. He was interested in people, a quality that made him a good officer. He had been interested in Marshall and his crew, in all of them, because they seemed to him to be men of character who had an influence in his command, and because of the queer story of the fishing. Now they were very likely gone. Too bad.

Behind him the control officer came out on to the balcony. "Nice night," said Dobbie quietly. "Anything from Robert yet?"

"Not yet, sir. When shall I put the lights on?"

"Two-fifteen." The Wing Commander paused. "Is that

Section Officer in there behaving all right?"

"Yes, sir." The Squadron Leader added: "She's engaged to Marshall or something, isn't she?"

"Or something," said Dobbie. "She's not officially engaged. Nobody on this station is officially engaged till they've stood me a glass of sherry, and I haven't had a sherry out of them. But I'm afraid it looks as if I shan't get one now."

"It doesn't look so good," said the control officer.

They turned and went back into the control-room. "Any tea going?" said Dobbie, brightly cheerful. "I could do something to a cup of tea." A cup of tea, he thought, would do her good; girls liked tea.

"I'll get a pot made in a minute, sir," said Gervase. She turned to the corporal; there would be no more work now for her at the blackboard. "Go through and make tea," she said quietly. "Three cups."

She sat on at her little desk, writing up the signal log from her rough notes. It helped, to have something to do. Already she had become accustomed to the thought that Robert was gone. Sitting in that same chair before that telephone, with that same blackboard at her back, she had known so many aircraft to be lost that she had herself lost the faculty for easy grief; that nerve had been so hammered in the last few months that now it hardly hurt at all. Peter was gone, had followed Drummond and Forbes and Bobbie Fraser and Sawyer and all the others she had known at Hartley Magna. It was so unobtrusive, the manner of their going. A lot of aircraft took off in the night and were airborne one by one; a lot of aircraft came in one by one and taxied to dispersal in the darkness. It was only when you came to count them carefully to make a record in a log that you discovered one or two of them had slipped away and travelled to some other place.

Instinctively she felt that she must make a move; she must get a transfer to another aerodrome. She could not carry on at Hartley after this. She was all right for that night; she felt that she could carry on till morning. But after that she knew she would become unserviceable, like an exhausted battery or a tyre worn down to the canvas, no more use in the job. She would go to Group and see the Wing Commandant and ask for a transfer, if possible to the north country, nearer to her home, where she could re-plan her life.

She could re-plan her life. In the north country near her home she could forget the irrational, merry adventure that had touched her in Oxfordshire, so remote from the realities of ordinary life. She would regain the life that she had promised herself: to work hard as a signals officer for the remainder of the war, and then when the peace came to get a job of some sort in the radio business for six or seven years, and then marry somebody or other. It was what she had wanted to do so recently as a couple of months ago; when the distress was over, surely she could get back, and want to live a life like that again. Surely?

The tea came, and biscuits, and the two officers made conversations with each other, bringing her into it from time to time. She played her part as well as she could, because that was what you had to do, because if you made a scene that only made things difficult for everybody. And presently the Squadron Leader told a near-clean story of a parachutist who had happened to come down in a nunnery, and that made her laugh a little, and she was grateful.

They put the lights on presently, and shortly after half-past two they heard the beat of engines overhead. The men went out on to the balcony with the Aldis lamp; presently a winking light against the starlit sky spelled G for George. They gave it a green flash and it departed in a wide left-hand circuit towards the east; presently they saw the navigation lights sink down towards the runway's end, and heard the rumble. The lights ran on upon the ground; over the wide expanse they heard the squeal of brakes. The Squadron Leader put his head in at the door and spoke to Gervase; she called the corporal and they started a fresh set of markings on the board.

Soon there were several aircraft making circuits of the aerodrome, winking their identification letters, waiting their signal to land. The Wing Commander and the control officer were busy with the Aldis lamp; in the control office Gervase and the W.A.A.F. corporal were busy logging them in. In the middle of all this they had a call from the W.A.A.F. signal sergeant in the radio-room next door.

"R/T from Robert, ma'am." Gervase shot through into the other office like a scalded cat. The W.A.A.F. sergeant, a plain, horse-faced woman, was writing busily at her table before the set, head-phones upon her ears; hearing her officer come through she put up one hand and switched on the loudspeaker, and resumed her writing.

Into the silence of the room there came the message, endless in repetition. "——have sustained some damage to structure, we have sustain some damage to structure. This is Robert calling Zebra, Robert calling Zebra, E.T.A. three five, E.T.A. three five, Robert calling Zebra, Robert calling Zebra. Emergency routine, please, emergency routine, Robert calling Zebra. We cannot receive R/T or W/T, cannot receive R/T or W/T, Robert calling Zebra."

Gervase swung round to the corporal. "Go and tell the Wing Commander Robert is transmitting R/T," she said.

Endlessly the message continued: "Emergency routine, please, emergency routine, please; Robert calling Zebra. Our navigation lights and identification lights are U/S, navigation and identity lights U/S, Robert calling Zebra. We are approaching at four thousand, approaching at four thousand, E.T.A. three five, E.T.A. three five, Robert calling Zebra."

The door of the light trap slapped shut, and Wing Commander Dobbie came through. "Robert?"

Gervase took the pad from the sergeant and gave it to him; he ran his eye over it quickly. Over the speaker came the monotonous voice. "———at four thousand, approaching at four thousand, all lights unserviceable, all lights unserviceable, Robert calling Zebra. When overhead we shall fire a red light, when overhead we shall fire a red, Robert calling Zebra. Please give me a green if this message is received and understood, please give me a green if this message is received and understood. Emergency routine please, emergency routine, Robert calling Zebra."

Dobbie said: "All right. Reserve that frequency for him, and take all others on the other set. He'll probably keep talking to prevent them breaking in."

Gervase said: "Very good, sir. We are listening on the other frequency. Nobody has tried to use it yet." She indicated a leading aircraftwoman at the spare receiver.

The Wing Commander glanced at the clock. "I'll get outside and be ready with his green." He handed back the pad. "Log everything he says."

He went out with the Very pistol in his hand; in the office Gervase stood behind the sergeant, listening to the repetition. She was feeling rather sick; Peter was safe and nearing home. The thought did not bring her joy or any conscious feeling of relief. All it brought to her was a sudden and immense feeling of fatigue, and the thought that she might have to leave the office for a minute to go out and be sick.

"Robert calling Zebra, Robert calling Zebra. We are now

passing over at four thousand, now passing over at four thousand. If this message is received and understood will you please fire a green. If this message is received and understood will you please fire a green. Robert calling Zebra."

Gervase ran through the control office and through the light trap, out into the fresh darkness of the night. "Robert is asking for the green, sir. Says he's overhead."

"Okay. He's just fired a red." There was a flash and a report close by her, and a green star burst up in the deep blue sky. She did not stay to watch it, but went back into the radio-room.

"Okay, Zebra, Robert calling Zebra. Your green received, we have received your green. Thank you. Robert calling Zebra. I am now transferring to Captain via intercom, now transferring to Captain."

There was a pause, and several clicks and scratches; the level of the background noise rose higher. In the small office they stood waiting in silence. Dobbie came through and Gervase turned to him. "They got the green all right, sir. They're just switching over for the Captain to speak."

"Marshall ? What on earth for ?"

"They didn't say, sir."

They waited, and presently the speaker spoke again. It was Marshall speaking this time. Her breath of fresh air had made Gervase feel better, but now the nausea returned, and with it a hard lump in the middle of her throat.

"Robert calling Zebra, Captain speaking, Captain speaking." The voice was clear, and young, and confident. "We're in a bloody awful mess and minus half of our port wing. We have lost half our port wing. My rear-gunner is seriously wounded and unable to bale out, rear-gunner seriously wounded. Will you give me a green when the aerodrome is clear, give me a green when the aerodrome is clear. My flight engineer and navigator and wireless operator will then bale out, and I shall land the aircraft. Please give me a white if this is understood."

He proceeded to repeat the message; Dobbie turned and went out to the balcony. Gervase heard the crack of the pistol, and then Marshall's voice.

"Robert calling Zebra; your white has been seen and understood. I shall proceed on left-hand circuits at four thousand till I receive your green. I shall then come down to two thousand and fly across up wind, and three members of my crew will bale out. Flood lights, please, for them to land. Wireless operator is wounded in the right hand. This thing's a cow to handle, so you'd better make it snappy with that green."

Gervase went out to Dobbie with this message; he came back into the control room, and they became furiously busy. There were eight aircraft still in the air and approaching to land; already T for Tommy was winking at them in the sky. They set to work to get through on the W/T to the seven others to divert them to Wittington and Charwick; in the meantime they brought in Tommy. For ten minutes the three telephones were going at full blast; then they were clear, and ready to put up the green for Robert.

"Okay Zebra, Robert calling Zebra. Your green seen and understood, your green seen and understood. I am now coming down to two thousand and will fly straight over while my crew bale out. Coming down to two thousand and will fly straight over while my crew bale out. Stand by with the flood lights, please, stand by with flood lights."

There was a silence. Gervase stood at the door of the radio-room, white and sick. Waves of nausea were sweeping over her, but it was impossible for her to leave the control at this moment. Nevertheless, her body was letting her down; her mind could take it, but her stomach couldn't. In a very few seconds she was going to be sick.

Desperately, she thought it would be horrible to be sick in the office; the lavatory was far away. It would have to be the balcony; at the far end it was quiet and dark and only grass below; she could creep out there for a moment and nobody would know. She slipped out through the light trap past Dobbie and the Squadron Leader, and went to the far end, finishing with a little run up to the railing.

Over the loud-speaker came the voice of her beloved. "Robert calling Zebra, lights please. Flood lights, please—Robert calling Zebra."

The control officer spoke into his telephone; from three sides of the aerodrome the flood lights blazed out from their trailers, making the whole scene as light as day. Dobbie with one glance noted his signals officer being sick over the railing, then turned and scrutinised the sky. Presently, drifting down into the light, he saw three parachutes spaced about a quarter of a mile apart. Two fell within the aerodrome; he saw the men collapse and the fluted silk shrivel and sink down; the other fell outside the boundary.

He turned and went inside. The Section Officer was in the radio-room, a little pale and with beads of perspiration showing on her forehead, but at her job. He said to her: "Are you all right?"

Gervase said: "I'm better now, thank you, sir." She was rather afraid of Dobbie. She did not mind that he had seen her being sick, because that was something that might happen to anybody, but she was terrified that he would find fault with her work.

Over their heads the loud-speaker said: "Robert calling Zebra. I haven't had this thing below two hundred since we lost our bit of wing. I'm going to slow her down a bit and see what she's like. I think she'll be very difficult to hold level at anything like landing speed. Think I'll get up to four thousand again and try it there."

The background noise increased. In the office the Wing Commander looked at the control officer. "Bit of test flying now," he said quietly.

The Squadron Leader said: "He'll never land it, sir, not if it's really got half one wing missing. It'll fall over sideways, in a roll."

Dobbie said: "There *is* a minimum speed . . ."

"Would you like me to make him a signal on the Aldis, sir, and tell him to bale out?"

"Let him handle it his own way."

Over the loud-speaker the background noise died slowly. "Robert calling Zebra. Just slowing her down now."

In the office they stood tense and motionless. Somewhere up above them in the darkness, not very far away, Marshall was sitting at the controls without light, alone but for his wounded gunner. In the dim starlight he was straining at the wheel as the speed gradually dropped, his eyes fixed upon the violet glow of the horizon bar, the hand and dots of the air speed indicator. They could do nothing to help him; they stood silent in suspense, waiting for a word.

In the soft hissing from the loud-speaker a note of music grew, incongruous and unbearable. It grew in volume till they could catch the words:

"The moon that lingered over London Town,
    Poor puzzled moon, he wore a frown—
How could he know we two were so in love,
    The whole darned world seemed upside down . . ."

The volume was sufficient to drown anything the pilot said. Dobbie swung round to the W.A.A.F. sergeant at the set, vehement with the strain. "Get that damned broadcasting tuned out, can't you?"

Gervase leaped across the room to her aid, but aid was not required. The horse-faced woman raised her head and gave the Wing Commander a glance of withering scorn.

"That ain't broadcasting," she said disdainfully. "That's 'im."

They turned and stared open-mouthed at the loud-speaker. It went on, with deep feeling:

"The streets of Town were paved with stars,
    It was such a romantic affair—
And as we kissed and said good night,
    A nightingale sang in Berkeley Square."

The background noise swelled suddenly in volume as the pilot opened up his engines, and the song stopped. "Robert calling Zebra, Robert calling. I got down to about a hundred and forty, but that's the limit of control. She's bloody heavy, and my wrists are getting tired. I shall put down at about a hundred and fifty. Robert calling Zebra. I shall have to put her down at about a hundred and fifty."

There was silence in the office, broken only by the hissing from the loud-speaker. The Squadron Leader broke it. "He'll never get away with that, sir," he said quietly. "I think we ought to tell him to bale out."

"Let the gunner go?" said Dobbie.

The control officer nodded. "Would you mind stepping outside, sir?" It was intolerable to have to talk a matter like this over before the signallers.

They went out on to the balcony. The control officer said: "What I feel is this, sir. The gunner is badly wounded, too badly to bale out. He may very likely die in any case. If we let Marshall try and put her down at that speed, even on the runway, he'll almost certainly be killed. If we tell him to bale out, we save a good pilot."

"No we don't," the Wing Commander said. "He'd never be a good pilot again."

There was a short pause. "Besides," said Dobbie, "he'd never obey an order of that sort. I know that crew. If Marshall's got to be killed, I'd just as soon he wasn't killed while disobeying orders. Anyway, he may get away with it. He's got very good hands."

They came back into the office, in time to hear the loud-speaker start up again. "Robert calling Zebra, Robert calling Zebra. I have fuel for forty minutes, I have fuel for forty minutes. I shall cruise around to burn up some of it. I shall land at oh three three five. Robert calling Zebra, I shall land at oh three three five. I shall require all lights, and crash wagons at the intersection of runways two and four. I shall require all lights, and crash wagons at the intersection of runways two and four. Please send up a green now if this message is received and understood. Please send up a green now if this message is received and understood."

Dobbie said: "Give him his green." The control officer went out of the light trap; from the balcony they heard the report of the pistol.

The loud-speaker said: "Okay, Zebra, your green seen and understood, your green seen and understood. I shall get away now over towards Kingslake to avoid other aircraft landing, I shall go towards Kingslake. I shall return to land at oh three three five, I shall return and land at oh three three five. Robert calling Zebra."

Dobbie turned to the control officer as he came back into the office. "Where's Kingslake?"

"Never heard of it."

From the door of the radio-room Gervase spoke up, rather timidly. "I know where Kingslake is, sir. It's over towards Chipping Hinton."

Dobbie glanced at the map on the wall. "Chipping Hinton —I see. What is this Kingslake place—a village?"

"No. It's a house—a house with a lake."

Dobbie laid his finger on a little blue spot on the map. "Is this the place?"

Gervase approached and looked at it. "That's it, sir."

The Wing Commander grunted. "I suppose that's where you get the trout."

"Yes." There was nothing else to say, except the urgent question. "Is Flight Lieutenant Marshall going to bale out, sir?"

"I haven't told him to." He looked down at her, noting a damp streak of hair sticking to her forehead, unbecoming. "You can go off if you want to," he said kindly. "The sergeant can carry on."

Gervase said: "I'm quite all right."

Dobbie nodded. "Good."

Over their heads the hissing of the loud-speaker merged to a half-tone of reminiscent melody:

> "That certain night, the night we met,
>   There was magic abroad in the air.
> There were angels dining at the Ritz,
>   And a nightingale sang in Berkeley Square."

"You'd think this was a bloody ENSA concert," said Dobbie.

There was the sound of a truck outside the office, and the outer door opened. Sergeant Cobbett and Sergeant Pilot Franck thrust their way in, still clumsy in their flying-suits and boots. They checked when they saw the Wing Commander. "Crew of Robert, sir," said Cobbett. "We sent the wireless operator along to hospital."

Dobbie asked: "Is he bad?"

"Only his hand." The flight engineer hesitated, and then said: "Is Robert still up, sir?"

The Wing Commander jerked his head at the loud-speaker, smiling a little. "That's him."

> "The moon that lingered over London Town,
>   Poor puzzled moon, he wore a frown . . ."

"Aye," said the flight engineer. "He was singing that song most of the way home."

"He's going to land at three thirty-five," said Dobbie. "What's the matter with the gunner?"

Sergeant Franck said: "There was a shell, sir. I think it burst not in the turret but underneath. Both legs is broken, one above and one below his knee. I have made splints and bandages, with wads of gauze, and I have given dope in the same way that it says in the book."

Gervase, listening, noticed for the first time that the Dane's hands were dark and stained, and that there was blood in smears all over his flying-suit. You couldn't help that, she reflected, when you were doing for a friend what Gunnar had done in the darkness and the wind blast of the shattered fuselage, tearing along in the black night.

"Where is he now?"

Cobbett said: "We got him all comfy on the floor, sir, right back in the rear fuselage, feet forward, with his head about two feet forward of the tail wheel jack. We got him lashed down there all ways, so he won't shift whatever sort of landing the Cap makes. The Cap, he come along while Gunnar here was flying, and he see to that himself."

"Did you help lash him down?"

"Yes, sir. Me and the Cap did it."

"You'd better go with the Headquarters crash wagon and get him out, quick as you can. Look sharp about it, in case there's a fire. You should be able to get him out of that in time."

"It won't take long to get him out of it," the flight engineer said. "There's a hole in the rear fuselage you could walk through."

"All right—you go for the gunner. Sergeant Franck, you go with the south bay crash wagon, and get the pilot out."

"Ver' good, sir."

"Take both crash wagons to the intersection of two and four," said Dobbie. "Get out there as soon as you can. There are no other aircraft landing. He'll be putting down at three thirty-five—that gives you fourteen minutes to get out there. Do your best for him."

They turned to go. By the door they noticed Gervase, white and tired. Gunnar checked for a moment by her. "I think that this will be okay," he said. "He is ver' good pilot."

She smiled weakly, but said nothing. Into the room there came the reminiscent melody, sung absently as an accompaniment to other occupations:

> "I may be right, I may be wrong,
>   But I'm perfectly willing to swear,
>   That when you turned and smiled at me,
>   A nightingale sang in Berkeley Square."

Sergeant Cobbett grinned at her. "Sounds happy, don't he?" he remarked.

*　　*　　*

In the machine, peering through the starred windscreen into the starlit blackness of the night, Marshall sat singing softly to himself. He had tied a piece of cod line round the right-hand side of the half-wheel and taken it down to his thigh, so that the weight of his leg helped to ease the strain upon his wrists. Beside him and below, the hatch was open from which his crew had jumped; he could not reach to close it and a great blast of cold air came sweeping in around him and out through the window at his side. He did not mind. This rush of cold air was the very substance of the night, the quiet, deep blue serenity sifted with a thousand stars.

He was happy, sitting there in the machine. He had found the Kingslake lake, or thought he had; once or twice in the deep blackness of the woods he had seen starlight reflected upon water. Rough bearings from the beacon at Nottingdene and the beacon at Gonsall indicated he was somewhere near his fishing. It made the serenity complete for him to be there.

Presently, very soon, he would return to Hartley Magna to put down. Either you got away with these things or you didn't; it didn't seem to mean much either way. He had been very near to death in Germany only three hours before; he now had a sporting chance of life at Hartley, and he only felt relief. Whatever happened, he would be on his own runway, tended by his friends, with everybody working to help him. And Gervase would be there.

He sat there staring forward at the stars, and singing quietly to himself.

★　　　★　　　★

In the control office Gervase sat down at her little table, and tried to work upon her signal log. There was nothing to do now for the next few minutes, and she must not fuss about, because that put people off. She sat there staring at her own handwriting, listening to the low repetition of the song from the loud-speaker. Whatever anybody else might be feeling, she knew that Flight Lieutenant Marshall was happy, and she was glad for him, and comforted herself. And, sitting there, she knew that she was always glad when he was happy, and she was always miserable when he was worried; it was like that between them, and would be, whatever they might do or say. He had been right, she felt, and she had been quite wrong; there was something wonderful for them if they gave themselves a chance. Within the next few minutes, Peter might be killed in putting down at that colossal speed upon the runway. If he was not killed, she would find herself married to him very soon. It wasn't fair to keep him hanging round now that she had made her mind up, nor did she want to hang around herself.

On the loud-speaker the song broke off, and the background noise diminished. "Robert calling Zebra, Robert calling Zebra. I am approaching from the west and dropping off some height, approaching from the west and losing height. If you are ready for me, please, put on all lights. Robert calling Zebra."

Dobbie nodded to the control officer, who spoke into his telephone. Outside the Chance lights blazed out from the lee boundaries of the aerodrome, so that everything was as bright as day. The control officer told Gervase to get the speaker to full volume, and went out on to the balcony with Dobbie, propping the light trap doors open behind them. Gervase went to the balcony door and stood in the doorway looking out, ready to get back to her signallers immediately.

"Okay Zebra, Robert calling Zebra, thank you for lights. I am now south of you, now south of you, and turning to come in, turning to come in."

On the balcony they stood tense. On the grass beside the office Gervase saw a little group of men in flying kit; she recognised Pat Johnson, and Davy, and Lines, and Sergeant Pilot Nutter, amongst others. There was nothing they could do to help, but they could not stay away. They were standing motionless, straining their eyes into the sky beyond the blinding lights.

From the lit office behind Gervase the loud-speaker said: "Robert calling Zebra. I am now coming in to land, coming in to land, bringing her in at about a hundred and eighty. Here we go. Robert calling Zebra. Here we go."

Staring straight into the searchlights, Gervase could not see a thing beyond the middle of the aerodrome. She could see the two crash wagons at the intersection of the runways, one on each side of the main runway, facing each other, ready to spring to the crash the instant the machine came to rest. Each truck was crowded with men hanging on to it, and some of these were ghostly in white-cowled asbestos overalls. A hundred yards behind the near crash wagon was the ambulance, its medical crew by it, staring at the sky.

Suddenly everybody exclaimed, and everybody saw the aircraft. It was about thirty feet up over the runway's end. Its under-carriage was retracted and no flaps were down; its tail was high, both engines going hard, and it was moving very fast. Gervase had time to note that one wing seemed little better than a stub beyond the engine, and time to see a spurt of white fumes from each engine. For an instant she thought miserably that it was on fire. Beside her she heard Dobbie say quietly: "Good man. He's remembered his Graviners," and realised that the pilot had set off fire extinguishers.

Then, quite deliberately, the aircraft flew on to the ground. A great shower of sparks flew up behind it from the runway. It held its course for three or four seconds, its tail high above the wing, unnatural and terrifying. Then it fell over sideways, still travelling at an enormous speed. The stub of the port wing touched ground and the tail dropped low; the undamaged starboard wing rose up vertically till the whole plan of the aircraft was presented to them, the body high above the ground. The port tail plane spun free up in the air behind, and the whole aircraft pirouetted round upon the broken wing, still travelling at an immense speed down the runway. It hung vertically on edge for an instant, the undamaged wing pointing to the sky. Then it fell back with a great crash on to the runway, right side up, and slid tail-first to rest two hundred yards beyond the crash wagons.

The control officer turned to the Wing Commander. "Right side up," he cried. "He should have got away with it."

Dobbie nodded. "I was afraid it was going on its back."

They stood for a moment, watching the crash wagons spurt up to the wreck, watching the men leap off and get to work. A cloud of smoke and dust masked what was going on, but there was no fire. Dobbie turned away. "I'm going out there in my Jeep," he said. "Get the lights out as soon as the ambulance is away."

In the control office he passed the Section Officer. "You can go off duty now," he said. "There'll be no more in your line to-night." He hesitated. "You'll get the news you want up at the hospital," he said. "I should get up there."

Gervase wanted to say: "Thank you, sir," but the words would not come. She just looked at him dumbly and nodded, and he glanced at her, and went on out to his Jeep, and jumped into it, and drove it straight out over the rough grass towards the wreck.

Gervase put on her coat and cap, told the W.A.A.F. sergeant to carry on, and went out of the office. At the road intersection with the runway she ran into a group of pilots still in flying-suits; their eyes, used to the darkness, could recognise her, though she could not distinguish them. Pat Johnson said: "We're just hanging round till someone comes up to

216

tell us what happened."

She moved towards him; he was someone friendly, that she knew well. "Winco told me to go up to the hospital. He said I'd find out there."

"Not a bad idea."

They turned, and walked together in the starlit night; as they went the ambulance spun past them smoothly and quietly; they could not see who was in it. It took them ten minutes to reach the hospital; as they got there, the ambulance was moving off again. At the door they found an orderly and asked him about it.

"Rear-gunner," he said. "Taking him straight into hospital at Oxford. The M.O. said not to take him off the stretcher here or anything—just take him right along to Oxford."

Johnson asked: "Did the pilot come up with the ambulance?"

"Aye, he's inside with the M.O. Got his face cut about a bit, but that's all."

It was odd, Gervase thought, that whenever good news came she wanted to be sick.

"Born to be hanged," said Mr. Johnson cheerfully. "You can't dodge Fate."

They stood in the corridor outside the surgery for a time, waiting for something to happen. Presently the door opened and the medical officer came out. "Hullo," he said, "Are you waiting for Marshall?"

"Just like to know what sort of a state he's in," said Johnson.

"He's all right. He wants to sleep in his own bed. If you like, you can take him over and put him to bed. I'll be along in about a quarter of an hour with some tablets for him. My truck's outside; you can take him in that."

They went into the surgery, and Gervase saw Marshall sitting in a chair grinning at her; he had white strapping and lint over the right side of his forehead and his eyebrow. She said shyly: "Hullo, Peter. How are you feeling?"

He said: "I'm fine, only I can't use my hands." His hands were lying on his knees, palm upwards; as they looked, the finger-tips twitched very slightly. "Look, I'm trying to bend them. Isn't that bloody funny?"

"That all you can do?" asked Mr. Johnson, interested.

"That's all."

"It's going to make a lot of difference to the beer situation in the mess," said Mr. Johnson thoughtfully. "The medical officer says we've got to take you and put you to bed."

Marshall looked up at Gervase. "That doesn't sound quite nice," he said smiling.

"It's not," she said. "We'll kick Pat out as soon as he's helped you upstairs."

Their eyes met and they laughed.

CHAPTER NINE

In the white-flowered hawthorn brake,
    Love, be merry for my sake;
Twine the blossoms in my hair,
    Kiss me where I am most fair—
Kiss me, love, for who knoweth
What thing cometh after death?
                                        WILLIAM MORRIS

Gervase slept late next day. She had not got to bed till about half-past five, when it was full grey dawn. She had been hungry, not unnaturally, and had visited the kitchen of the mess at about five o'clock with Pat Johnson; they had discovered some lukewarm cocoa and three dozen plates of bread and butter cut ready for breakfast, and they had eaten themselves full. She slept till noon, and only got up then because she was hungry again and if she got up she would be in time to have some lunch.

She got into the ante-room just before the medical officer, a Flight Lieutenant called Proctor. Davy asked the question before she could. "How's our nightingale?"

"Asleep. He won't wake up just yet. Don't any of you go and wake him; I want him to have a good long sleep."

Pat Johnson said: "What's wrong with his hands?"

"Nothing functional. Last night it was just nervous reaction. He'll probably be all right when he wakes up."

Lines said: "That's what you told us about Tommy Broadhead. It took him four months."

"That's right," the surgeon said easily. "I have to shoot a line to keep up your morale."

There were matters that were tacitly avoided in the mess, and nervous trouble was one of them. Gervase changed the subject by asking: "How is Sergeant Phillips?"

"I rang up this morning, but it's too early to say much. They think they'll save his legs."

"Marshall will want to know about that as soon as he wakes," said Gervase.

"Yes—of course. I'll ring up again about tea time."

They went in to lunch. Gervase sat long in the ante-room afterwards, drowsily looking at the *Illustrated London News*.

She roused at about half-past three and went out, thinking to walk round the aerodrome. But in the hall she met the medical officer coming down from the bedrooms, and she stopped to speak to him.

"Is Flight Lieutenant Marshall awake yet?"

He shook his head. "He's sleeping more lightly." He looked at her thoughtfully, thinking of the fish that this Section Officer had brought home with his patient only a few days before. "You're a great friend of his, aren't you?"

There was nobody else within hearing; it was the middle of the afternoon and the mess was deserted. She said: "Yes."

"Are you going to marry him, or anything like that?"

"He asked me to some time ago," she said. She knew this to be a purely medical enquiry. "I think we'll be announcing it pretty soon."

He nodded. "I thought so. Would you like to take him up a cup of tea in an hour's time, and wake him up?"

"All right."

"I think that might be a good thing." He hesitated, and then said: "If he has any difficulty with his hands, do what you can to make him use them. But don't let him get worried or panicky about it if they aren't quite right at first. He may have to have some leave."

She met his eyes. "He couldn't use them at all last night. We had to do everything for him."

"I know. See if you can get him to use them. I always think it's a great pity to have to start electrical treatment, or massage, excepting in the last resort. I've known that start a hospital psychosis before now. Just see if you can make him use them naturally."

"All right. Ought he to get up?"

"Give me a ring if he wants to, and I'll slip over from the surgery and see him. Otherwise he's just as well in bed."

She went out for a little walk along the ring runway; out in the middle of the aerodrome there were still trucks and cranes disposing of the scrap duralumin that had been R for Robert, and towing it to the knackers' yard right over on the far side by the hedge. She did not get so far as that, but turned back to the mess, and took two cups of tea furtively from the dining-room, and slipped away with them upstairs to the bedroom floor, where no W.A.A.F. officer would dream of going normally if she valued her commission.

She opened the door carefully, with two cups of tea in her

hand. Marshall was awake in bed; he turned his head as she came in. "I say," he said. "There'll be a stinking row if anybody catches you in here, Gervase."

She said: "I brought you up a cup of tea, Peter."

"Thanks awfully. Put it down, and come and give me a kiss, and then nip out quietly. I'm going to get up. I'll see you downstairs."

He looked very like a little boy, she felt, lying there in bed and worrying about her. She put the cups down carefully upon the chest of drawers. "It's all right," she said. "This wasn't my idea. The M.O. said I was to bring you up a cup of tea and wake you up."

"Did he ? Damn decent of him. How long do you think it would take to wake me up ?"

"About as long as it takes me to drink this cup of tea." She sat down on the edge of his bed. "How are you feeling, Peter ? How's your head ?"

He struggled up into a sitting attitude. "My head's all right. But I can't do anything with my hands." He sounded worried and incredulous. "Look—they just won't work."

The finger-tips flexed very slightly. She took one of his hands in her own, and stroked it. "Feel that ?"

"Sort of. It feels all kind of numb inside."

She bent impulsively and kissed the back of his hand. He put the other hand up and stroked her hair clumsily, and they were silent for a minute or two. Presently she drew back. "You'll have to take it easy for a bit," she said. "You said your wrists were tired, over the R/T."

"Did I ? Were you listening in ?"

She nodded. "You said your wrists were tired quite early on, and that was a long time before you landed."

"So they were," he said. "She was frightfully heavy to hold. I was afraid they weren't going to last out, and that I wouldn't be able to hold the wheel any longer."

She massaged his wrist gently. "It'll come back as soon as the muscles are rested," she said. "It's a sort of sprain." She got up and fetched the tea over, and put both cups on the floor beside the bed. "I'll hold the cup for you while you drink."

He said: "Do you know how Phillips is getting on ?"

She told him what she knew, and she gave him his tea in little sips, holding the cup for him. And presently she said: "I've been thinking about things, Peter—about us. Do you still want to marry me ?"

He put out his hand and stroked her arm clumsily to the elbow. "I want that frightfully," he said. "But only if it's going to be as good for you as it would be for me."

She said: "If we didn't get married, I don't think I'd ever be happy again."

A shade of apprehension came into his eyes. "You're really sure, Gervase? I mean, this isn't because you think it was a good show, what I did last night?"

She shook her head. "It *was* a good show, Peter, and I'm frightfully proud. But it was before that, when you didn't send 'Mission completed', that I knew. You see—I thought you were dead, Peter, and you wouldn't come back at all. That's when I knew what I really felt about you, and what it would mean, sort of going on alone."

Medical officer or no, if the Queen W.A.A.F. had happened to look into Bedroom 16 in the next few minutes, Gervase would have been out of the Service within half an hour. But she didn't, and presently they broke away and sat quiet for a minute, looking at each other.

Marshall said: "Got any ideas about when?"

She said: "Let's have it soon, Peter. You've only got two more ops to do, and then you'll be sent away. If we're going to be married, I'd like to be married before you go."

He said: "We ought to meet each other's people. Mine won't worry, but I'd like to keep them sweet."

She said: "It's the same with me. But we could get a week's leave, and go and see them both."

He nodded. "It takes about three weeks to get married, anyway, unless you pay out about forty quid for a special licence."

"We're not going to do that," she said. "We'll be glad of forty quid when the peace comes."

They talked until the lapse of time scared them. Gervase gathered up the cups. "I'll go down and ring the M.O. and he'll come and tell you if you can get up," she said.

He smiled at her. "It'll be rotten if I get transferred away as soon as we're married," he said. "You'll have to get a shift, too."

Gervase said vaguely: "I expect I could do that."

She went out, walking in a dream. Because of that, she did not go with caution. In the hall, at the foot of the stairs, she ran into Flight Officer Stevens, and Mrs. Stevens was in one of her more difficult moods.

She stared at Gervase, and at the tea cups in her hands. "Have you been up on the bedroom floor?" she demanded.

Gervase started, and flushed. "I took Flight Lieutenant Marshall up a cup of tea," she said.

"In his bedroom?"

Her tone angered the girl. "In his bedroom," she replied. "What's more, he was in bed."

The Flight Officer stared at her. "You know perfectly well that that's against the rules," she said. "You could be cashiered for that."

The girl said angrily: "Do you mean you think I've been doing something wrong?"

Her anger spread to the Flight Officer. "I mean I'm going to report you to the Adjutant for insubordination and indiscipline," she said. "You'd better get back to your quarters now."

Gervase flushed scarlet. "All right," she said, "report me. I'm engaged to Peter Marshall, and we're going to be married very soon, so I want to get out of the W.A.A.F.s so that we can be together. I was going to do the usual. If you get me chucked out for misconduct it'll save me a lot of trouble."

The grey-haired Flight Officer looked at her thoughtfully. "You're not officially engaged," she said.

"I am," said Gervase hotly. "I wasn't when I went upstairs, but I am now. I don't know if that makes a difference in the rules—whether an engaged officer may go and see her fiancé in bed after a crash, and what happens to an officer who's not engaged when she goes up and is when she comes down. But anyway, the M.O. told me to take him a cup of tea."

"He did? He shouldn't have told you to do anything of the sort. You shouldn't have gone."

Gervase said angrily: "I don't agree with you. If you feel you've got to report me, go ahead and do it, and let's have a bit of fun."

She marched off, carrying her cups. The Flight Officer went off to find the Adjutant.

Gervase was still very angry when Marshall came downstairs three-quarters of an hour later, escorted by the young M.O. Gervase met them in the hall. "He says I can go out a bit," said Marshall. "I want to go and see what's left of Robert."

Proctor said: "You'd better go in my truck. Don't go and

get tired. I'll expect to see you back here in an hour."

He walked out with them to the truck; Gervase got into the driving seat and they drove off towards the runway. The medical officer turned and went to the Headquarters office, and went in to Wing Commander Dobbie. The C.O. was talking to the Adjutant; they looked up as the M.O. poked his head around the door.

"Sorry, sir," said Proctor. "Could I have a word when you're free?"

"Is this about Marshall?"

The medical officer said: "Yes."

"Come on in," said Dobbie. "Let's have your story."

Faintly surprised, the Surgeon Flight Lieutenant said: "There's no story, sir. His head is quite all right—just one deep scar that will need dressing every day. His hands are semi-paralysed, but that's only nervous strain, together with muscular fatigue; it'll go off in a short time. I was going to suggest you send him home on leave for a few days. He lives quite close to an R.A.F. hospital, and he can have his scar dressed there."

"I don't mind," said Dobbie. "You don't want to take him into hospital?"

"Not if I can help it. I don't like hospital with these slight nervous troubles." He hesitated. "He's just got himself engaged," he said. "If Section Officer Robertson wants leave at the same time I'd think it was a very good thing for him."

Dobbie laughed, and turned to Chesterton. "He's the nigger in the wood pile." He turned back to the surgeon, still laughing. "Did you send Section Officer Robertson up to Marshall with a cup of tea?" he said.

The surgeon looked surprised. "Yes, I did. Why?"

"You started something. Old Mother Stevens has just been in to report her for indiscipline—to wit, visiting an officer in his bedroom."

"For Christ's sake!" said the surgeon irritably.

Dobbie turned more serious. "All very well," he said, "but we can't slur over it like that. The W.A.A.F.s are very strict about these things, you know."

Proctor said: "I'm strict about my job as well, sir. I do my duty by the air crews to the best of my ability. I told that girl to go and wake him up because I thought it would be helpful to that pilot. I'm sorry if I acted thoughtlessly about the W.A.A.F.s, but I still think it was the right thing to do."

"I don't doubt you in the least," said Dobbie. "The only thing I'm worried about is, what to do with Flight Officer Stevens and her moan."

Chesterton leaned forward. "Send both of them off on leave for a week," he said, "and stall Mother Stevens. I'll see her this evening and tell her all the circumstances, and see if I can calm her down. She's all right if you take her the right way."

Dobbie nodded. "I'll come into the mess and take a glass of sherry off them before dinner," he said. "That'll put it all on an official basis for the W.A.A.F.s."

In the truck, halted by the side of the ring runway, Gervase was telling Peter all about it. "It was awful," she said. "I think I'm going to get into a frightful row, but the M.O. told me to take tea up to you."

"It's crackers," said the pilot. "They can't possibly do anything to you for that."

Gervase said timidly: "Would you like to sort of tell people in the mess this evening, Peter? It might spike their guns a bit."

He drew her to him clumsily in the truck and kissed her, regardless of an interested A.C.2 approaching in the middle distance. "Suits me," he said. "It makes it harder for you to get out of it."

Presently, feeling some slight stir of Service decency and aerodrome behaviour, they disentangled and drove on round the runway. In the warm sunlight of the summer afternoon they got out of the truck and walked over the grass to the remains of what had once been R for Robert. The fuselage was broken by the crash and shattered by cannon fire; the turret was crushed and stained with blood. "Proctor said Sergeant Phillips is going on all right," said Marshall. "He's been asking about me. I'd like to drive into Oxford to-morrow and see him, if they'll let me."

They walked forward to the broken cockpit. The wheel was still intact, a piece of cod line hanging from the right-hand side. For the rest, it was just smelly, bent, and tangled wreckage waiting to be carted to some dump to lie and rot.

"Poor old Robert," said the pilot thoughtfully. "I did a lot of hours in her." They got into the truck and went back to the hospital.

Proctor came out to meet them at the door. "I've just had a word with Winco about you," he said to Marshall. "Like to go on leave a bit?"

Marshall hesitated, and involuntarily glanced at Gervase. "Think I ought to?"

"Might be a good thing." He hesitated in turn. "I told Winco you two were engaged," he said diffidently. "I hope you don't mind. Matter of fact, there's a bit of a hoo-hah on about your tea-party."

"Well, that's your fault," said Marshall directly. "You told her to come up."

"I know it's my fault," said the surgeon. "I told Winco so. Matter of fact, I think he wants to get you both off the station on leave till the heat goes off."

Gervase said: "Does he want me to go on leave as well?"

"I think so. Chesterton put that idea into his mind. I said I thought it would be good for Marshall if you went together."

Gervase turned to Peter, troubled and distressed. "It's awful," she said. "I've never been mixed up in anything like this before."

He smiled down at her. "You've never been engaged before."

"Does getting engaged always land you in a blazing row?"

"Always," said the surgeon firmly. "I've never known it miss."

Gervase said: "I do think someone might have told me."

Marshall turned to the surgeon. "Is Winco in his office still?"

"I think he is."

"I'd better go along and see him. I'm not going off on leave until I've seen my rear-gunner. Can I go and see him to-morrow?"

"I should think so. I'll ring up and ask if that will be all right."

They left the truck before the hospital, and walked on up the road towards Headquarters. The Wing Commander came out as they approached; he saw them and turned briskly towards them.

"Evening, Marshall," he said. "How are you feeling?"

The pilot grinned at him. "Okay, sir," he said. "I've just been down to have a look at Robert."

"Not much of it left."

"No. I'm sorry about that; I thought I'd get her down more in one piece."

"Bloody lucky to get her down at all," said Dobbie. "How are your hands?"

"I can't do much with them. Proctor says I've got to go on leave."

"He told me that. You'd better get away first thing to-morrow."

The pilot said: "I would like to go into Oxford first to see Sergeant Phillips, sir. I don't suppose I'll be able to see him till the afternoon. Could I go the day after?"

"All right." He spoke for a few minutes about hospital treatment for the cuts upon the pilot's face, and about a Medical Board before resuming flying. Then the Wing Commander glanced at Gervase; there was a momentary pause.

She said diffidently: "Could I take a week's leave at the same time, sir?" She coloured a little. "We've decided to get married."

Dobbie grinned. "Thank God for that."

"Why?"

"There'd have been the father and mother of a row if you hadn't," said the Wing Commander. "Yes, you can go off. I'll see Mrs. Stevens. You'd better try and make your peace with her before you go, but for God's sake don't upset her any more."

Marshall said seriously: "That was Proctor's doing, sir. It was his idea that she should bring me up a cup of tea."

"I know," said Dobbie. "The whole tea-party was most unpleasant for you both, and must have caused you a great deal of embarrassment. All I say is, don't do it again. Are you going to stand me a glass of sherry in the mess to-night?"

"We'd like that, sir."

"All right. I'll see if I can get Mrs. Stevens to come too."

He strode off up the road; in the calm evening sunlight Marshall and Gervase turned and walked slowly to the mess. In the porch they met Flight Lieutenant Johnson, returning from the links.

"How's Nightingale?" he asked.

Marshall grinned weakly. "Not so bad." He hesitated; it was as well to get it over. "Got a bit of news," he said. "Give you three guesses."

Mr. Johnson cocked an eye at them. "They're sending you back to F.T.S. to learn to land an aircraft?" he said.

"No," said Gervase. "That's one."

"You've pulled another of those things out of the main drain?"

"No," said Gervase. "Now just try, Pat. Think very, very hard."

He turned to her and said innocently: "Somebody's caught up with him with an affiliation order?"

The meeting became confused. "We'll have to tell him," Gervase said at last. "We're going to be married, Pat."

Mr. Johnson said: "I *am* surprised." He glanced at them. "It all started with that fish. I always said no good would come of that fish."

Gervase said: "Well, anyway, you get a glass of sherry out of it."

That night the name Nightingale descended upon Marshall and adhered; he was known for the remainder of his service in the R.A.F. as Nightingale Marshall. Gervase before long was to grow accustomed to being addressed by young men and women as Mrs. Nightingale, who had never heard her real married name. That first night it was all a great joke for an hour or two, terminating when Proctor sent Marshall up to bed and Gervase went over to her own mess in the W.A.A.F. officers' quarters. In the sitting-room she found Mrs. Stevens alone, smoking and reading.

She hesitated at the door. "I asked Wing Commander Dobbie if I might go off on a week's leave," she said. "Did he mention it to you?"

The older woman looked up. "That's all right. Come in and sit down a bit."

Gervase went and sat down rather awkwardly. "I'm sorry I was rude this afternoon," she said. "I was a bit excited, I suppose."

The Flight Officer said dryly: "I imagine so." And then she smiled. "Are you very happy?"

"Frightfully," said Gervase soberly.

"Well, you'd better get off the station before we have another row. W.A.A.F. rules aren't made to cope with people like you and Peter Marshall, in your state."

The girl looked up in wonder. "I suppose they're not. One seems to look at things so differently."

They stayed talking together for a quarter of an hour. Then Gervase went to bed at nine o'clock and slept the whole night through.

She was early in her office next morning, cleaning up her work and handing over to Section Officer Millington, in readiness for going off on leave. In the middle of the morning

Marshall came into her office. "It's all right to go and see Phillips this afternoon," he said. "Proctor says we can take his truck. Will you be able to drive me?"

"I think so, Peter. There's nothing much to stay for." She thought for a minute. "You won't be very long with him, will you?"

He shook his head. "They won't let me stay more than a few minutes, I should think."

She said: "Do you think it would be nice to take some stuff for tea and have it somewhere? I mean, if Proctor's lending us his truck . . ."

He grinned. "I think that's a wizard idea." They settled that she should get some tea put up into a thermos-flask, and sandwiches, and they would try and get some cakes and fruit in Oxford. "If we get enough," said Gervase, "we can cut supper and stay out till quite late."

"Okay. I'll tell Proctor he can kiss his truck good-bye for the rest of the day."

"Get somebody to fill it up, Peter."

He nodded. "I'm just going in to see Winco about Phillips. I think he ought to get a D.F.M., even if he did shoot the thing down on top of us."

"It's the second one he's shot down, isn't it?"

The pilot nodded. "The point is, he was wounded before he got this one. He got shot up in the first attack."

"I didn't know that, Peter." She had not asked for any details of the night's work, fearing to revive memories that would upset him.

"Sorry, Gervase—I thought you knew. I'll tell you about it this afternoon."

He went off to the Wing Commander's office and Gervase sat down at her desk to write a letter to her mother in Thirsk, breaking the news that she was going to be married. She did not write very logically. Having described her young man, she went on: "We'll try and get up to Thirsk in a few days before I have to come back here as soon as they will let Peter travel, but I'll let you know again as soon as we know. We want to be married quite soon because Peter's going to be shifted probably to Scotland, so I want to leave the W.A.A.F.s so that we can be together, so we'll have to get busy." She ended up by saying: "I'm terribly happy, darling mother, and I hope you and Daddy will be too."

She posted this before lunch, and lunched with Peter in the

mess, cutting up his roast lamb for him so that he could eat it with a spoon, to the accompaniment of a running commentary from Mr. Johnson. They got off afterwards in the small Austin truck with the canvas canopy over the rear body and drove out of the station in good spirits, Gervase at the wheel.

They got to Oxford in about half an hour and drove straight to the hospital. They came out twenty minutes later considerably sobered; there had been nothing funny in the pathetic gratitude of a very sick young man lying stretched upon a complicated rack of weights and pulleys made up into a bed. The incongruity of life in England struck Gervase very forcibly as they went out into the crowded streets of Oxford to buy buns and fruit if they could find any. The streets were cheerful and busy, remote from any element of war except the uniforms. But they had come straight from the bedside of a young man who had been shot up over Hamburg only thirty-six hours before, and Peter walking with her could not use his hands.

They bought some gooseberries in a bag and a few tired-looking rock-cakes and four doubtful sausage-rolls, all the food that they could find in Oxford in the middle of the afternoon. Then they walked around and looked at engagement-rings in shop windows, and came to the conclusion that they would do better in London. And then, because they were tired of being in the company of other people, they went back to the truck and got out on the road again.

They discussed where they should go to have their tea as they drove out of Oxford. Kingslake was ruled out because Marshall could not use his hands enough for fishing, and because Gunnar Franck and Cobbett were most likely to be there, and they wanted to be alone.

"What about Coldstone Mill?" asked Gervase. "It's nice there."

"I caught a pike there once," said Marshall. "Did I ever tell you?"

"Not properly," said Gervase. "We'll go there and have tea and you shall tell me all about it. It's not much out of our way."

It was very pleasant out at Coldstone Mill that afternoon in May. Chestnut and hawthorn were in bloom; in the millpool the water slipped translucent over the gravelly shallows and the new pale green weed, brilliant in the sunlight. They drove the truck a few yards off the road down to the grass beside the water and went on for fifty yards carrying their thermos and their paper bags till they found a place that suited them beside the running stream. There they sat down very close together and began to talk, but not about fishing.

Presently Gervase said: "You'd like us to get married pretty soon, Peter, wouldn't you?"

He drew her a little more comfortably close to him. "I would," he said. "I don't want to hurry you, Gervase."

She smiled up at him. "I'd like to. If we're going to do it, let's do it right away. I don't see that we've got anything to wait for." She felt, although she would not put it into words, that it would be better for him to be married, that if she wanted to keep Peter Marshall safe she must reduce the nervous strain upon him to the utmost that she could. "I'd like to be married before you go on ops again," she said.

"I believe we could do that," said Marshall thoughtfully, "if we went at it right away. I don't see myself going again for the thick end of a month."

She caressed his hand gently. "Nor do I."

Presently he said: "There's one thing, though. I've only got two more ops to do. Then I'll be transferred away from here, Gervase." He looked down at her, worried. "That means that I get buzzed off somewhere else just after we've got married, leaving you here. Have you thought of that?"

She nodded. "I've thought of that one, Peter. I think I'd like to leave the W.A.A.F.s."

"Honestly?"

"Honestly, if we're going to get married."

There was silence for a little. Gervase, resting against his shoulder, thought how quickly she had changed her views about her work. Only a few months before she had thought that her work in the R.A.F. mattered more than anything else. Work in the R.A.F. still mattered in her life, but it was Peter's work.

He was troubled. "I don't want you to give up too much," he said. "It seems a bit one-sided."

She sat up a little. "I've loved being in the W.A.A.F.s," she said. "I don't think specially because I like the Service. I've been very unhappy in it at times. I was miserable when first I came to Hartley. But I've loved learning to do an important job really well—that's been the real fun. And you can get that in other ways."

"What sort of ways?"

"Being a wife," said Gervase simply. "I don't know the

first thing about it, Peter. But if I'm going to do it, then I want to do it well. And that's not staying on at Hartley as a married W.A.A.F. while you're in Scotland flying Liberators." She paused. "I'd like to leave the W.A.A.F.s now, honestly."

They sat quiet together for a while, watching the water running past over the weir. And presently he said: "I've always understood that there were one or two minor formalities before you can get out of the W.A.A.F.s."

She glanced up at him; his face was solemn but his eyes were dancing. "I know," she said. "You have to get chucked out for misbehaviour, or else you have to start a family."

Their eyes met, laughing. "I'll help you misbehave at any time," he said obligingly. "Just say the word and I'll bring out my rude suggestion."

"There doesn't seem to be much difference, does there ?" she said thoughtfully. "But if I'm going to leave the W.A.A.F.s I don't want to finish up like that. I'd rather start the family and go out gracefully."

They sat for some time quietly together, planning their progeny; four seemed to them to be a good round number as a first objective. "Four kids ought to be able to support us in our declining years," said Marshall. "I mean after all, one of the four ought to make some money."

"You might make some yourself," she pointed out. "That makes five chances."

He stared out across the millpool soberly. "I was only making four pounds ten a week in the insurance racket," he said quietly. "If the war ends, I may have to go back to that, and you'll have a baby, Gervase. If it goes on long enough you might have two. Have you thought of that side of it ?"

She turned and faced him, as serious as he was. "I've thought of that, Peter. I suppose we're being foolish and improvident to talk of starting up a family in times like this. But it's a risk I think we ought to take, and if we're bold enough I think we'll get away with it. I'm ready to chance it, anyway."

"Supposing I got killed ?"

"I'd have to go to work," she said. "I'd want to, anyway, if that should happen. We're safe enough, Peter, to do what we want. We're healthy and we're young. You can't be safer than that."

In the sound of the wood-pigeons calling in the trees behind them, and in the sound of running water at their feet, they unpacked their tea. "It's not much of a tea," said Gervase ruefully. "Do you think it'll keep you going till breakfast, Peter?"

He grinned. "We'll look in at the 'Horse' and get a can of beer and a snack on the way back to the station."

She said: "Oh, let's do that, Peter. I've never been to the 'Horse'." She filled the plastic cup with tea from the thermos. "Want a drink?"

He did not answer. She looked up at him, and he was staring over her shoulder towards the road and the truck behind her back. "What are you looking at?" she asked, and turned to see.

There was a large, camouflaged R.A.F. saloon car stopped upon the road. The W.A.A.F. driver was still in her seat. The door of the rear seat was open, and an officer in Air Force blue was walking down across the meadow to their truck parked by the water-side. He was a tall, thick-set man about fifty years of age. He wore two rows of medal ribbons beneath the wings upon his chest. He wore one broad band of light blue braid upon each cuff, with a black band each side of it. Gervase stared at him aghast.

Marshall said very quietly: "Christ, it's the Air Commodore!" and scrambled to his feet. His tunic was unbuttoned and he could not work his hands sufficiently to button it, but he went forward to the truck, leaving Gervase sitting on the ground holding the thermos-flask. He had picked up his cap and managed to put that upon his head, and he achieved a parody of a salute.

Air Commodore Baxter was not generally a fussy man, but he had little use for insolence; an officer who saluted awkwardly with his cap on crooked and his coat unbuttoned was not the sort of officer he liked to have about him. "Is this your truck?" he demanded.

Marshall flushed. "Yes, sir."

"What's it doing here?"

The pilot said: "I've been to Oxford on a Service trip, sir. I'm on my way back to the station." It was no good, he thought; it was a fair cop, if ever there was one.

"Where are you stationed?"

"At Hartley Magna."

The Air Commodore said: "This isn't the road from Oxford to Hartley."

Marshall was silent. He knew that he was six or seven miles

out of his course, and it was clear the Air Commodore knew too.

"Who is that young woman? Is she stationed at Hartley?"

"Yes, sir. She's my fiancée."

Air Commodore Baxter fixed him with a cold, grey eye. "If you think you can use Service transport for this sort of thing you're very much mistaken." He looked the pilot up and down. "Button up your jacket."

Marshall began to fumble with the buttons impotently. In the background Gervase scrambled to her feet, straightening out her skirt.

"Do you know who I am?" the Air Commodore demanded.

"Yes, sir."

"Report to me at Group Headquarters, Charwick, to-morrow morning at ten o'clock. What's your name?"

"Flight Lieutenant Marshall, sir."

There was a momentary pause.

"Nightingale Marshall?" the Air Commodore demanded.

The pilot hesitated. "Yes, sir." Gervase slipped up behind him, reached round, and did his buttons up one by one from the top. Marshall said: "I'm sorry, sir. I can't button things yet."

"I see." The Air Commodore thought for a moment, and then turned to Gervase. "What's your name?"

She said in a small voice: "Section Officer Robertson, sir."

Baxter stood looking out over the millpool at the chestnut trees in bloom, at the thermos and the paper bags upon the grass. They had picked a pleasant place, he thought, He turned to them again. "Finish your tea and then take that truck back to Hartley," he said. "You ought to know better. I think you're a couple of damn fools. If you'd run it in behind those bushes I'd never have seen it."

The pilot grinned faintly.

"Come and see me at Group, ten o'clock to-morrow morning, Marshall."

"Very good, sir."

The Air Commodore turned and walked back to his car, and got in, and drove off. Gervase and Peter stood and watched it go, the pilot white and shaken. "First time I've ever had a thing like that happen to me," he said.

Gervase said, "He won't do anything, Peter. It made a difference when you told him who you were."

"I'm not so sure," the pilot said gloomily. They turned and

walked back over the short grass to their tea. "Conduct unbecoming to an officer and a gentleman, and conduct unbecoming to an officer and a gentlewoman," he said.

"It was pretty unbecoming," said Gervase. "I had to stop behind and do my tie, or I'd have come with you. I never knew that people did such silly things when they were in love."

He laughed and took her arm. She glanced up at him. "Anyway, Peter," she said, "your hands are much better . . ."

They sat on for an hour beside the stream and finished all their food, and then, still hungry, they took the truck and Gervase drove it back on to the road. They were only three miles from the station by the lanes, but the direct road from Oxford to the aerodrome passed by the "Black Horse" in Hartley Magna, so a halt at the "Black Horse" was clearly permissible upon a Service journey from Oxford to the station. It only made a detour of ten miles or so to get back on the Oxford Road, and they drew up in the market-place at about half-past seven.

At the bar Marshall asked Nellie to ask Mrs. Simpson if he could have a word with her, and when the fat landlady came he asked her to take a glass of sherry with them, because they had got engaged. And while all that was going on he asked if she could do them bacon and eggs because Gervase was feeling a little faint, and presently they were sitting down to quite a comprehensive supper in the back parlour.

On their way out they looked into the lounge bar, and Proctor was there, and Pat Johnson, and Davy. They went in to thank the surgeon for his truck. "It was terribly nice of you to let us have it," said Gervase. "It got us into a most frightful row, but that's not your fault."

"Another row?"

They nodded and told him. "That makes two in two days," said Marshall.

Davy said: "And if you stay here to-morrow it'll be three in three days, old boy."

Proctor said: "I told you what happens when you get engaged. It's just row after row."

Gervase said thoughtfully: "Ma Stevens told me the same thing. But it's all right—we're going off on leave to-morrow."

Marshall said. "I'd like to use the truck again to-morrow morning, if I may. I've got to go to Group to get my raspberry before going off on leave."

They drove back to the station in the truck and parked it in the transport yard. In the close privacy of the little cab they said good night in suitable manner; then they got out and went each to their own quarters.

Next morning Gervase drove Marshall over to Group Headquarters at Charwick. She parked the truck outside the Headquarters office; Marshall got out and went into the offices simultaneously with a civilian who arrived in a car labelled Ministry of Aircraft Production. Both deferred to each other at the door of the Secretary's office; the civilian went in first.

"Air Commodore Baxter?" he enquired.

The W.A.A.F. Flight Officer evidently knew him. "He's expecting you, sir." She turned to Marshall. "Who is it you want to see?"

The pilot said: "The Air Commodore told me to report to him at ten o'clock. Flight Lieutenant Marshall."

She said: "Just one minute." She went through into the inner office, closing the door quietly behind her. In a minute she came out again and said to the civilian: "Would you mind waiting for a few minutes, sir? The Air Commodore will see this officer; then he's free for the rest of the morning."

Marshall went forward into the inner office; the door closed behind him. Air Commodore Baxter was writing at his desk. He laid down his pen and looked up at the young man standing on the carpet in the middle of the room.

"Morning," he said. "First, about that truck. I'm not going to have Service transport used for personal excursions, and you chaps may as well understand that right away. There's been a good deal of slackness about that recently, and it's got to stop. The Battle of the Atlantic isn't fought to bring oil to this country so that you can use it to go courting. I'm sending a reminder out to all commanding officers to-day. I hope I shan't have to make an example. Understand?"

Marshall said: "Yes, sir."

"All right. Now about yourself. Wing Commander Dobbie tells me that you've done twenty-eight operations of your second tour of duty, and that you're going off on sick leave. I understand you'll have to go before a Board before you fly again."

"That's what the medical officer told me, sir."

"That may take some time. Do you want to do a third tour in bombers?"

"Not very much. I'd like to be transferred to Coastal if I could. I was in Coastal before."

"All right. Any particular preference in Coastal? I don't promise that you'll get what you want, you know."

"I'd like to be on Liberators, sir. And I'd like to be in Scotland or the north somewhere. I don't want to go overseas much." He hesitated. "I'm just getting married."

"So I observed." The Air Commodore made a pencilled note upon his pad. "Do you want to finish off your tour in bombers—two more operations?"

Marshall looked up in surprise. "Not specially. I've done fifty-eight."

"Wing Commander Dobbie tells me that your crew will have to be re-formed. It's hardly worth coming back to form up a new crew for only two operations, and then break it up again. You can go to Coastal right away, as soon as you are through your Board, if you like. You'll have three months ground duty before operations, of course, after this tour."

"I'd like to do that, sir."

"All right, Marshall. Anything you want to see me about?"

"I don't think so."

Air Commodore Baxter got up from his desk. "How are your hands now?"

"Oh, they're getting better. I can move them a bit more each day."

"I'm sorry we're going to lose you. That was a good show you put up the other night. I'm having it marked up on your record."

"Thank you, sir."

The Air Commodore moved forward and held out his hand. "Good-bye, Marshall. Best of luck in Coastal. We shall miss you here."

*　　　*　　　*

The pilot came out through the door. I got up from the chair where I had been sitting with my brief-case on my knee, subconsciously uneasy that I might lose the beastly thing. The secretary said: "The Air Commodore will see you now, sir."

I went through into the inner office. Air Commodore Baxter was standing by the window looking out; he turned as I came in.

"Very good of you to come down," he said. "You've brought the drawings with you?"

"I've brought the installation drawings," I said. "I didn't think you'd want the manufacturing details, and they're rather a responsibility to have about the place. The first three equipments should be here to-morrow."

I put my brief-case down upon the table, and unlocked it, and unfolded my white prints and sheets of typescript. When I looked up again he had moved back to the window, presenting his back to me as he studied something outside.

I hesitated, then moved up the room to see what he was looking at. All I saw was a little Service truck, and the young pilot who had come out of the room before me standing by it, talking eagerly to a W.A.A.F. Section Officer in the sunlight. There was nothing else but that.

Baxter turned from the window. "The very stuff of England," he said quietly.

I smiled. "Those two?"

He nodded.

I was intrigued. "Is there anything particular about them?" I enquired.

"Nothing particular," he said. "Just an average good pilot, marrying one of the girls from his station. He did quite well the other night. I'm putting him in for a D.F.C."

I glanced back at the couple by the truck. "I'd like to hear about that," I said.

The Air Commodore picked up one of my white prints. "Is this the bit that sticks down under the rear fuselage?" And then he glanced back at the window. "Remind me, and I'll tell you about that chap some time," he said.

We turned to the drawings.

*This book
designed by William B. Taylor
is a production of
Heron Books, London*

*Printed in England by
Hazell Watson and Viney Limited
Aylesbury, Bucks*